# MIND
# HOSTAGE

## EMILY W. SKINNER

Editor and Book Formatter: Lisa DeSpain
www.book2bestseller.com

Book Cover: www.Labelschmiede.com
ISBN: 978-1736191125 (Hardcover)
ISBN: 978-1736191118 (Paperback)

For the elderly, the vulnerable, and their advocates.

Inspired by true events.

# CHAPTER 1

Suzy loosened the cloth straps tying her mother Virginia to the hospital bed. *What the hell is going on?* The room smelled like a mixture of urine and floor wax. She couldn't believe what she was seeing. Why would a rehabilitation center tie a patient down? And why was her mother wearing a sleep mask? She looked like a prisoner of war, not a knee-replacement patient.

"Mom!" Suzy was infuriated. "What have they done to you?"

Suzy pulled off her tan sweater, rolled it up, and stuffed it into her backpack. A sleeveless olive top, brown skirt, and black ballerina flats were her uniform of sorts. All solids. She trusted solids and loathed wardrobe mistakes. Suzy smoothed her shoulder-length, rust-water blonde hair and put the pack on the floor. She didn't need this now. Her shoulders were tight, her neck tense.

"Suzy," Ginny grumbled, "I need you to write my story."

"What's going on, Mom?" She removed the cloth ties around her mother's shaking wrists and tossed them into the garbage. Her mother's hands were ice. She began massaging them.

Virginia Compton, Ginny to her friends, was a 76-year-old former produce stand owner. She'd inherited the business from her parents, Monica Woodson Compton and Edward Compton. Together, the three had raised Ginny's only child, Suzy Lennox, in their rural Romeo, Florida home. They were a foursome.

In the predawn hours, they would pick up surplus citrus and vegetables at neighboring farms and bring them to the palm-thatched roof hut Edward had constructed along Highway 41. Every morning, Monday through Saturday, they'd arrange their produce in wooden crates and containers made of the discarded furniture Edward had salvaged from dresser drawers, small cribs, and the pieces he had repurposed for the price of the nails he needed to cobble them into workable orchard bins.

Crops that didn't sell became preserves, pickled items, ingredients for baked goods, or compost.

There was not much time, between school and the grove stand, for young Ginny to have a social life. She managed to sneak out on Sundays with her friend Mabel to meet boys.

When Ginny became pregnant, Monica demanded she give her granddaughter the surname of the child's biological father, Lennox, to provide legitimacy to Suzy's birth certificate. Suzy Lennox.

"Lennox" was a man Suzy would know only by his last name. He was a man no one would discuss.

Now a 47-year-old full-figured data analyst, Suzy financially supported Ginny and her own out-of-wedlock daughter, Chloe Lennox.

Suzy was joint owner in Ginny's Florida Cracker home in Romeo, a co-signer on Chloe's student housing, and the owner of her own mobile home in Palm Breeze.

When Ginny retired, she had continued living in the only home she had ever known, the home her grandparents Catherine and Joseph Woodson had built in the late 1800s. Ginny's parents Monica and Edward had raised her in this house, and together they had raised Suzy; later Suzy and Ginny raised little Chloe, until Suzy pushed herself out of the nest at 23.

Though Ginny lived alone, she never felt alone. In recent years, she had scooted around on an office chair to avoid pressure to her right knee and entertained herself with QVC purchases. When her mobility issues became falling accidents, Suzy temporarily moved her mother into her Palm Breeze mobile home.

The goal was to get Ginny's knee replaced, get her back on her feet, and back to her Romeo, Florida residence with home health if needed.

Suzy and Ginny were not ideal roommates.

Suzy was the neatnik. Ginny, not so much.

Suzy had too much on her mind; Ginny had not a care in the world.

Suzy wanted a love life; Ginny wanted to talk to on-air hosts of home shopping.

Suzy stared at the eye mask on Ginny. She had done her due diligence: a thorough background check of The Lily of the Valley Rehab. She had read online reviews, checked their infection rate, toured the facility before booking Ginny's surgery, and even interviewed a few patients *without* staff consent. *So, what the hell?*

"Suzy," Ginny moaned again, "I need you to write my story."

"What happened to you?" Suzy's patience was wearing thin. Her compassion came and went in waves, depending on her stress level.

None of this made any sense. Her mother had only been transferred to The Valley a mere 24 hours ago, three days after a full knee replacement in Gulf Terrace Hospital.

Ginny's lips quivered. "Write my story."

*Would Chloe be there for her someday?* "I will," Suzy appeased. "Just tell me what you can."

The lights were off in Ginny's room. Aside from an occasional burst of sunlight casting tree branch shadows on the room's white fabric curtain, the only illumination in the shared room came from her roommate's television on the other side of the cloth divider.

"Suzy." Ginny squeezed her hand.

Suzy whispered, realizing the roommate could be sleeping, "What?"

Her mother repeated, "Write my story."

Suzy leaned over and pulled the eye mask down.

Ginny flinched. "Too bright." She rolled her head back and forth and squeezed her eyelids tight.

Suzy cupped her hand over her mother's eyes and held her chin. She attempted to get a look by holding Ginny's eyelid open. Ginny looked blind. Literally, like she didn't see Suzy.

"Maybe it's a side effect of medication?" Suzy talked to herself. "When did your eyes start bothering you?" Suzy replaced the eye mask. "I can't help you if you don't explain. Tell me something," she stressed.

Suzy dissected the last four days:

- She helped her mother prep for surgery.
- She stayed at the hospital the day of the surgery.
- She went back to work.
- Ginny had a lot of confusion after surgery which seemed understandable.
- Suzy wasn't there much day two because she had left Ginny in the care of a freakin' hospital!
- The knee surgeon, Graham Smithson, was frustrated that Ginny wouldn't stand or even try to stand before she was discharged from the hospital on day three.
- Smithson shipped Ginny off to The Valley Rehab so they could help her start walking again.
- Smithson would be in to check on her.

"Has Smithson been in?" Suzy spoke into her mother's ear.

"Who?" Ginny reached her hand into the air, searching for Suzy.

A gravelly Brooklyn accent spat from behind the room divider, "No one should have to put up with that." It had a smoker cough and a rasp.

Ginny continued to search the air for Suzy.

"What?" Suzy stood up straight and pulled the curtain back.

An elegant troll in a gray bouffant, buttoned-up-to-the neck yellow sweater, white pleated skirt, and white Velcro sneakers sat in a recliner. She had crocodile leather hands, face, and short legs. Her dangling feet were unable to reach the floor. "She's awful." The troll hacked a throaty cough.

"Did they do something to you, too?" Maybe Suzy could finally get a straight answer.

"Is that your mother?" The troll asked.

"Yes," Suzy replied.

"God love you." The troll pointed toward Ginny.

"What are you saying?"

"She's awful...your mother."

Suzy didn't bother to respond. She yanked the drape divider back in place. The beaded chain hissed to a close. Suzy turned back to Ginny. "Mom, I need answers! What's going on?"

Ginny muttered to Suzy, "Ignore her."

The troll shouted, "I heard that."

Ginny whispered, "She's crazy."

"She's the crazy one," the troll screamed back. "She's making everyone work double time. She doesn't cooperate."

Ginny whispered, "Write my story."

"Why?" Suzy asked.

They were interrupted by squishing.

A short, heavy nurse in oversized green cotton scrubs squished into the room. Her rolled-up pant legs ended with black Crocs. "I need you to sign some forms. You're the surrogate." This was delivered more as a designation than a question. She handed a pen and clipboard to Suzy.

Suzy read the nametag: *Becky Larsen, RN*. Her bright pink face sported black cat-eyeglasses and a lavender bob.

*Finally!* Suzy thought.

The troll stayed quiet.

Suzy remained calm. *More bees from honey.* "Becky, why was my mother tied down?"

The nurse stood a moment with her short arms dangling at each side. She crossed them into a fleshy pink pretzel.

Suzy stared hard at Nurse Larsen.

Larsen pulled a lollipop out of her pocket and began unwrapping it. "Would you like to go in for her exercises?" Cat-eyes placed the sucker in her mouth. "She doesn't trust us."

*I'm not sure I do.* "Why are you ignoring my question?" Suzy asked.

Larsen looked dumbfounded. "Why are you ignoring mine?"

*More bees from honey.* Suzy took a cleansing breath and looked at the forms. One thing at a time. Suzy looked back at Ginny, who was motionless. Her mother could easily be mistaken for dead—except that she had a restless ankle twitch on the non-operated leg. Ginny was flat on her back with no pillow. She looked like a thick wax mold of a gray-haired woman in a pilled purple skirt and a dingy white knit top. These were Ginny's comfort clothes. Her nice clothes were in her closet for special occasions that never happened.

"Return the paperwork to the nurse's station on your way out. Do you want to attend Ginny's exercise session with her or not?" Larsen half-turned to leave.

"Is this necessary?" Suzy pointed to the papers, tapping the clipboard with the pen. She didn't want to sign anything until she knew what the hell these people were doing to the elderly.

The nurse took the clipboard and indicated the highlights on the papers. "You are the power of attorney." Another statement.

"Yes," Suzy sighed.

The nurse sucked the lollipop intermittently as she began her oral argument. "Your mother gets government benefits." She paused to give Suzy a chance to let that sink in.

Larsen continued, "She's enrolled in government programs." Pause. "The Valley needs to be **paid.**"

*Paid* hung in the air like a sermon as the next lines sped up. "The government won't pay unless the necessary forms are approved --and --if --you --don't sign --services cannot be rendered. If services cannot be rendered your mother will be discharged --and --can go elsewhere." Larsen handed the clipboard back to Suzy.

Suzy flipped the pages and tried to read them. *Discharged? Do your damn job!* She saw *Lennox* on one form. "Why's my name on this form?"

"You signed forms at the hospital last week." The nurse stepped into Suzy's personal space. "This is standard." Cat-eyes continued to suck and chew. She waited.

Suzy stepped back and held the clipboard to her chest in defiance. "Answer me. Why the mask and the ties?"

The nurse looked confused.

"Why was my mother tied down!?" Suzy felt her blood pressure rising. Larsen's cherry lollipop was making her hungry. She hadn't eaten much that day, other than four cups of coffee in the last two hours.

*Why wasn't her mother chiming in?* Ginny had great hearing.

"She asked for it," the nurse said.

Suzy threw the clipboard down. "What the fuck does that mean?! Are you saying that if she doesn't cooperate, she's asking to be bound and blinded into submission!"

The nurse's middle section didn't bend. She struggled to pick up the clipboard, and when she finally got it, she thrust it back at Suzy. "Ginny asked us to restrain her in the bed and to block out the light! She said it made her feel secure."

The troll grumbled, "She did."

Larsen continued, "We closed the curtain. She wasn't satisfied, so we found a sleep mask."

Suzy's mind was reeling. "I'm supposed to believe *my mother* wanted to be restrained! The woman who can't sleep with a top sheet because it's too confining!?"

"Keep your voice down." The nurse pointed to the clipboard. She chucked the sucker into the trash and rested her crossed arms on her stomach. "You know you'll get more bees with honey instead of vinegar."

Suzy's mouth dropped open. "Why'd you say that?"

"Restraints are not something we do..." Larsen started.

Suzy stopped her, "The bees part!"

The nurse looked at Suzy and her mother as if to say, the apple doesn't fall far from the tree. "Restraints are not what we do. They were not tight. Ginny did not make much sense. And no one has been in until now. We don't know her."

Suzy wasn't buying it.

The nurse sighed. "We didn't want something to happen, so we played along. She seemed to like it if you ask me…Maybe you don't really know your mother?"

Suzy gasped.

Larsen shook her head. "Show up…She hasn't fallen or been deprived of attention." Larsen pushed the glasses up the bridge of her pug nose.

"She gets ALL the attention," the troll spat.

Suzy took the clipboard. "Mom"—Suzy turned to her mother—"is this true? You wanted to be restrained?"

Ginny didn't answer.

Suzy signed the forms and handed the clipboard and pen back to Larsen. "I'll take some time off for the exercises."

Larsen nodded and *squished* out.

Suzy anticipated the troll.

To her mother, "I know damn well you heard every word. Why didn't you defend yourself? I looked like an ass! You said *nothing*. You asked to be RESTRAINED? So, help me God if you ask me one more time to write your story!"

There was a soft knock at the open door.

Suzy held her breath. *Now what?* She turned.

A handsome 50-ish man in a blue long-sleeve dress shirt, Rolling Stones tie, and khaki slacks asked, "Where's the workout room? I'm trying to find my father."

Suzy felt heat rise from her face to the top of her head.

He was handsome.

*Why was she so angry?* Suzy took inventory:

- Mom looks like a P.O.W.
- Troll roommate
- Wax mother
- Squishy nurse
- Lollipop
- Handsome guy

"It's closed." Suzy couldn't believe how hot her face felt. "Well. Right now." Did her voice sound robotic? "Likely. Ask. Where… he is?" Her voice trailed off. Her cheeks were experiencing nuclear fusion and her mind was alarmingly calm.

He seemed to understand her. His soft brown eyes were saying, *You're overwhelmed.* His hair was saying, *I'm real.*

He was:

- Six-foot-tall
- Olive-complected
- Slightly crooked nose
- Big tan hands
- Slim
- Brown-eyed
- Thin-lipped
- Italian, Spanish, Indian guy?

13

"Got it," he nodded.

Suzy felt a new flood of cranberries take over her face and arms. Her core reactor needed water to cool down. Maybe she was catching something? "My mother. Rehab. Good luck."

He leaned in and offered his hand to Suzy. "Frank Wisner, nice to meet you."

Suzy took his hand. It covered hers and felt like warm silk.

Her mother blurted, "Suzy Lennox."

Frank and Suzy both turned to look at Ginny.

"Thanks," Suzy muttered. *Now she wants to talk.*

The troll grumbled at the sound of Ginny's voice.

Frank's brows knit together at the growl.

Suzy rolled her eyes and gave a head click in the direction of the troll while she mouthed to Frank, "My mother's roommate." She let go of his nice bear paw. "I'm Suzy Lennox and this is my mother, Ginny Compton."

Frank nodded.

"Seen the Stones?" Suzy pointed to his tie.

Frank slapped a paw on his tie. "Yes. You?"

"More of a Zeppelin fan."

He nodded again. "Seen them?"

"No." Suzy wagged her thumb back at her mother. She couldn't think of anything to say.

"Right." He leaned in, brushing Suzy's thigh with his slacks. He grabbed Ginny's dead hand and shook it. "Nice to meet you, Ginny." He stepped back and avoided physical contact the second time.

Suzy wondered when a man had last touched her thigh.

Frank gave Suzy another nod.

Suzy was still deep in thought.

He waited a beat to be polite, then left.

Suzy's heart raced. Her face was warm. *What time was it?*

He was gone.

*Probably married. Or gay. Or gay married.* She checked the hallway twice, pulled the drape back, and gave the troll a stare, dared her to comment, then snapped it closed.

She turned to her mother. *Write her story?* She pulled Ginny's eye mask down.

Ginny didn't flinch this time.

Suzy whispered, "You're gonna talk."

# CHAPTER 2

**1920 Sulphur Springs, Florida**

Monica fluttered her long, black eyelashes at two men, who gave her a flirtatious nod. She and her church group had made the day's journey by train to the famous Sulphur Springs bathing resort and adjacent Tampa Alligator Farm. The shorter man tipped his striped-band boater hat and elbowed his friend. Both were clad in worsted wool sleeveless bathing tops that partially shrouded wool shorts. Their shorts stopped just above the knee but didn't hide calf-length socks held up by men's sock garters. Their shoes were buffed and shined. They were regular fish out of water.

The taller, swarthy fellow made long strides toward Monica and conveniently pushed his shorter competition into the resort's pool. He had a dimpled chin, wide grin, and a sharp straight nose. Aggressive and confident, his strong pine cologne greeted her.

She breathed him in. He was no farmer.

"Hey!" His short companion pushed himself up from the side of the crowded, noisy pool. To Monica, "Lou's the bee's knees alright, but you want a sheik, baby. You want me." He leaned back into the pool and fished his hat out. He dumped the water right over his head, slapping the hat down on his auburn locks. His shook each leg and didn't bother to remove his socks and shoes. Grinning widely, he put his fists up like a prize fighter. He began dancing around Lou. "Let's duke it out."

Monica twirled her white parasol and chuckled, "Oh my." Her thin brunette hair was tucked into a bathing cap that emphasized her pink summer complexion. Heat radiated from her cheeks, giving her daisy-petal skin a rose quartz hue. She wore a long red- and white-striped one-piece bathing suit of the latest knit fabric. Although it was dry, it hugged her body's soft curves.

"My friends call me Lou. That's my cousin, Joe." Lou wagged a thumb at his sopping counterpart. He shook a fist at Joe and gave him a wink.

"Monica." Her pastor waved her over.

She was startled to hear her name. "I'll be right over." She gave them a pout. "Nice meeting you, Lou and…"

"Joe." The shorter man held out his hand. "And if you play your cards right, I'll buy you one of those baby alligators to take home."

She continued to twirl her parasol. "You're not from around here." She cast her eyes down.

"That obvious, eh?" He withdrew his hand. "You're a native."

She blushed. "Little gators are cute, but they grow up. Is it true you city folk flush them into the sewer?"

Joe put his hands on his hips and said with exaggerated glee, "You're saying something can appear innocent, but grow into a monster?"

"Or becomes someone else's problem," she said softly. "Toodle loo." She hurried toward her group.

Lou punched Joe in the arm. "You scared her off, old sport."

Joe held his fists up again and started to shadow box. "You wouldn't last five rounds," Joe clowned. "If you weren't family, I'd cold-cock you here and now."

They paused and turned to look at Monica. Lou wolf whistled as she made her way to the Toboggan Water Slide with her church group.

"May the best man win." Lou gave Joe another shove into the 60,000-gallon pool and ran toward Monica.

Suzy rushed into her office, throwing her keys and backpack on the desk. Her fellow analyst, Arnold Welch, was eating a turkey leg and playing on her computer.

"Degrease the keyboard!" She was not amused.

He saluted her with the leg. "Said the woman with Cheetos locking up her spacebar. How's your mom?"

Suzy rubbed her face with the palms of both hands. "Oh my God, rehab's a nightmare!"

"Should have listened to Amy Winehouse. She said, no, no, no!" Arnold's soft blue eyes darted back and forth, a comedic thing he did to make her laugh.

She gritted her teeth.

Arnold floated between needing laughs to validate his existence and saying whatever popped into his head. Forty-five and fair-skinned, he exploited his weaknesses for drinks, sex, and football tickets.

"I need you to hear me out." Suzy was serious.

He turned off the joker. He was almost handsome when he wasn't playing cocky and insecure. His wolfman beard grew in patches of red-brown, divided by a sea of black ingrown hairs. He tossed the turkey leg into her trash can.

"Hell, no!" She grabbed a tissue and pulled it out of the can and handed it back to him. "It'll smell like something died in here if the trash isn't emptied tonight."

"That's chicken," Arnold scoffed. "Turkey smells like rotting Thanksgiving dinner. Chicken is like a dead rat in the wall, a whole different decaying process." Arnold smacked his mouth. "I'm gonna be sick."

She opened her drawer and pulled out a plastic bag.

He glanced down at the handmade dispenser stuffed with recycled plastic bags. "Dispose of animal carcasses often?"

"Shut up." She held open the bag and he dropped the leg in. She tied the bag. "I'm going to place this in the lunchroom freezer. That way if I forget to take it to the dumpster, the whole place won't smell."

Arnold did the eye thing again. "Jeffery Dahmer's got nothing on you."

Suzy grumbled, "I'll be right back." She squirted hand sanitizer into his palms.

He pretended to be sad. He worked the gel into his hands.

They rented a space with two offices and a small boardroom. The main office of each unit had a large window that looked out into the complex's hallway. Windows in some units were tinted, but each tenant could see what was going on across the hall or know who was working late, got in early, was bored, or raging. It provided an extra measure of visibility for the building's security officers and a sense of community for the occupants.

Suzy's office was exposed to the hall. Arnold's office had a window but was tucked back into a corner and only Suzy could see him.

She came back in and shut the door. "Can you be serious? I need some advice." She sat on the couch.

They were both generalist workaholics with private, corporate, and government clients. Their current project was a study of vacant city lots for conversion to "tiny home" parks for the homeless.

Arnold moved to the couch beside her. He crossed his long legs and stretched one arm across the back of the aged leather. He could be charming at times. He was forever in golf shirts, black jeans, ball caps, and loafers. His beer bump was his latest accomplishment. He prided himself on his ability to let go. He removed his worn Devilrays cap and scratched his dry scalp. "I'm all in." He put the cap back on.

"She was tied down by her wrists and had an eye mask over her eyes." Suzy turned toward him. "The lights were off in her room ..."

"Sounds romantic." He grinned, then made a mime wipe to a straight face.

"Fuck you, Arnold." She stood.

He tapped the seat next to him. "You set that up. Sit back down."

"Forget it." She moved to her desk and took a damp towelette out of her other desk drawer and worked on cleaning her keyboard. "Where's the latest survey?"

Arnold huffed. He knew she wasn't going to talk now.

"The park?" He gave her what she wanted. "We tested it across all platforms for medium demos with kids. The social shares were zip. No one wants to admit the homeless make them uncomfortable." Arnold crossed the other leg. "The click through rate was high. People want to know what will affect their neighborhood, but they're not willing to stick their neck out and say anything."

Suzy nodded. "Can you do the focus group this weekend? I've got to be with Ginny."

Arnold yawned. "The Planet Family Group is managing it. Video-taping everything. We're free as lizards."

"Oh, that reminds me," Suzy smiled. "There's a Led Zeppelin tribute band at the Hungry Lizard."

Arnold shrugged. "I'm not available."

"I was actually talking to myself." Suzy suddenly felt inspired.

"I'm unavailable, because..." Arnold waved his hands like a musical conductor. He continued to call in trombones and cymbals and other instruments.

Suzy ignored him.

"All right. All right. If you must know." He paused.

She wasn't playing along.

"I'm going to a John Williams Star Wars concert."

*Why did her mother want her to write her story?* "Good for you. Good for John Williams."

Arnold nodded. "It is good for me." He made an air exclamation point.

She held up her hand to stop him. She decided to take another stab at talking it out. "Okay.... I'm going to talk about my mom."

Arnold zipped his mouth.

"This is crazy. She was tied down. Had a black out mask on. And the nurse said Mom wanted it to feel secure. Mom didn't deny it. She just kept asking me to write her story."

Arnold leaned in.

Suzy grabbed a pen, placed the point over the towelette, and cleaned between the keys.

"Then, a guy looking for his dad wandered into the room… and my mother decided to introduce me, mask on, flat on her back!"

"Matchmaking under the influence," Arnold bobbed. "I like it."

"Influence?" Suzy asked. She started working on the groove in the spacebar.

"Drugs." Arnold looked at Suzy like she was nuts. "She was cut open and had a Terminator knee put in. Napping in a blackout mask sounds right to me. And tied down if the nurses promised many happy endings… But drugs… the drugs are talking, Suzy."

Suzy felt dumb. "Oh." *How did she always miss the obvious?*

"She's old. It's time," Arnold continued. "She could die. A lightweight with heavy drugs in her. She wants to tell her story. Sounds reasonable. Not that she's going to tell you something you don't already know. Am I right? Well, other than the tied down thing." He stopped himself from the eye dart. He watched her.

Suzy exhaled. "But seriously, it's strange…"

Arnold nodded sincerely. "Yeah, for sure. Tied down is the only part that sets off alarms. Not cool. I'd be pissed, too. You likely need to talk to the head nurse or supervisor on the floor."

*I would have, but "handsome hair" messed with my thinking.* "You're right." She felt better. Where was her empathy? But tied down?!

Arnold knew Suzy was overthinking. "Hey, I'm interested in hearing Ginny's story. Seriously."

Suzy smiled. He wasn't always a dick. "But let's say she really did want to be tied down... Why?"

"Start with that," Arnold nodded. "She wasn't always your mother. She was young once." He arched his eyebrows rapidly.

*Damn it. He's right!*

# CHAPTER 3

**6 a.m.**

Suzy drove to her favorite coffee shop on the way to the rehab facility. Her mother loved coffee cake. She'd get her a treat and start over. Catch the staff off guard. Blow the whistle. Or maybe things would be normal?

She turned her radio to a talk program. The newscaster was discussing local weather forecasts and upcoming news stories. A possible hurricane. She turned it off. She didn't need any distractions. She pulled forward and placed her order.

Traffic was light.

Once she got to The Valley, Suzy walked swiftly past check-in. A volunteer watched her, then went back to reading her magazine.

Backpack over her right shoulder, coffee in hand, and cake bag in the other, she pushed the second-floor button. Before the door closed, a doctor jumped in, then pushed the button for the same floor. He smelled really good. His white coat was ironed, and he wore a stethoscope around his neck. He was also carrying a coffee and looking at his cellphone. Text messages were dinging on his phone. He stepped to the left of Suzy and continued to scroll his phone.

Once they got to the second floor, he moved to let her out. *The hair!* She recognized him from the other day. Embroidered in blue on his coat was the name, Frank Wisner, M.D.

She stepped out and gave him the eye. "You knew EXACTLY where the gym was." *What was his game?*

He didn't recognize her at first, then he smiled with perfect Chicklet-cubed teeth. "Guilty."

*This didn't make sense.* "You work here." Suzy stared at his name.

"Well... my practice is down the road, and I see a few patients on rounds. But I'm actually here to see my dad."

Suzy eyed him suspiciously. "Why did you lie?"

He didn't follow.

"When you stopped in my mother's room, you asked where the gym was." Suzy took a sip of her coffee.

He thought a moment. "Right. I'm going to come clean. I heard you. I wasn't sure if everything was okay. So, I stuck my head in."

Suzy turned red, and her eyes watered. That stung. Suzy walked away. *Shit! Shit! Shit!*

He followed her. "I'm sorry. I am. I could tell you were having a moment. I just wanted to be sure, for Ginny's sake."

Suzy stopped. A tear spilled from her left eye. She had thought this jerk was handsome. "Wow. Ginny! Are you her doctor? Are you going to come clean about that?"

He looked shocked. He held up both hands, almost pouring his coffee out. "Let's remain calm. I fill in for doctors on this floor."

Suzy looked at the ceiling, then back at him. She felt her nose start to run. "Did you have my mother tied down? Did you order that!?"

He shook his head no. "I have no idea what you're talking about. Restrained? Have you discussed this...?"

Suzy couldn't believe him. "The nurse was no help. When you walked in, I was trying to get a straight answer from my mother, Dr. Wisner."

His smile was gone, and he looked confused. "Is there anything I can do?" He placed his phone in his lab coat. He held his coffee, waiting for an appropriate moment to take a sip.

"Yes, find out what really happened!" She rushed past him, knocking her shoulder into his. It had not been a planned move, but it felt appropriate. She kept going.

He almost lost his coffee. He watched her walk away, then took several sips.

Suzy walked into Ginny's room. *The nerve.*

Her mother was in a hospital gown, and her sleep mask was on. A machine was rotating the operated leg. She had a cotton blanket over her, and there were no ties on her wrists. The bed rails were up.

Suzy stuck her head around the curtain to see if the troll was still there. The small woman was asleep in her recliner. Her beehive looked like the Leaning Tower. She was in the same outfit as the day prior.

Suzy came back to Ginny and whispered in her ear, "I've got coffeecake."

Ginny was matter of fact. "Are you ready to write?"

"Mom, since when do you want to write?"

Ginny shook her head. "I can't. You have the education."

The troll hissed.

"I'll write your story." Suzy gave her mother a kiss on the forehead. *If only Dr. Wisner would walk in now, would he think she was being nice to Ginny? Of course not. Don't be silly.* She put her coffee and things down and sat next to Ginny.

Ginny smiled.

"Take a bite." Suzy fed Ginny the cinnamon coffeecake. "Let's take the eye mask off."

Ginny placed a shaky hand on top of the mask. "They made me have you."

*Who?* "Mom, what are you talking about?"

Ginny kept her hand on the mask. "The people." She chewed the cake and opened her mouth for another bite.

"What people?" Suzy fed Ginny.

Ginny coughed.

Suzy grabbed the Styrofoam cup on Ginny's bedside stand and swished it. She lifted her mother's head and gave her a sip of water.

Ginny swallowed, then put her head back. "Write this down."

"Are you saying grandma and grandpa made you have me?"

Ginny stifled a soft cry.

Suzy took her mother's hand. "You must have experienced trauma when you were young. Maybe the meds are dredging things up."

Ginny whimpered, waking the troll.

"For the love of God," her roommate protested.

Suzy felt her shoulders tighten. She whispered to Ginny, "Promise you'll do the exercises, so we can get you out of here."

Ginny nodded.

Suzy raised Ginny's bed a bit and handed her the remaining cake. "I've got to go. I just stopped by before work. We'll write later and you can explain everything." She kissed Ginny on the head.

Ginny blew her a kiss.

Suzy heard the hum of fluorescent lights overhead as she left her mother's room. She looked left and right into the other patients' rooms. Most were still sleeping. She spied the workout room to see if he was there. There were only a few therapists talking and doing whatever morning routine she supposed they did before patients were brought in. It was early. She could smell coffee brewing and looked at the activity board. The breakfast, lunch, and dinner menus were posted, as well as some motivational posters, fall prevention tips, occupational therapy guidelines, and warnings that cellphone use during visits was strongly discouraged.

The nurse's station was vacated at the moment. She wondered if there was a team meeting happening. Did they do that at hospitals or rehabilitation centers?

A chill ran down her spine. Most of the patients were easily in their 70s and 80s, with a few exceptions. *Don't old people wake up at the crack of dawn? Who was taking care of them?*

She suddenly thought of puppy mills and the pet stores she visited that had groggy, sleepy little dogs that rarely barked. The first few times she had seen this, she thought puppies were just like babies who needed sleep to grow and develop. But then she noticed each circle fence had as many as four or five little furballs napping, and the room was filled with fifteen to twenty round enclosures, yet barely a puppy yawned.

In a similar way, the employees were not visible or available, unless you called out or snooped around a corner. *What's going on?*

"Can I help you?" a voice called out.

Suzy turned to see a very chipper African American male nurse in blue scrubs approach. He was tall, fit, and had a gorgeous Afro man-bun. *Thanks for debunking my house of horrors suspicion.*

"Are you lost?" He placed his hands on his hips.

*Power poser.* "I just stopped to see my mother and I'm curious. How are all these older patients still asleep? My grandparents were always up before the roosters," she generalized.

"Stick around. They'll be in the gym after breakfast. It's a regular Grand Central Station." He nodded, "Anything else?"

"No, just leaving." Suzy gawked at him. "I love your hair."

"Thanks."

An awkward silence passed, and they both left. Suzy moved toward the elevator, he down the hallway. "Thank you." She turned and tried to sound upbeat. *Is he walking toward mom's room?*

The elevator door opened, and she backed into it. She continued to gaze down the hallway to see where the nurse went, but he was already out of view. An elevator maintenance man exited out around her.

She jumped. *Where did he come from?*

"Beep. Beep." He smirked. "You need to turn on your reversing indicator."

Her face became beet red. "Haha. Need more coffee."

"Don't I know it." He was gone before she pushed the first-floor button.

# CHAPTER 4

The security guard at the office building nodded to Suzy as she walked past. "Preparing for the hurricane, Miss Lennox?"

*Hurricane?* She spun around. "Jamal, what hurricane?" Her backpack dropped off her shoulder. She hoisted it back up.

The 80-year-old guard kept watching his screens as he spoke. He was pleasant and knew the latest on all the leaseholders and random world news. "Cat 5 possibly. Could still turn and head to Louisiana. Best make plans. The Weather Channel says it could pass through the middle of the state this weekend."

Suzy didn't need this. She lived in a low elevation, prone to flooding. Mobile homes were always the first to evacuate. She would need to go to Romeo and put Ginny's storm shutters up. She may need to stay there. The hundred-year-old frame home had long-survived other threats. Chloe would shelter at the college.

"She's just intensified," Jamal exclaimed. "Hurricane Virginia," he read from his screen. "Looks like the offices will be closed by Thursday."

The realization hit her, and she started to chuckle. She almost believed him. "Nice try, Jamal. Arnold put you up to this?" *Hurricane Virginia.*

Jamal turned around, irritated. "Lord knows Mr. Welch has made my job harder at times, but I don't joke about danger."

She hadn't seen the security guard this angry before. "Virginia… Hurricane Virginia?" she repeated. *Seriously?*

"Get informed." Jamal was curt. He turned around. "The complex will be sending emails to all tenants in preparation."

*How could the National Weather Service name a storm after her mother at this particular time? Why was Virginia such a threat?* "Sorry, Jamal," Suzy sighed. "My mother's in rehab."

"They will keep her safe. The hospitals and medical centers have back-up generators." Jamal's tone was less terse. "You need to protect yourself, Miss Lennox. Nobody's looking out for you, but you."

Suzy froze. She nodded.

Jamal got up from the desk and stretched. "Be grateful for warnings."

Suzy drove into The Valley's parking garage. The sky was bright blue, and the clouds were marshmallow white. The world appeared to be normal. How was it that storm threats never seemed real? They never happened on gloomy, rainy weeks. Instead, they always happened on bright muggy weeks that were the Florida norm, and crept up like an untreated infection, becoming windy, charcoal skies of doom. And always on a weekend. Or was that her imagination?

And why was she always in a rush? It felt like the world was finally catching up.

She found a space almost immediately. She parked, grabbed her backpack, and jogged across the parking garage. A shiny white van with no windows was parked at the garage exit. She made a wide sweep around it, thankful it was daylight. She, Ginny, and Chloe all watched way too many true crime shows. They knew what a white panel van meant.

Suzy noticed the wheelchair lift on the back and the words, "Wisner Family Practice."

"Dr. Creepy... Oh my God." She powerwalked to the rehab entrance. The humidity was thick, and her clothes felt heavy. Suzy defiantly walked past the check-in again. *Nope, not checking in.*

When she got upstairs, she found Ginny in the workout room. Her mother was sitting in a wheelchair with her eye mask on, wearing the dingy purple skirt again and a long-sleeved black knit short top, possibly with no bra. Ginny's small, droopy water-balloon breasts were almost hanging out under the short top. Suzy sighed. What was a matter with these people? The top must have belonged to the troll, or maybe they shrank what Suzy had packed for Ginny. Her mother's white Velcro sneakers hugged her swollen tennis-socked feet. Her physical therapist was asking her questions and filling out a form.

"Hi, Mom." Suzy kissed the top of Ginny's head. She peeked inside her mother's shirt and discovered a flesh-colored ill-fitting sports bra. Relief.

Ginny reached out like Frankenstein's monster trying to grab a small child. Her bra was showing.

Suzy took her mother's hands and moved them lower. "I'm here to watch you exercise."

The 1000-square foot room was buzzing with all ages of the injured and disabled. Some had encouraging loved ones with them, while others were dependent on their therapists. Fluorescent lighting covered every inch of ceiling, it seemed. It was way too bright. Mirrors wrapped around three walls. Every piece of exercise equipment was occupied. Patients talked loudly, therapists talked loudly, and the noise was giving her a headache. Suzy wanted her mother to do well but couldn't blame Ginny for wanting to close her eyes.

Ginny, eye mask on, hands clasped in her lap, directed Suzy, "Tell her I need my eye mask."

Suzy looked at the therapist, who shrugged. *Great assist. So, it is my job to encourage her?* "Mom, you can't walk with your eyes covered." Suzy kneaded her mother's hands. They were like ice.

"Blind people walk," Ginny complained.

"And you're not blind." Suzy turned to the therapist. "What's she supposed to do?"

"We've reassured Ginny we will not let her fall," the petite therapist said.

"She's too small," Ginny disagreed. "She can't catch me if I fall."

"You peeked at your therapist?" Suzy was slightly amused.

"She made me take my mask off." Ginny pulled away.

The therapist chimed in, "And, I let her put it back on. Anyway, two of us will be walking her." The small woman pointed to the equipment.

"Excuse me?" Suzy felt her shoulders tighten. "Am I one of the two?"

The therapist looked confused. "Two therapists will walk her."

*Damnit.* Suzy took a deep breath. *Wrong conclusion, again.*

"Ginny is to walk through that path, holding onto the bars," the petite woman explained. "We've got a gait belt around her waist. She's not going to fall."

Ginny pushed her mask up to her forehead, just over her eyebrows like a visor. "I can wear it like this." Ginny wanted it her way. "Suzy, watch me."

Suzy's backpack was beginning to stress her shoulders more. *Where were the spectator chairs?* She sat on the floor next to her mother. Suzy was in black slacks, a blue blouse, and a black sweater to hide her weight gain. *This is a mistake,* she realized, almost as soon as she sat on the waxed surface. Hunched over in an Indian squat, her ankles rubbing the hard floor, she felt ape-like. She tried to move both legs to one side. That was worse. She felt a muscle pull and briskly went back to the cross-legged squat. She glanced up at Ginny. She appeared to be wheezing. Suzy hadn't noticed that before.

"Mom, are you breathing okay?" Suzy inquired.

The therapist touched Ginny's back. "We're next."

Suzy looked at the clock. "How long?"

Ginny's mouth gaped, childlike. "You promised."

"I'm here." Suzy observed the other determined patients. She was certain her ankles, along with her butt bone, were denting the floor. She watched Ginny. Her mother was winded even when she was just sitting.

Ginny's therapist looked up from her phone and stood. She didn't wait for Suzy. She pushed Ginny's wheelchair to the entry of the bars and waved a male therapist over.

Suzy got on her hands and knees to try to get up. She looked across the room and saw Wisner wave. He was next to an elderly man who had barely moved the pedals of a stationary bicycle. *Fucking hell.* She wanted to shoot him the bird, but he seemed genuine. She took a deep breath and prayed to God she could get up. Quickly. *Maybe she needed rehab?* There was nothing to grab. She was certain at this angle and momentum she might fall forward and take a patient down with her. Plan B: crawl to the nearest wall for support.

"Are you watching, Suzy?" Ginny called out.

*Are you?* "Yes," Suzy grunted as she stood. She was up. *Where are the Olympic judges? That was a solid 8.* She tried not to look at Wisner as she shuffled over to her mother. A walker looked great right about now.

The two therapists got Ginny to her feet. They pulled the wheelchair away. Ginny panicked and tried to sit back down. They held her belt up and encouraged her to take a step.

"I'm watching," Suzy emphasized.

Ginny took her first steps. She paused. The whole room stopped to watch.

Wisner came over. "Great job, Ginny."

Ginny perked up.

Suzy wanted to deck him. Her own legs were finally recovering.

"Suzy, are you watching?" Her mother's voice sounded especially feeble now that she had an audience.

"Yes, Mom," droned Suzy. Wisner was in her personal space. "You're almost to the end," came out sounding morbid instead of encouraging.

Wisner turned and gave Suzy an "atta girl, Ginny" wink.

This made Suzy's nostrils flair. She wanted to punch him in the face.

Ginny's reward was a wheelchair break.

"Are you okay?" Dr. Wisner asked Suzy.

"Why do people say that?" Suzy glared at him. "I'm a little out of shape."

His eyes searched hers. She felt an awkward blush take hold.

"I meant from the other day," he said.

Suzy held a hand up. She pointed to her mother. Eagle ears was listening.

He nodded.

Suzy turned to Ginny's therapists. "Are we done?"

"No," the therapists said in unison.

Wisner walked away.

Ginny called for Suzy, "Is that the nice man who came to my room?"

Suzy didn't bother to fake nice. "It is."

"What's wrong, Suzy? He sounds so nice." Ginny's tone was now Olivia de Haviland's Miriam in *Hush, Hush Sweet Charlotte*, which made Suzy, Charlotte. Bette Davis crazy.

*Not taking the bait.* Suzy grit her teeth.

The therapists reminded Ginny it was time to stand again.

*Perfect.* "I've got to get back to work." Suzy gave Ginny a pat on top of her head. "I'll come tonight. We'll write your story."

Ginny reached for Suzy. "I'm afraid."

"Of what?" Suzy rolled her eyes. The other families in the room found Suzy unkind, or so Suzy thought. She wanted to hiss at all of them.

Ginny whispered, but Suzy couldn't make out what her mother said.

This time, Suzy caught Wisner's concern. He seemed to understand Ginny.

Suzy mumbled to her mother, "See you later."

She left with a lump in her throat. Her eyes watered. Why couldn't she be calm and enjoy a moment?

Wisner caught Suzy by the elevator. "How about a coffee?"

*Really. And answer 50 questions about elder abuse?* "No, thank you." She stepped into the elevator and pushed the button to go down. She felt ugly, mean, misunderstood, and now her neck was turning to concrete.

When she finally reached the outside, Florida humidity hit her in the face. It brought the realization that Ginny was not normal. Granted, her mother got on her nerves at times, but where was the fun woman who loved home shopping, reading historical novels, watching *America's Most Wanted*, and playing rummy? Could she get the old Ginny back?

She passed Dr. Wisner's stalker van, grateful she had turned down the coffee. *Who are you? A coffee date?* Surely he wasn't attracted to the grunting gorilla who could barely get off the floor.

Suzy's cellphone rang. She answered. It seemed she was always working, driving, eating on the run, or managing her mother's needs. She got into her car.

"Hey, daughter." She loved it when Chloe called. "What are you doing?"

Suzy put the call on speaker and placed the cellphone in the console. Suzy's 1999 silver Honda Civic had once belonged to a teenager, Blair Carlisle. The Carlisle family sold the car to Suzy before they moved to New York. They told Suzy they had the car blessed when Blair bought it secondhand in 2007. Suzy wasn't particularly religious, but she figured it certainly couldn't hurt. But where was God now? Was he watching out for Ginny?

The sedan's paint was fading. It had 115,000 miles, give or take, an automatic transmission, and only needed oil changes, tires, brakes, and A/C repairs. She considered giving the car to Chloe but bought her daughter a new vehicle with a warranty. Suzy didn't need another loan, but Chloe needed reliable transportation.

Suzy drove the backstreets. She never understood the fascination with getting somewhere fast. Safety was underrated.

She bit into a stale French fry. A grease-soaked white paper bag contained the remnants of her lunch.

"Amazing"—Suzy was impressed with Chloe's maturity—"a full scholarship!" She was addled, but also relieved by Chloe's news. Suzy had just refinanced Ginny's place to get Chloe's first-year tuition. Maybe she could put that money back into paying off the loan. "What foundation or charity is behind your scholarship?"

Chloe rambled. She wasn't exactly sure. She'd find out. The counselor told her, but she really didn't pay much attention. She also had a new boyfriend, and they were going to take a road trip for Thanksgiving.

That was news to Suzy. "Tell me his name." Suzy was excited, but also concerned. "Send me his address and phone number, too. I want to run a background check on him."

Chloe laughed. "No. He goes by Damien and he's a nice guy. You have to have confidence in my judgement."

*Damien! The Omen!* Suzy slammed on her brakes. She had almost rear-ended the car in front of her. The remains of her fries scattered on the passenger side floor, along with her phone. She knew Chloe. Her daughter wouldn't reveal anything now. "How old is he?" Suzy shouted. She knew she couldn't reach the phone with her seatbelt on. "What's he studying?"

Chloe went silent. Suzy assumed she disconnected the call.

Chloe came back with, "Hey, I can barely hear you. We're together. I've got to go."

*Damn it!* Suzy understood. "Okay."

"You're breaking up," Chloe said.

*I wish you were. You don't need a boyfriend now.* Suzy shouted, "My phone is on the floor of the car. Call me later. Love you."

Chloe mumbled, or it sounded that way, "You, too."

Suzy looked for a place to pull off and grab her phone. *Now what?*

# CHAPTER 5

Arnold pulled up a chair and patted it. "I've been looking at public assistance in Romeo." He wanted Suzy to have a look at his computer.

"Why?" Suzy walked over. "If you show me some Marx Brothers clip, I'm going to kill you."

"You ruined the surprise," Arnold pouted.

He gave her the darting eye and his best Groucho impression: "Wouldn't you like to know, Ms. Lennox."

Suzy sat in the vacant chair and looked at the screen. "I don't follow. What am I looking at?"

Arnold nodded. "It mentions Romeo, Florida."

Suzy's eyes narrowed. "That's a Google search for 'public assistance in Romeo, Florida.'" She hit enter. The screen scrolled with results.

Arnold watched Suzy. Neither spoke; it was as if one had touched the other inappropriately.

"You're not really reading, are you?" he mumbled.

Neighboring city searches listed clinics. Suzy glanced at the results. "Not much there. But I knew that."

Arnold closed his laptop. "Isn't Ginny heading home soon?"

*Was he trying to refocus her? What exactly was he getting at? Implying?* She pursed her lips, then scratched her head with both hands exasperatedly.

"Stop, Suzy." Arnold placed a hand over his mouth and gushed, "That tousled hair pouty face is too much."

She ignored him. "Are you hinting at something related to Ginny? Spit it out."

He slapped playfully at her hand. "How's Ginny's story coming along?"

*Please. I know your diversion tactics.*

Arnold gave her a big grin. "We can discuss over an empanada. They say there's nothing a good empanada can't cure. You'd think the cancer doctors would catch on."

Suzy got up and walked out. "I'm not in the mood today."

"For empanadas?"

"For you."

"Then you *really* need an empanada."

Ginny was tucked in bed with her hospital gown and eye mask on. Suzy had brought her iPad and some snacks. The troll had been discharged, and a nice, quiet, sedated woman about Suzy's age was now sharing the room with Ginny.

Suzy sat and tried to keep her voice down. She shook her mother. "How do you feel? I'm ready to write your story. I brought my tablet."

She put her backpack on the floor, pulled the tablet out, grabbed a few almonds from a Ziplock bag, and began to chew. *How do I gain weight? I barely eat anything.*

Ginny's feeble hands pushed the mask up part of the way. She stared past Suzy. She sounded frail, but sweeter, more like the Ginny who had taught her to crochet and embroider. "Something's wrong," she whisper-talked.

Suzy could see by her mother's lack of expression that this wasn't recovery.

Ginny's eyes were a little bloodshot. Her breathing was shallow, and her lips trembled. There was no smile in her.

"How do you feel?" Suzy asked.

"Like I will lose my mind."

Suzy took her mother's left hand and kissed it. "How could you lose your mind?" She tried a lighthearted tone, hoping Ginny would mirror her.

"The Snake Pit." Ginny held Suzy's hand.

A tear spotted Suzy's pink t-shirt. Her nose was running. "Snake Pit?" There was something innately wrong. Suzy felt it in her mother's grip. Something was crushing her spirit.

"The movie..." Ginny motioned with her right hand. Her long semi-arthritic fingers brushed the air. "Olivia de Haviland, she plays a woman... who goes the hospital and loses her mind."

Suzy felt a tremor in her own smile. She wasn't certain why her mother always drew comparisons with the actress, but it was apparent they both did. "I've never seen it."

"They wouldn't let her out." Ginny squeezed Suzy's hand tighter. "They tricked her."

"Mom, how do you remember this movie, and not remember being tied down?"

Ginny shook her head. "The medicine," she whispered. "Don't leave me here."

Her mother was usually directing things, fun and demanding, but not vulnerable. Suzy needed to distract her mother and get answers.

"Did something happen a long time ago? Tell me about that." Suzy brushed the hair from her mother's face. "I'm going to type on my tablet like you asked me to."

Ginny pushed the mask down with her bruised right I.V. hand. "Your birth," Ginny muttered.

Suzy found an outlet for the tablet. She didn't want to search for it if the battery needed to be charged later.

She heard a familiar squishing sound. Nurse Larsen came in with a small tray of Ginny and her roommate's meds.

"What are you giving her?" Suzy tried to sound nice, but it came off as accusing.

The nurse rattled off a fast list.

"What are they for?" Suzy wanted an explanation of each.

Her mother barely took more than a blood pressure med, an aspirin, and a multi-vitamin. Ginny obsessively read warning labels and avoided anything that sounded even remotely like it would maim or debilitate her. Suzy thought it was an absurd habit.

Eight or more jeweled caplets and opaque stone pills made up the tray of pharmaceuticals.

"That's a lot." Suzy's brows knit together.

"You can have a list. Just come to the nurse's station." Larsen positioned Ginny's bed upright for easier swallowing. She dumped the gems into a thimble-sized paper cup and opened an unrefrigerated pudding pack. The manufactured pills were poured into the artificially sweetened pudding and fed to Ginny.

*A regular Mary Poppins,* Suzy thought. *Just a spoonful of…*

When Larsen finished, she put a straw to Ginny's mouth. "You need to drink more water," Larsen encouraged.

"Thank you," Suzy said when the nurse finished. *More bees with honey.* She needed that med list!

Larsen mumbled, *You're welcome,* or so Suzy assumed. The nurse lowered Ginny's bed and took the remaining meds to the woman in the next bed.

Suzy patted Ginny on the hand. "Let's get to writing."

Ginny muttered, "Don't leave me in the snake pit."

Suzy heard the lady in the next bed laughing and lauding the pain meds. She and the nurse sounded like best friends.

*When had she stopped being fun? A lifetime ago.*

Ginny yawned. "I don't know if this is a good idea, Suzy. I'm feeling sleepy."

Suzy wondered about the meds. "If you fall asleep, we'll do more tomorrow."

Ginny stammered, "I never knew your father..." She sobbed softly. "It happened so fast."

Suzy felt a hot knot form in her throat. She understood. She didn't know Chloe's biological father, either. She and Ginny had never really talked about it. Fun Suzy had met a guy at an Ocala Econo Motel bar. Too many Tom Collins led to a musty-smelling motel room. Sweet cocktails were her drug of choice, which made her dance seductively and crave sex way too much. She remembered going to the room with him. She sang Donna Summer's *Last Dance* as they walked down the stained patterned carpet leading to room 111. He carried her shoes and purse. She felt dizzy. Once in the room, he took off his clothes, hers, then got on top of her. She woke up alone the next day.

The clerk said Mr. Lennox paid for the room. She didn't ask for Mr. Lennox's full name. It didn't make any sense. Suzy had probably given her own name to the clerk in a drunken stupor. She drove home and never told Ginny what happened.

Nine months later, Chloe was born.

"It's okay, Mom. We both let a one-night stand change our life. It's not all bad. We have each other, and I have Chloe."

Ginny wailed loudly.

"Shh!" Suzy fully expected Frank Wisner, M.D., to show up in a Superman cape.

The roommate snored loudly. Suzy was grateful she hadn't been startled awake.

Ginny's mouth hung open in a voiceless cry.

"Breathe." Suzy patted her mother's hand and closed Ginny's mouth. "Breathe through your nose. Deep breaths."

Ginny complied. It seemed like an eternity, the deep breaths. Suzy listened for squishing or knocking. All she heard was the roommates snoring. Her own head began to ache.

Ginny's breathing became even.

"Okay, Mom, I need to understand." She shook Ginny to keep her from dozing. "There will be no snake pits and no shame or guilt. We are both single mothers." Suzy typed out what had just transpired.

Ginny went from emotional to frank. "I was part of a government experiment."

Suzy's head flew back. "What?" She stopped typing.

"You are, too." Ginny put her hand on her heart.

"Wait." Suzy wanted to get this straight.

"I'm the second Virginia," her mother blurted.

*Two Virginias?*

"I replaced her dead baby." Ginny was inconsolable now. Her cries were muted as she choked back emotion. She covered her face with feeble hands.

Suzy stared. *Need that med list. Stat!* "Breathe, mom." Suzy typed. "Who is *her*? Grandma? You replaced what baby?" Suzy paused, put the tablet on the chair, and hugged her mother. She stayed in a stooped position until she felt Ginny relax. A new rope-like tension rose in Suzy's spine. She needed a massage in the worst way. *Or a pudding cup of pills.* The roommate snored on cue. Suzy sighed.

Just like that, Ginny was calm again, as if a naughty secret had made her joyful. "I've never told a soul." A tear escaped her mask and streamed down her thin pale temple. "I feel so much better."

*I don't.* Suzy had never experienced a migraine before. Was that what she was experiencing now? Her eyes wouldn't focus. She saw jagged starbursts. She blinked several times. "Who is the *her* you mentioned. The other Virgina? How am I part of ...? I do government data. This makes no sense."

"I'm sorry, Suzy. Your father was a Vietnam Vet."

Suzy wasn't sure what the military had to do with any of this.

"They are watching you." Ginny reached out for Suzy's hand. She found her forearm and patted it.

Suzy sat back down and closed the tablet. She had heard "watching you" in a burst of clarity, like a movie zoom-in realization.

"Desert Storm," Suzy said. She was having a moment of déjà vu.

Ginny shook her head. "Vietnam, Suzy. Are you listening?" Her mother had the accusing tone of an inconvenienced parent listening to the nightly news being suddenly interrupted by her high schooler wanting homework assistance.

Suzy was transported to a slow dance at The Econo Motel Bar when he spoke. "I was in Desert Storm," Suzy recalled out loud. Her heart raced. *I don't know his name. Oh my God! How did I dredge that up?*

"You were not in Desert Storm, Suzy."

Suzy was having a multi-dimensional experience. She was here and yet she was at the Econo Motel. Now she wanted to cry.

Ginny blathered on with dry facts, "I consented to have you."

*Stop talking. I'm not listening.* Suzy tried to see Chloe's dad. It wasn't working.

"I wanted you and, I didn't." Ginny was business-like now. "Are you typing?"

"You wanted an abortion?" Suzy muttered. *I wouldn't be dealing with this if you had.* All she could think about was Desert Storm and trying to see his face.

Ginny nodded. "You're not typing."

"Who are *they*?" Suzy asked.

Ginny shivered. "I'm not supposed to say. I don't want *you* to get hurt. Are you writing?" She pulled the mask up to squint at Suzy.

*I thought the pills were making you drowsy, Miss Demanding.* Suzy moved out of the Econo Motel to the present. "I'm here. I was born.

No one is going to hurt me. Remember, I work on government contracts…I think you are right. The meds are messing with you."

Ginny pulled the mask down. "You need to write…"

Suzy mocked, "You need to write. Give me a chance to understand."

Ginny whimpered, "You're going to leave me here."

*I might. Not really.* Suzy turned around, fully expecting someone to be there. "You're mixing up what I do for a living with whatever you and my biological dad did." She turned back to Ginny. *Arnold was right, the meds are talking.*

"The first Virginia died," Ginny sobbed. "They wanted another. I don't deserve my own name. I'm Virginia's ghost."

Suzy tried to make sense of it. "If there were two of you, she would be the ghost. You're here."

Ginny was quiet, then a smile formed. "You're right."

Suzy had no clue what her mother was talking about. "Were you a twin?'

"I was born 23 years after her!" Ginny was now indignant. "Aren't you listening?"

Suzy threw her hands up.

"You think this is comical." Ginny's voice shifted to a stronger, angrier tone.

*No, I don't.* "Mom, you act like I somehow know what you're talking about. Give me a break."

Ginny was incensed. "Women didn't talk about these things."

"Grandma had two daughters named Virgina. It does suck that you were named after the first one."

Ginny crossed her arms. "I'm sorry I brought this up."

"Mom, I'm not. Let's continue. I'm hearing this for the first time, and you have to admit this is kind of weird circumstances."

"Go home, Suzy."

"Ok, soon enough. I'll let you sleep this off." Suzy got her phone out and took some pictures of Ginny. She needed to document this. Her phone dinged.

Chloe's text: `I'm considering one of those DNA tests. We should get one for you and grandma, too.`

Suzy really had a headache now. She looked at her mother.

Suzy's text: `You sure?`

Chloe's text: `Why not?`

Suzy's text: `Let's talk later. I'm with Grandma.`

"Did you ask the nurse to tie you down?" Suzy wanted a straight answer from her mother.

Ginny nodded.

"When was the first time you were tied down?"

"I was pregnant with you. They didn't want me to run off." Ginny sobbed loudly.

*That's disgusting!* "Who are *they*?"

Ginny reached for Suzy's hand. "I can't."

"Breathe, Mom. It will free your mind."

Suzy opened her tablet and typed. "Where did this happen?"

Ginny covered her mask with both hands. She whispered, "The clinic for unwed mothers. Near Panther Creek. The government watched us."

"You told me when I was old enough to drive that grandmother took you to a clinic in Panther Creek. Grandmother Monica also went there, but it wasn't a clinic for unwed mothers. It was for the poor."

"We were poor. Poor women."

"You mean poor people?" Suzy clarified.

"They studied poor women... the doctors, with their medicines, their foods... to raise our children." Ginny grabbed for Suzy's hand. "I'm sorry, honey."

*People knew me before I was born?*

Ginny whispered, "They're watching you."

Suzy whispered back, "No, they aren't."

She could see how guilty thoughts might surface under heavy meds. "Do the exercises, Mom, so you can go home."

Ginny whispered, "Dr. Smith's son said I have to rest before I can walk."

"His name is Smithson."

"What did I say?" Ginny asked.

"You said Dr. Smith's son. It's Smithson."

"That's what I said." Ginny was agitated.

"Never mind, when did you see him?" Suzy heard nothing from the doctor or anyone about this.

"He came to see me exercise." Ginny rested her arms by her sides. "You were gone."

Suzy was suspicious. *I'll call him in the morning.* "Do you want to keep writing?"

Ginny yawned. "Tomorrow."

# CHAPTER 6

**1920 Victory Theatre, Tampa**

Monica and her fellow David's Church parishioners were gathered at the corner of Tampa and Zack Street outside the newly opened Victory Theatre. Lou and Joe wanted to take Monica to the cinema, but her church's elders wouldn't hear of it. Instead, the pair treated their whole group. The men coordinated the trolley fare from Sulphur Springs to downtown Tampa, as well as their movie tickets to the newly released silent film, *Way Down East*.

Monica eyed the poster. It showed an unconscious woman on a rapid flowing sheet of ice, one hand in the river, being pursued by a man on an approaching ice block.

"I've never been to the picture show," Monica spoke softly. Her hair was up, and she had changed back into her mid-length cotton day dress with a lace hem. She had only packed for their picnic lunch and swimming.

Lou ribbed Joe and muttered, "This one's got to be a virgin."

Joe nodded his head. "Shh! You are talking about my future wife. She'd better be."

Lou slapped Joe's back. "The pastor's right there. Whenever you're ready."

Monica walked over. "Boys?" She smiled quizzically.

Lou leaned on Joe. "Joe's sweet on you."

She blushed.

Harlan Welch, the church deacon, abruptly turned and approached Joe. "I beg your pardon." He motioned for Monica to join the women.

Lou sighed. "Joe's harmless." He apologized to the elder.

"He's not." Joe pointed to Lou. They both snickered but stopped when they saw several of the womenfolk shaking their heads.

Lou cleared his throat. "Deacon, forgive me for any offense. Joe and I are family, businessmen, and often clowns. We mean no disrespect." Lou dug his hands into his pockets and gave his sharp focus to Deacon Welch.

Monica cleared her throat and moved closer to the church leader. "Deacon, I told the boys I've not seen motion pictures." She turned to face the cousins. "I've been to tent rivals and the circus." Her wide soulful eyes were hopeful. "Thank you for sharing your kindness with our church."

Welch shook a finger at the guys. "No funny business, you hear. We can just as easily return home now as accept your generosity. Monica, you'll sit with the women. Men, you'll join me."

Joe crossed his eyes at Monica.

She giggled.

Lou pretended to strangle Joe when Harlan wasn't looking.

"Absolutely." Lou followed the deacon. "Joe, here, was just saying he felt a religious stirring. Didn't you?"

Joe didn't miss a beat. "As a matter of fact, I did." He did his best Charlie Chaplin tramp walk behind Harlan. He winked at Monica.

Suzy munched on a Dove dark chocolate as she ran a bath. She needed to unwind with her magazines and distract herself. She read the side of the Epsom salt container. A cup should: Reduce tension and inflammation. Relieve swelling. May have a laxative effect. *Great, tense people are full of shit.*

She grabbed a bath pillow package and bit through the cellophane. The new plastic smell reached her nostrils as she squeezed the nipple and began blowing. She wished she had two pillows or one large one. It seemed she was either pitching forward or trying to stretch backward.

She caught her naked Rubenesque figure in the mirror. *Were Baroque women pressured to look full-figured?*

She tossed the inflated pillow into the running water, then walked to her den for a footstool. Her vertical blinds were drawn. It was dark, no lights on. Ginny had always warned her to keep the lights off if she didn't want people to see her moving around the house at night, especially if the drapes were open. *Was that the people who were watching?*

Her coffee table was a newsstand of evenly stacked magazines: *Woman's World, Wired, U.S. News, Smithsonian, Money, Home & Garden, Ancient Archaeology, Time,* and *People.*

*Smithson-ian. Dr. Smithson. Hmm.*

Many were still wrapped in plastic and collecting dust. Only four issues of *Home & Garden* left. That was bummer. She grabbed a *Woman's World* and *People*. The rest would have to wait. She didn't need depressing reports, current or ancient. Each vacation she swore to spend the whole time reading, but only seemed to thumb through the gossips and toss them into the recycling as she completed each. She never renewed a subscription, just let it run out. She only bought them when she was guilted by the neighboring office tenants' kids' fundraisers. She just stacked them up as they arrived, with the most recent edition on top.

She stopped in the kitchen and filled a Solo cup with Chablis. She carried it all to the bathroom. She put the stool next to the tub as her table, then put the wine and magazines on top. Hot steam danced on the mirror. The pillow floated on the bath's surface, ready to blow off.

She gulped her white wine. It tasted medicinal versus enjoyable. Bitter wine had replaced the cocktail confections that were her downfall.

She grabbed a washcloth so she could dry her hands while she read. She shut the door and locked it by habit. The tub was too full, and her displacement would flood the trailer floor. She let some water out. The drain instantaneously drank its fill of her Epsom salt solution. She got another cup of salts and plugged the drain. She lowered herself into the tub and started stirring the crystals. The heat felt good. She enjoyed the searing temperature the way she imagined tattoo fanatics relished their pain.

Positioning the pillow behind her neck, she closed her eyes. The darkness was comforting. She thought about Ginny's eye mask fixation. *Where did that really come from?*

The med list! She needed that list. Larsen had left before she had made her way to the nurse's station. The next nurse didn't believe she was Ginny's healthcare surrogate. They argued. Suzy had tossed her driver's license at the woman like a poker player going out. *Okay. That was rude.*

The nurse slowly fished through Ginny's notebook, looking for legal documents. Every patient had a binder. When the nurse finally found Suzy's power of attorney in the reams of papers, she offered to let Suzy copy the med info longhand. *That was total bullshit!*

Jeannette Sanders, LPN, Nurse Number 2, explained that she would photocopy the documents for Suzy to pick up the next day.

*No thanks.* Suzy would take photos with her phone.

Jeannette pointed to the signs that said no cameras allowed in the building, per patient privacy.

The chess match continued.

Suzy agreed to write the info down and fished through her backpack for a receipt or anything to write on.

Sanders placed the thick notebook on the counter and stood next to Suzy. A buzzer rang. Sanders needed to check on a patient.

Suzy assured her that she was trustworthy, but Sanders wouldn't have it. *Poor buzzer patient*, Suzy thought. The buzzing continued. Suzy agreed to pick up a photocopy the next day.

*Check.*

Suzy opened her eyes. *Why the games? What did the nurses have to hide? Why was everything a mystery?* She grabbed the washcloth, dried her hands, and picked up *People Magazine*. Thumbing through the style photos, she marveled at the outlandish prints some actors wore. *Attention hounds. Prints! Eck!*

Which brought her back to LPN Sanders. *Sanders didn't crave attention. She was protecting information. What was that about?*

Suzy thumbed through more photos.

Why was The Valley facility so strange? Or making her feel strange? Or was this modern medicine? Gestapo-like. Where was Florence Nightingale? And Dr. Creepy!

She grabbed her wine and took a gulp. *He was kind of cute.* That was the wine talking. She tossed the magazine and closed her eyes again. The alcohol was working, or the Epsom salts, or both. She focused on the hum of the air conditioning.

She awoke snoring. The water was cold, and she felt goosebumps rising across her bare flesh. She stretched her foot to release the drain.

Her brain connected with a sound in the distance. She looked around. Where was her phone? She sat up. The tub was nearly empty. She grabbed a terrycloth robe and wiped her feet on the bathmat. Her body felt like it had absorbed the tubful of water. It was exhausting to consider a walk across the house.

The ringing stopped. She unlocked and opened the bathroom door and heard a beep. Someone left a message. She persisted. The phone sounded a reminder beep. It was on the counter, next to the wine.

She looked at her phone. Voicemail: `Smithson, Graham 2 min.` It could wait.

She slipped the phone into her robe pocket and shuffled her feet toward the bedroom. Her bedroom was mostly white with black accents. She didn't want to have anything resembling the room she grew up in. It had been a hodgepodge of thrift store items Ginny had collected thrown together with her music posters.

She pulled back the New York, New York comforter. It was her vision board. She had never been there, but she loved the glamourous images of the skyline. Her comforter was just black words in a fancy font on a white overstuffed comforter she'd picked up at a home accessories store.

Fishing out the phone, she played back the recording.

Recording: `Hello Ms. Lennox. This is Dr. Smithson, your mother's doctor. I am returning your call. I missed you on my rounds at The Valley Rehab. I'm happy to discuss your mother's progress and answer any questions you might have. I also ran into a colleague, Dr. Frank Wisner, who alerted me to a concern of yours. Please call me at your earliest convenience on the office line. The afterhours service will connect us.`

*Wisner! Was Ginny telling the truth?* She listened again. She needed to write out her concerns. It wasn't a good idea to wing it. Her work taught her that the unprepared were easily sidetracked.

She grabbed the TV remote. The television screen showed a storm tracker alert of Virginia's progression. *Seriously! Was everything Virginia?* The weatherman reminded all to get their preparations in order. Her mobile home was destined to blow away, according to the meteorologists and hurricane center. Nothing was different from any other storm season.

She turned the TV off.

*What was Wisner up to?*

# CHAPTER 7

Suzy entered the Hungry Lizard. Led Zeppelin's "D'yer Mak'er" was pulsing.

She mouthed the words and scanned the room. This felt like home. She knew a few of the waitresses which made it comfortable for her to go alone. She didn't want a hookup, just a chat with a few barflies and to listen to music.

Gretchen waved at her. She and Gretchen had met during a dental waiting room layover. Neither could find anything to read among the horrid selection of golf, weightlifting, motorsports, home repair, and dental trade publications.

"Hey lady," Gretchen happily shouted over the music.

The brunette barmaid exposed her mid-forties' cheerleader assets with a bend here and a hint of cheek there. She reserved the peek-a-boo cleavage for the big tippers. Her regulars were straight twenty percenters. Gretchen was fit, seductive, ate healthy, and landed dates with articulate, skinny, long-haired vegan bicyclists who modeled for Zen retreats or possibly dabbled in human trafficking.

Suzy and Gretchen air kissed. Time to let her hair down, not think about Ginny or Chloe.

She glanced at the band. A middle-aged Robert Plant-ish lead singer in lowcut hip huggers and an open shirt belted out a convincing falsetto. His gut was a little too full, but he had the voice. The other members were bodily challenged, too, but vocally spot-on.

Gretchen yelled, "There's someone who wants to meet you."

Suzy shook her head. "No thanks."

"He's super cute," Gretchen bounced. "He's your type."

Suzy kinda sorta trusted Gretchen. "Seriously?"

Not that they hung out, other than at 3 a.m. breakfasts with other sobering Lizard patrons.

"Actually, he asked for you." Gretchen nodded.

"The CPA, again?" Suzy sighed.

"Oh, he's here, too!" Gretchen made a baby clap. "Someone else." She was so excited for Suzy.

Suzy looked across the crowded bar and the dark shadows of people gathered at tables. "Who am I looking for?"

"He's waving at you." Gretchen pointed again.

The Budweiser neon was all Suzy could see.

To pacify Gretchen, "How about I say…"—talking super-loud as the band finished—"HELLO." Suzy's *hello* seemed to echo.

A drunk shouted back, "Hello!"

In her peripheral vision, she saw *him*, his thick dark espresso tresses, and short peninsula sideburns. *Wisner!*

Gretchen looped Suzy by the arm before she could turn toward the door.

"How do you know him?" Suzy attempted another tug as Gretchen energetically walked her to Wisner.

He was grinning big. Tipsy. "I figured it was worth a tie."

Wisner seemed very different from the attractive doctor/elder advocate/father encourager she'd met at The Valley.

She was happy to smell him. "You mean try?" His cologne was performing an aroma therapy treatment on her.

Gretchen whispered in her ear, "He was here last night, too."

Suzy's heart raced. Gretchen winked and moved to grab a drink order from the next table.

"Tie," he slapped his paw on the Rolling Stones tie. "I need a Zeppelin."

He sounded super sweet, and she wasn't sure what to think. His smile was infectious.

How had she missed the stalker van in the Lizard parking lot? Not that she was looking for it. She turned around, trying to see her reflection in something. Thankfully, she was wearing her good bra, a slimming long sleeve black knit top, and black jeans. A thin-*ner* appearance for sure. Her hair was freshly washed and flat ironed. Her eyelashes were brushed with two coats of waterproof black mascara and pinched into a reverse umbrella of firmness.

At a loss for what to say, she thought she may as well get down to business. "Dr. Smithson said you spoke with him."

He closed his eyes and nodded.

"Am I supposed to clap or shake your hand?" Suzy shook her head. *Are you trying to look noble? Because you look wasted.*

He gave a sincere belly laugh. A handsome, fun, and thankfully not maniacal one.

Her heart fluttered. She didn't expect it. "What exactly did you say to him?"

Wisner waved his empty glass at Gretchen. He was shaking his head and smiling.

Gretchen nodded to them. She held up two fingers to ask if they both wanted a drink. Suzy gave her a thumbs up.

Suzy squinted as she looked back at him. She wanted to like him, but she felt played. "Did you mention my mother was tied down?"

He touched Suzy's shoulder and leaned in to avoid shouting. "I did. And I couldn't stop thinking about you."

*You're drunk.* Suzy's eyes got big.

He couldn't see her expression. He was breathing on her neck as he spoke. His musk scent and shoulder caresses were firing dormant nerve endings.

*God, you smell good.*

Gretchen squeezed in and handed them their drinks. She pinched Suzy's arm fat.

Suzy gritted her teeth. She hated when Gretchen did that. She loved Gretchen, but the woman had a way of making her feel less attractive.

"Thinking about Ginny?" Suzy corrected Wisner. "You said thinking about *you*, as in me."

Wisner looked her in the eyes and said nothing. Suzy reciprocated by searching his. The microphone squealed and broke the moment. Suzy was not sure if he was feeling remorseful or concerned.

Wisner leaned in again and said, "Not Ginny."

*Drunk.* Now she needed to sit down. His touch. His scent. His voice. His breathing. Suzy sipped her Chablis. "You flirting with me or is this a make-good for how we met?"

He smiled. "Both."

His relaxed body language made her give him the once over. She wondered if he noticed. Suzy looked around, expecting to see a pool of doctors hooting at a dare. She really needed to sit. This was not what she expected, but then again, she didn't expect him to admit he was flirting with her.

The band started.

"Stairway to Heaven," Suzy called out.

He motioned toward the band. "Do you want to dance?"

*God, no.* "No." She was sure. Where the hell was Gretchen?

It was too early for a mating dance.

He spied a small table in the corner of the bar well away from the speakers. He pointed and Suzy followed. They listened to the music awhile, just sipping and grooving. Then a thought popped in her head.

"Malpractice," she blurted.

He looked confused.

She clarified, tapping the table, "Was tying Mom down malpractice?" She was shouting in his ear.

"Excuse me." This broke his cheer.

Suzy looked into his sad eyes. "Put yourself in my shoes."

"I have." He took a long pull of his drink. "If you feel there's been a breech in care, please, do what you have to do," he punctuated. "I've not witnessed anything but your frustration with your mother."

*Damn!* That stung. Her eyes watered. *Protect your profession.*

Gretchen popped over and squatted down. Ever cheerful, "What's shakin, guys?"

Wisner gave her a sweet smile. He was able to switch gears easily, but that was always the case when males encountered Gretchen. "Getting to know Suzy. How about you?"

Gretchen loved to talk about herself and the room. "Well, a senator guy tipped me $100 for sharing my opinion on some women's issues. Not like I'm voting for him or actually vote."

"Could be a nice guy, even though he is a senator." Wisner finished his drink and gave Suzy a half sneer. "How about a water?" He pushed the short tumbler to Gretchen.

Gretchen stood, grabbed the glass, and laughed. "He could buy the whole place a round if he wanted."

"That sounds like a group DUI-in-the-making," Suzy scoffed.

Wisner sighed. "Gretchen, I've got an early morning. Skip the water." He loosened his tie, grabbed a couple of twenties, and pushed them to Gretchen. "Good night, Suzy. Gretchen." He got up to leave.

Suzy held up her Chablis. *Whatever.* "See you around The Valley."

Gretchen left them to it.

He half smiled, took it in stride. "I suppose." He turned.

"Black Dog" started, and Suzy let the wine take her. She began singing and bouncing to the tune, not realizing he was still there. He didn't leave, just watched the transformation.

Suzy belted back the rest of her drink and looked for Gretchen but didn't miss a Zeppelin beat. She began snapping her fingers and lap dancing her chair. Wisner was mesmerized but dodged out as the song ended.

On her break, Gretchen sat in his spot and gave Suzy a *holy shit* look. "You tied him in knots!"

By then Suzy needed a taxi. "Huh?"

Gretchen was dying. "He watched you get off on 'Black Dog' before he left."

Suzy rolled her head and thought. "No, he didn't."

"Oh yes, he did." Gretchen slapped the table. "It's game on."

Suzy squinted.

Gretchen pinched Suzy's arm fat. "I'm getting horny just thinking about you two."

Suzy pulled away. "You need to calm down."

Gretchen squealed, "Oh my God, he's the one!"

Suzy pointed to her chest. "I'm the one."

Gretchen's mouth flew open. "You are! He ate you up grinding that chair."

Suzy thought about it. Gretchen always exaggerated.

Gretchen looked at the clock. "Are we doing breakfast?"

Suzy needed to sober up. It was hours from closing time. "I gotta go."

"Get an Uber."

"I can't." Suzy frowned. "I threw up the last time. Not pretty."

Gretchen winked. "The CPA is barely drinking. He could give you a ride. You know he would!"

"I'd rather walk." Suzy sobered a tad. "Do you have a cot in the office or something?"

"I'll walk you to your car and take the keys." Gretchen was inspired. "Just kick the seat back and sleep it off. I'll get you up when we go to IHOP."

Suzy shrugged.

Arnold walked in. "The complex said we need to leave while they do storm prep."

Suzy fidgeted with her desk phone, awaiting a connection with Smithson. She held up a finger. She thought she heard a click connecting her, then it went to music. "What's the plan?"

Arnold wore his laptop bag, a Marlins cap, a Hawaiian shirt, and plaid shorts. "Going to a hotel. No one is going to talk to us. They're all prepping, too. Virginia is headed straight for us."

Suzy shook her head. *Virginia!*

Arnold moved the bag to his other shoulder. "She's supposed to cut across the state and head to the Carolinas. If you haven't bought water, snacks, or gas, you're going to be relying on Domino's. There's nothing. The whole county freaked as usual. But you can always count on the pie guys."

"Hello," the speaker called out.

Relief. Suzy picked up.

Arnold saluted and left.

"Dr. Smithson"—Suzy tried to sound cheerful—"I feel like I won the lottery."

He chuckled. "How can I help?"

"Where to begin?" Suzy fished around for her list of questions, realizing she dialed before she pulled them out of her bag. She didn't expect him to answer this soon. She grabbed her bag and tried to wing it.

"What's the plan for Mom's recovery?" She tried each zipper and found no questions.

"She's not recovering as fast as we'd like. She does have Medicare and Medicaid, so she's good for up to 21 days, if need be, to work on rehabbing the knee." He went on with exercise options for when she returned home or went to assisted living.

"Assisted living?" Suzy wasn't sure why he said that.

"She lives alone?" Smithson questioned.

"Yes, but we're going to have someone come in."

"Her social worker will make an in-home assessment then."

*In home assessment? You should have done that before she had the surgery.* Suzy's mind was reeling. *Snake Pit.* What did her mother say? She jotted on a Post-it, *Order Snake Pit.* "What about her light sensitivity and wearing a blackout mask?"

"That should pass. It's not something we've seen in other patients, but your mother does seem anxious. The physician on-call ordered something to help that subside." Smithson was confident.

*On-call?* "Who is the on-call physician?"

"Depends on the shift and day. This was Dr. Pham."

Suzy fished around again. Still no paper in her bag. "What did Dr. Wisner recommend?"

Smithson cleared his throat. She felt there was an inside joke she was missing. "He mentioned some of your same concerns. Said he was on the floor to see his father and assisted you. Felt obliged to share."

*Right. You're both so reasonable.*

"Our office staff will check in with The Valley during the storm, so feel free to reach out. Your mother is in the best hands. The Valley has generators, elevation, and hurricane windows. We should *all* be so safe. I'll check back before our next assessment. Anything else?" Smithson closed the call.

Suzy hung up and saw the questions tucked into the corner of her desk mat. First question. *Why was Mom tied down?* "Seriously?!" She wadded the whole thing up and pitched it.

Chloe texted Suzy that she and Damien were hosting a hurricane party. They would go to the student union hall if things got bad over the weekend.

Where would Suzy go?

Romeo. She needed to put Ginny's storm panels up. She'd stay there. *What did Arnold say about gas and water?*

Jamal knocked on her office's window. He pressed a paper on the glass for her to read. "Vacate The Premises. Make Your Storm Preparations. Offices Should Reopen Monday."

Suzy held up her keys and nodded. She would be leaving soon.

He gave her a thumbs up.

She then looked at the Post-it, pulled out her phone, and ordered the movie *Snake Pit* from Amazon.

## 1920 Victory Theatre, Tampa

C.D. Cooley, the Victory's President and General Manager recognized Lou and led their group to box seats on the right side of the elevated posh interior. "I understand you are staying at the Tampa Bay Hotel. Please let us know if your group would like to attend one of our vaudeville shows this week."

Deacon Harlan shook his head. "We'll be on our way after the show. Thank you."

Joe raised his eyebrows to Lou. They found the religious man rather stuffy.

Lou shook Cooley's hand. "Thank you for the kind offer. The deacon is correct. Their group will leave once the show is over." He gave Harlan a rigid nod. "However, I have business associates coming in from New York who look forward to Keith's show. I understand he has some new acts."

"The best vaudeville has to offer! You will be delighted. Very good sir, we look forward to accommodating you." Cooley grinned.

Lou introduced the theater proprietor to their party. The women sat in one box and the men in another. "Mr. Cooley runs this fine establishment. He would appreciate your undivided attention. Please." Lou sat.

"Welcome," Cooley acknowledged everyone sitting in the boxes, balcony, and mezzanine. "It is a privilege to welcome our esteemed guest"—he pointed to Lou—"visitors, and fellow Tampans to the very best in theatrical entertainment. Not only will we be bringing you first class live shows, but as theatergoers you'll experience today the newest silent film hit with a pipe organ and orchestra accompaniment like none in the south. For your comfort, the Victory's installed a typhoon ventilation system with ten-foot fans pulling air through ducts under each row of seats."

A murmuring of audience approval paused Cooley's presentation.

He continued with greater enthusiasm. "Sure to keep the Florida heat out, and if there are any questions about safety, the entire building is completely fire-proof. Please, look around, from the ceiling adornments to the balcony and mezzanine décor." He motioned. "Luxurious velour drapes in our boxes. No expense has been spared. And ladies, you'll want to check out the powder room with its dressing tables, comfortable lounge seating, opulent mirrors and complimentary toiletries should you need to refresh your pretty nose," he said directly to Monica. "And there's more. We even have lavatories." He chuckled heartily and the group chimed in.

Monica blushed and waved to Joe. They were in separate tiered boxes.

Joe put two fingers behind the deacon's head.

Monica mouthed, "Rabbit ears." She giggled. She wasn't certain what made Lou important, as they never got around to discussing serious things when they were careening down the water toboggan, but she was certain to ask before she went home. As it was, he and Joe were amusingly handsome suitors, and she was feeling quite smitten with Joe.

She looked at the blue, gray, and gold interior design elements Mr. Cooley had pointed out. Tall columns supported the 1600-seat auditorium. This was a place meant for royalty, she was certain. And she'd never seen a real orchestra before. There were so many more instruments than the small bands that performed at town squares. This was like a place she'd read about in a romantic English novel, where kings and queens entertained the country folk, from the honored to the common to the completely naïve. At present, they were all together to take their minds off the worries of the day, the heat, and to connect for an intriguing Hollywood show.

Monica whispered to the woman next her, "Did you see the marquee poster? The damsel in distress. It's incredibly remarkable. I just can't imagine a woman alone in such harrowing circumstances."

Suzy went home and grabbed a jar of peanut butter, some crackers, nuts, a six pack of Gatorade, and put some tap water in a wine carafe. She also stuffed a few outfits in a tote: pajamas and a couple of changes of clothes. Something to get dirty in, something to wait it out in, something to go home in, plus a stack of magazines. Done.

As she drove to Romeo, the rain and wind started picking up. She passed long lines at gas stations. She looked at her gas gauge. *Half empty.* She'd find gas or figure it out in a few days. Half would get her there. If the power went out and the gas ran out, she'd be cleaning Ginny's yard and reading for a few days. Nothing she hadn't experienced before. AAA could bring gas.

Flashing lights and brake lights dotted the long highway exodus. She turned the radio on. Repetitious storm news.

Everyone stopped, and she turned off the car. The Civic was one unlit piece on the U.S. 19 Lite-Brite board.

Smithson's comment chided her. He said Ginny needed time to recover. Ginny had misinterpreted it as, "Dr. Smith's son said I have to rest before I can walk."

Maybe the nurses misjudged Ginny? Maybe Smithson's patient interaction differed from his orders to the nurses? *Maybe they all needed to work from the same damn translation.*

Suzy's phone rang. "Gretchen" lit her phone display.

"Hi, Gretch."

"Hey." Gretchen was at the bar. Suzy could hear the crowd. "He's back."

Suzy rolled her window down and let a little rain in. "Good for him." She knew Gretchen meant Wisner.

Gretchen loved relationship melodrama. "The senator guy is here, too."

"I'm stuck on 19. Heading out to board up my mother's place." She let the rain wash over her face, holding the phone inside.

"He's having dinner at the bar. Sooo damn cute," Gretch shouted.

*What's he eating?* She was so hungry. "The doctor or the senator? Don't tell me what he's eating, or you'll be responsible for road rage." A downpour blasted Suzy's face. She coughed. Closed the window. Restarted the car. Wiped her face with her shirt.

Gretchen shouted, "Frankie."

Suzy hated cute nicknames. Frank Wisner was good enough for her.

"Turn around," Gretchen pleaded. "We're having a hurricane party."

No one was moving. Now she was below half, but above a quarter tank.

"Tell Dr. Creepy I said hello," Suzy snarked. "He's really there to see you, Gretch. Everyone is."

"Creepy here," Wisner said. "She handed me the phone."

"Your stalker van earned you the Creepy title… in case you're wondering. I saw it at The Valley." She cranked up the A/C, then immediately shut it off, realizing she might run out of gas.

"You think the wheelchair lift is a ruse?" He laughed.

Lightning streaked across the highway in the distance. "Don't get me overthinking." Suzy hadn't considered that.

He shouted as the background noise grew, "Are you on your way?"

"Stuck in traffic. Someone's got to board up Ginny's place."

"Can I help?" Wisner shot back.

*Awe.* Suzy's heart started a conga with her lungs. "Heading to Romeo."

"That a person or place?"

*Helpful men are not attracted to me. Who the hell do you think you are?*

"My phone's about to die," Gretchen shouted at Suzy. "I'll …"
Then nothing.

Suzy's phone rang back. Unlisted.

If it were Wisner, he'd just have to leave a message. Two can play
that game. She waited for a voicemail alert.

Nothing.

*Asshole.*

A car horn startled her into the realization everyone was moving. It
was now getting darker, and the ditches were filling up.

# CHAPTER 8

When she arrived at Ginny's, it was several hours later than she had expected, and she couldn't wait to stretch on the sofa. Her headlights swept the house as she pulled into the gravel drive.

"What the...?" She saw the windows were shuttered and two wide green boards were nailed across the doorway in an X. "Fuck!" she screamed.

*Was she at the right house?* She looked around. It was Ginny's.

Lightning shot across the sky. Thunderclaps sent her arms upward. She got out. Rain pelted her in stabbing sheets as she ran to the porch. She tugged at the boards. "Shit." They wouldn't budge. She went around the back, but not before one foot sank in sludge and gave her ankle a turn. The back door was nailed shut, too. She shrieked, "What the fuck!?"

Suzy turned to see Ginny's yeti neighbor Minnie.

The name defied her 6 ft. 2 magnitude. Clad in faded coveralls, tank top, and weather-appropriate rubber boots, Minnie held out a patio-sized umbrella. "Been boarding Ginny's for years." Sheet lightning illuminated Minnie's eminence.

Suzy sighed, "It's coming back to me." She stepped under the umbrella.

"Come on," Minnie chuckled.

Minnie San Pedro was, for lack of a better term, a Frankenstein's monstress, as Grandpa Compton used to say. It was a term of endearment for a badass. Ten years older than Suzy, she had lived in Romeo her whole life. Her family was a mix of Timucua Indian, Spanish, West Indies, and perhaps Middle Earth. She was a giant, stronger than most men, and had a mystical presence, turquoise eyes, an enviable tan, and a face that sported a deep scar on her right cheek from jumping chicken wire as a teen.

"How's your momma?"

They trudged through the puddles and weeds, Suzy limping. "Mom's a long story. Can I take a shower?"

"This not enough?" Minnie could be profound in her observations.

"Warm shower," Suzy clarified. They moved toward the Civic.

"It'd be a warm bath." Minnie held the ginormous umbrella as Suzy pulled food items from the car. "You can toss all that." Lightning sizzled behind the towering woman. "Soup's on."

Suzy let the snack items dump to the ground. "Works for me."

"What's more debris?" Minnie waited patiently as Suzy decided what to do.

Embarrassed, Suzy picked up the carafe, peanut butter, and Gatorade bottles. "These could be projectiles."

They both turned toward Minnie's. The cracker cabin had the warm glow of a Thomas Kinkade painting on a foreboding Highwaymen landscape. Her incandescent lamps were 60 watts at best to save on electricity.

Suzy's ankle gave a little as she mounted the shotgun porch.

Minnie's screen door clapped behind her and Suzy.

Suzy wondered if Minnie had ever had a boyfriend or girlfriend? She was certainly one of the most caring people Suzy knew.

Suzy took off her wet clothes in Minnie's white honeycomb-tiled bathroom. The sink, a porcelain pedestal with spoked hot and cold knobs, sat beside a modern toilet and a large clawfoot tub that showed its age in soap and well water rust rings. *Not a comfortable fit for a gargantuan woman,* Suzy surmised.

She grabbed one of Minnie's beach towels and wrapped herself. She'd forgotten to grab her clothing from the car. She pulled the white muslin nightgown draped over a towel bar and tried it on. Perfect fit, other than the length. *Minnie and I can't be the same size, can we?* Suzy tried to look at herself in the medicine cabinet mirror and couldn't see past her breasts.

She rolled her hair in the towel as she joined Minnie in the living room.

"Hope you don't mind. I'll grab my things in a bit."

"If you mean when the rain lets up. Tomorrow we hope." Minnie locked the screen door and placed a three-little-pigs cast iron doorstop in place to hold the interior door open.

"Hmm." Suzy hadn't thought of that. She wouldn't run out in the nightgown. *Oh well.*

The cabin's turn-of-the-century chairs and sofa were covered in chenille and flannel throws. Never air conditioned, the white noise of oscillating fans moved with the familiarity of a Tennessee Williams tragedy. The windows were open. An occasional gust of faintly cool air puffed the café curtains. The floors were unvarnished hardwood. Woven cotton rope rugs covered sections of the pioneer floor.

"When the winds pick up, we'll batten down." Minnie swept up the dirt they had tracked in.

The interior smelled of swamp cabbage and broccoli soup or a giant fart as Grandpa Compton called it.

A whirring howl followed by a bang sent Suzy jerking. "Sounds like a werewolf!" *Time to batten down.*

Minnie shrugged. She took her broom and dustpan into the kitchen and brought back two bowls of soup and heels of sourdough bread.

The lights went out.

Suzy took the bowls and bread from Minnie. Minnie lit an oil lamp and positioned it on a marble pie crust table near the window.

"That a good idea?" Suzy questioned. "It could blow over."

The tall woman blinked at her.

Suzy pressed her lips firmly together and kept her thoughts to herself. She handed Minnie her food and then sat in a barber's chair. Dunking her bread in the warm bowl, she let the sopping sourdough lightly burn her tongue. It tasted so good. "Thank you, Minnie." Suzy felt warm and sad. It was a familiar setting, a ghostly setting. Most of the people she knew in Romeo were dust and bones or their property was now owned by heirs who were a mix of horse and cattle people.

"Is Ginny coming home soon?" Minnie drank from her handled bowl.

Suzy pulled her legs up in a squat. But her right leg wasn't feeling it, so she dropped it to the footrest. "Might be 21 days or so. She's not being too cooperative."

Minnie nodded. "Doesn't surprise me." Minnie's tone was insightful.

Suzy sat her bowl in her lap. "Not sure I did the right thing or if she's even at the right place."

"You always do your best, Suzy." Minnie put her bowl down and pulled her bread apart.

"I'd like to agree, but I'm not so sure." Suzy unwrapped the towel around her hair and draped it over the back of her chair.

Minnie chewed her bread in round motions. "You drove here to protect your mom's house. You take care of everything. If it's not the right place, there's a reason."

Suzy looked at Minnie wondering if she heard her right. "What reason? If she's not in the right place?"

"You'll have to find out." Minnie took another gulp of her soup.

"You sound like Arnold." Suzy got up and took her bowl to the kitchen. "Mind if I have a more?"

"Made plenty."

Suzy came back, nearly tripping over the long hem of the nightgown. She put the bowl on the coffee table and tied the bottom of the gown in a knot. "Okay, tell me this." Suzy grabbed her soup and returned to the barber chair. "Ginny's claiming that she was part of a government program that watched women. A study of some kind. To control women."

Minnie was quiet.

"You're not saying anything."

Minnie belched. "We're all part of some program… ranchers or citrus growers out here, Suzy. We need subsidies and aid to get through the tough times, you know."

"Ginny was tied down when I came to see her at the rehab. They said she actually asked the rehab staff to tie her down."

"Why do you call her Ginny, not Mom?" Minnie wiped her wrist on her chin.

Suzy wondered if Minnie was listening. "Well… I call her Ginny when I talk to doctors and such."

"I'm not a doctor."

"I'm aware." Suzy felt her blood pressure rising. "What's your point?"

"I'm trying to understand. Are you a daughter or an analyst?"

"What difference does it make? I'm both."

"What are you going to do with this information?" Minnie grabbed a clove cigarette and lit it. "Want one?" She extended the pack toward Suzy.

"No." Suzy wondered if everyone was insane. Not a single person reacted to Ginny being tied down.

Minnie took a long drag and exhaled circles.

*What the fuck is going on?* "Does the tied-down thing not surprise you?"

Minnie was noncommittal.

"Care to expand on that silence, Minnie?"

"I've been through some shit, Suzy." Minnie was curt. She tapped her ashes into her soup bowl. "Think being a giant is easy? Like I haven't been tackled and chased down by rednecks with something to prove? Thank God I had the strength to earn their respect."

"Seriously?" Suzy couldn't believe her ears. "I hope you broke their legs."

"It's a way of earning respect." Minnie inhaled.

"What's happened to Romeo's women?!"

Minnie crushed her cigarette in the bowl. "Like you've forgotten your past?"

Wisner took the last sip of his scotch and water and shouted to Gretchen who was standing behind the bar, "Have you been to Romeo?" The band wailed some Van Halen in the background.

"What?" Gretchen didn't know what he meant. "Romeo?"

A blonde in a low-cut purple spandex tube dress tapped his shoulder. "We were wondering if the food's any good?" The blonde next to her was an equally attractive Spandex twin.

Gretchen leaned in. "Need a menu, girls? He's taken, by the way."

Wisner gave her a grateful smile.

Blonde number one's mouth dropped. "I don't see anyone with him. Is he your old man?"

Wisner shook his head to Gretchen and the women. "I'm flattered. And yes, the food is good." He motioned for his check.

"Aw. Don't go." The twins sulked.

He pushed his credit card to Gretchen.

She took it, tapped her screen, then swiped it. She handed each of the women a menu. "Ahi tuna salad's great."

They smiled.

Gretchen pushed the receipt and card to Wisner.

He signed. "Will you be checking to see if Suzy got to Romeo?"

The pair perked up. Blonde number one asked, "Who's Romeo?"

Wisner chuckled. "More like where's Romeo?"

Blonde number two laughed. "Exactly."

Gretchen grabbed a napkin. "Gotcha." She wrote down Suzy's number. "As you can see, I'm a little busy."

Wisner nodded. "Thank you."

A large crack of lightning sounded, and the generator lights came on. The twins screamed.

"Damn you, Virginia!" A voice cried out, followed by a drunken, "Fuckin' hurricane."

"Be safe." Wisner touched Gretchen's hand.

"You, too."

He gave the twins a smile.

"Don't go, Romeo." Blonde number one waved.

Wisner sat in his van, watching the rain blast his windshield. He ran his fingers through his soaking wet hair and shook his hands. He took off his shirt, grabbed his gym bag, and pulled out a dry t-shirt.

The wiper blades blew straight out and flapped backward to hit the opposite side of the windshield. The van shook as the weather intensified. No way was he driving in this.

He took the napkin out of his trouser pockets, wondering what Suzy had driven through. The sopping paper square almost ripped. He was lucky he could still make out the number. He grabbed his cell out of the other pocket. It was moist, the screen fogged. He pushed the starter to turn his vehicle on, then plugged his cellphone into the charger to dry it as best he could. His keys were deep in his pocket, his pants painted on with rainfall. He got the car fob out and rolled it in his tee, then tossed it in the console.

He added Suzy to his phone contacts. He pushed her number and waited. His pant hems dripped on the floorboard. He pushed off the Florsheim's and pulled off his socks.

Her phone rang and then went to voicemail: "This is Suzy Lennox. If you are a consulting client, please leave your name, number, and a brief message. If this is a healthcare provider for Ginny Compton, please include the aforementioned and the best time to reach you. I'll call you at my earliest convenience."

Wisner paused as the beep sounded. He couldn't decide if he wanted to leave a message or just hang up. He finally jumped in. "Hi Suzy, Frank Wisner, just checking to see if you got ..." The message cut off. He exhaled, balled up the napkin, and tossed it on the floor.

After pulling on his clean t-shirt, he dialed his service to check for messages. His mother's aid had left a brief message that her husband and children were at the house.

Wisner called his house. "Lana, I got your message. How's Mom?" Wisner waited for Svetlana to reply. The TV was loud in the background.

"She's sleeping," Lana yawned. "Not a care in the world. Can't hear a thing without her hearing aids. Would you pause it," she shouted to someone in the distance. "We're watching a movie, doc. Are you coming home?"

He could hear the hesitation in her voice. "I'm probably staying where I am. Not sure about the roads and flooding." Wisner watched some of the bar patrons make a run across the parking lot. *Why the hell did I come to the bar tonight? Suzy.*

"Dr. Wisner"—Svetlana's Russian accent had a lyrical quality—"the children want to sleep in the television room. They are afraid of the empty rooms." She referred to vacant resident rooms.

"That's fine. Glad you're all together. Tell Mom I love her when she wakes. Go into the hallway and grab some mattresses if there's a train sound. Wheel Mom there, too."

He heard the kids laughing.

"We will. Be safe, doc." The aide hung up.

She had been his parent's long-term care provider since he had bought the place. He had consolidated his and his parents' household assets to purchase a neighborhood assisted living facility. In his 30s and 40s he had enjoyed the single life and his sexual freedom. After 50, he noted his father's lack of understanding for his mother's diabetes and decided it would be best to enjoy the family he had. This brought him to a small eight-resident facility with a detached garage apartment for his privacy. The extra rooms were reserved for an elderly aunt, uncle, or a colleague's family members should the opportunity arise. He was in no rush to become a facility administrator.

He wondered if Suzy had made it to her destination. He couldn't imagine a more determined woman.

The winds gusted on the passenger side of the heavy wheelchair accessible vehicle. The Hungry Lizard was a waterfront bar on an elevated foundation with a dock that drew boaters and tourists alike. Its intercostal access wound westward to the mouth of the Gulf of Mexico.

Wisner put the vehicle in drive. He drove across the lot to a neighboring condo and parked next to the building, figuring it would be best to be pinned next the structure than tossed or flipped. He set his emergency brake.

He called the Lizard and was surprised to hear the band playing in the background. "Gretchen?"

"No. She's preparing the walk-in in case we all have to go in there," a feminine voice shouted.

"Sounds like you've done this before." Maybe he should have stayed?

"Yeah. It's not bad, depending on how long we're in there. There's food. The freezer gets warm the bigger the crowd, especially if the electric goes out again. But we do have a backup generator."

"Stay safe." Wisner closed the call. *Now what?*

The Valley's generator hummed loudly. Industrial fans were centered in the hallways to keep air circulating. The facility was fully powered but maintenance supervisors advised to spare the strain on the system by setting the air conditioning to 78.

A good majority of the elderly patients were asleep. Many preferred warmer temperatures and likely enjoyed baking in their burrito-rolled cotton blankets. Middle-aged patients were happy to take a sleep aid or swap storm stories with their roommates. The only signs of life and real buzz came from the staff scrolling Instagram on their phones, making required entries in patient logs, and snacking by the community televisions that looped continuous Weather Channel reports.

Nurse Larsen looked in on Ginny.

Ginny woke and stared at Larsen. "I need a bedpan," she said, as though coming to a stark realization.

"I'll take you to the bathroom, Ginny." Larsen approached.

"I don't think I can stand," she whispered.

Larsen positioned Ginny's bed up. "You are capable of using the toilet."

"I'm afraid."

Larsen pursed her lips. "I'll bring a bedside commode, Ginny. But you are getting up."

Ginny grabbed for her sleep mask, embarrassed by nurse's tone. "Dr. Smith's son said I should not get up," her voice tremored. Her hands struggled to put the mask on.

The nurse reached for Ginny's hand. "I'll help you. We have a walker here for you to grab hold of."

Ginny's age-spotted hands covered her eye mask. She trembled as she turned her head toward the wall.

Larsen groaned, "I'll get an aide." She squeezed the gray plunger on the bed's call bell. A ding sounded. Each room had a light on the ceiling just outside the patient room so the nursing staff could easily see who needed assistance.

"You need to make an effort, Ginny." Larsen squished out toward the nurse's station.

# CHAPTER 9

Minnie began lockdown procedures. Her windows were already boarded, all but a few that had aluminum awnings she could drop and lock in place at the last minute. The goal? Keep the roof on. She and Suzy closed all the interior doors in the house, shut off and unplugged small appliances that could catch fire easily, and moved supplies into the bathroom.

Suzy lined Minnie's clothes hamper with a garbage bag and put their hurricane supplies inside: yard gloves, batteries, flashlights, tarp, duct tape, scissors, tools, mosquito repellant, crank radio, sunscreen, can opener, canned vegetables, fruits, tuna, beef jerky, some bottled water, peanut butter, matches, cups, utensils, and paper plates.

Suzy checked the medicine cabinet. They were set. The bathroom would be their shelter in place for the night or until the storm passed. Suzy would sleep in the tub, Minnie on the floor. Then they'd alternate. They had water, a toilet, supplies, and electricity if it didn't go out.

Suzy dragged the hamper into the small bathroom. Minnie tossed Suzy's clothing in the hamper and handed Suzy her phone. Minnie had retrieved her things from the car.

The patio umbrella was now positioned to jam the back door in place along with several furniture items. Minnie's gun safe blocked the front door.

"When do we…" Suzy barely had time to ask before a loud *thud* hit the roof.

"Oak branch," Minnie speculated. "We go now."

Suzy looked at her phone. She saw a missed call from a number she didn't recognize. Then noticed she only had 50% battery. She turned the phone off. The charger was still in her car.

Minnie piled all the cushions in the house in the bathroom before she closed the door.

Suzy got in the tub to start her shift. "Has Ginny told you things she didn't want me to know?"

"Sure," Minnie laughed.

"Like?"

"She fostered a miniature horse for about two weeks."

"Oh my God, she said *you* were keeping the horse! I thought the house smelled funny that weekend."

"She befriended a young lawn guy, Charlie. He cut her grass, trimmed her trees. Helped her setup the iPad you got her for Christmas."

Suzy felt a shiver. "Minnie, you said you set up the iPad."

"I'm not technical. You know that. Besides, he stopped coming around after that."

*Because he probably has all of Ginny's personal info!* "Do you have his contact info?"

Minnie opened her cellphone. "I do. I'll call him. He put his number in my phone. Said to call if Ginny ever needed help."

Minnie hit the number and put the call on speaker. It went straight to a message that said it was no longer a working number. "That could be due to the storm. We'll try after the storm." Minnie turned her phone off.

Suzy felt her heart racing. "You should have told me about that."

Minnie said, "You're right."

"What did you mean before, about my past?"

"You were drinking. Blackout drunk spells. Thank God you had Chloe."

Suzy dissed Minnie's exaggeration. "Yes, I drank a lot coming out of high school. It was a rite of passage thing. I was bored to tears. I admit, I didn't have great control, but I'm not an alcoholic."

"You had potential."

"Okay, I suppose Chloe turned that bus around."

"Or her dad."

## 1920 Downtown Tampa

Monica pulled away from the men. She waved to her church group that had boarded the trolley to go back to Sulphur Springs. "The boys are walking me to the train station. See you tomorrow," she shouted.

"Best behavior!" The deacon pointed at the men.

"Scouts Promise." Lou held up his hand. "For Christ's sake"—he played along with the deacon's chaperon rubbish—"he knows who I am."

The three waved as the David's Church party departed.

"What did you think of his prayer after the show?" Joe continued waving. "Talk about fire and brimstone."

Monica stopped waving. "The moving picture story was scandalous."

The trolley moved further away until it was a speck in the distance.

She looped her arms into the gentlemen's arm on either side of her, Lou on her left and Joe on her right. Joe carried her tapestry bag over his forearm.

She squealed, "I've had the most exciting day!"

"Let's not stop now." Lou pulled free and pinched her bottom. "What do you say we head to Charlie Wall's in Ybor for a little throwing?"

Monica stopped. "That's rather ungentlemanly." She rubbed her buttocks.

Lou grinned. "But did you like it?"

"No." She looked at Joe. "What are you throwing?"

Lou roared, "Bolita. It's great fun to watch. A numbers game of chance. I'll get you a ticket." He caressed her ass. "You'll be my good luck charm."

Joe shoved his cousin. "You heard the lady. She doesn't like that."

Lou shoved Joe. "She doesn't know what she likes."

They roughhoused some more. Joe gave Monica her bag as he tried to pen Lou to a streetlamp.

"Boys!" Monica pleaded.

Lou pushed Joe away and pulled a pistol out of a shoulder holster in his jacket. Lou pointed it at his cousin. "I've had enough of your antics. Settle down. And don't pull any escapades when we get to Ybor or so help me God, you'll regret it."

Joe held his hands up. "Understood." He said to Monica, "I get a little carried away. Lou's right."

Monica's eyes teared up.

Lou leered at Monica, returning the gun to its holster. "While we're at it, 'boys' sounds delightful, but it's getting a little tired. You're a beautiful woman, and its high time you grew up. We're going to see some friends of mine, important men. They'll grab your ass if they choose, and you'll like the flattery intended. Understood? Watch the other women around you. Use your feminine resources of intrigue and make a guy feel special."

She took a deep breath. "What is it that you do?"

Arnold tried to call Suzy. It went to voicemail. "Now she turns off her phone."

He rolled over and turned the television on. He didn't believe in disaster prep. He preferred a chain hotel that had backup generators, procedures, and food. He chose one near his apartment, splurging on a bridal suite with a hot tub.

He chucked his phone next to an open bag of Dorito's. The bed was his war room. He had his tablet, charger, some favorite *Playboy* issues, moisturizer, snacks, and an old school three-ring binder Suzy insisted he keep in case the cloud and all backup hard drives failed. He mostly drew hateful cartoons in it and wrote a few cryptic notes. If he didn't use it, he'd never hear the end of it.

The Weather Channel showed the whole state. He switched to a local television station with an affable weatherman who would not likely sleep until the storm was over. Arnold loved local anchors. A meteorologist with a two-day stubble, bloodshot, dark-circled eyes on a joint marathon broadcast that included Facebook Live Q&A would not disappoint. He could even watch the repetitive spaghetti models from his vantage point in the hot tub and let the jets lull him to sleep.

The weather forecaster focused on the center of the state. It was getting pounded. He wondered if Suzy had lost her cell signal.

He changed channels and found a serial killer marathon on a cable network.

"Suzyland!" He grabbed the Suzy notebook and wrote this down: Killercane, a vortex of serial killers. "She'll love this!"

He wrote.

Pitch: A hurricane rips open Florida's death row, swooping up serial killers and residents along the way in low-lying zones, who choose to ride out the storm versus evacuate. Tough question: Would you rather be molested in an overcrowded evacuation shelter or die in the Killercane?! Think *Sharknado* but with serial killers.

Minnie ripped a giant fart that woke Suzy. She wanted to open the door. Her limbs were numb, and she couldn't move. She uncoiled herself from the fetal position to sit up in the tub. "Minnie, Minnie." Suzy reached for Minnie, then she gagged. She pulled the nightgown over her head, took a deep breath, then realized she needed some deodorant. She listened to the howling storm and the sounds of things crashing into the frame home and within the walls. She wondered if Ginny's roof was still on.

She grabbed a few extra pillows from the floor and sat them in the tub. There was barely any room to move with Minnie on the floor. Suzy needed to stretch her legs. She put her heels up on the tub rim.

She switched her phone on and tried to get a weather report. The internet buffered. She was now at 40% battery.

A firework sound exploded. "Jesus," Suzy screamed. The lights went out.

"Transformer," Minnie said in the blackness.

"Could it catch fire?" Suzy felt her heartbeat in her throat.

"Rain should put it out. Can't go out anyway." Minnie rolled to her back.

"I feel like I'm having a heart attack."

Minnie sat up and thought a moment. "I've got some valerian root in the cabinet." She grabbed a few flashlights and a water bottle from the hamper. She stood, turned on both flashlights, opened the medicine cabinet, and squinted. "Here it is." She put a few droppers full of the sleep herb into the water bottle. She recapped, shook the bottle, and handed it to Suzy, along with a flashlight.

Suzy stood up. "Want to switch places? I have to pee."

Minnie nodded.

Their flashlight beams crossed on the ceiling as they made their maneuvers. Suzy tapped her flashlight to Minnie's. "May the force be with us."

"Wise you are." Minnie got into the tub and turned toward the wall, snoring almost immediately.

Suzy stood on the cold tile and gulped down half the water bottle. She capped it and prepared to pee immediately. The orgasmic release of her bladder was heavenly. She grabbed the toilet paper, wiped, and flushed. As she did, she stood, dropped her nightgown, then heard a strange gurgling from the toilet.

Suzy looked for a plunger, fearing the toilet might back up. She found one behind the toilet. In her peripheral vision, she saw something float up. She tried to flush again, but the tank was still filling. Then she saw it move. *Old turds don't move.*

She stepped back and took another look. She shined her flashlight right on it. Then she let out a blood-curdling scream that echoed through the small bathroom. The plunger was airborne.

"Oh my god, oh my god, oh my god!" Suzy slammed the lid. The turd had ears, a twitching nose, and a tail!

Suzy let out another scream so horrific she was sure her throat was bleeding.

The plunger had landed on a snoring Minnie.

Suzy ran in place as she screamed. "How…" She shook Minnie. "There's…" she stifled.

Then she heard it swimming.

"Ohmygod… ohmygod… I can't…. MINNIE!"

Minnie snored louder.

Suzy shone her light into the giant woman's face. Minnie opened her bloodshot eyes and grabbed the flashlight from Suzy.

"I can't." Suzy mounted Minnie.

"Calm down." Minnie tried to push Suzy off her chest.

Suzy clung tighter. "I can't."

"I have Benadryl." Minnie shone Suzy's flashlight in her face. "Are you allergic to valerian root?"

"Oh my God, I'm going to faint. Or vomit." Suzy buried her face in Minnie's chest.

Scratching and splashing ensued.

Minnie stretched her long arm toward the toilet lid.

"Ohmygod… ohmygod." Suzy karate-chopped Minnie's forearm. "NO!"

"That hurt!" Minnie was now wide awake. "You need to calm down."

The splashing intensified with Suzy's hysteria.

"I can't… I can't…" Suzy mumbled. "I'm going to die."

"Is it a mouse or a rat?"

"I …don't know?" Suzy shone her light into Minnie's face. "Don't…"

"This… is uncomfortable." Minnie wiggled enough to sit up more. "A rat can swim a few days. A mouse can't." Minnie pushed Suzy up. "I'll take the floor."

Suzy shook violently. "Nononnononono. You can't." She clamped her hand over Minnie's mouth.

Lap swimming continued.

Minnie rolled her eyes.

"We've got to get out of here." Suzy's head shook, almost convulsing.

Minnie took a deep breath, then pulled Suzy's hand off her mouth. "The sewers…"

Suzy slapped her hand over Minnie's mouth, hard. "Don't."

Minnie wrestled her arm from Suzy.

Thus began a wrestling match for Suzy's light saber.

Minnie's was wedged under Suzy.

Suzy's shin gouged into the spicket.

They were both in pain.

The air was thick with stench and the sounds of rodent Olympics.

Then, suddenly, there was calm in the toilet bowl.

"Must be a mouse." Minnie reached toward the toilet with lightning speed and flushed.

Suzy's eyes got big. "Do it again."

Minnie flushed again.

"Again!"

They heard nothing.

Minnie flushed again.

Suzy collapsed on Minnie.

Minnie grabbed Suzy's shoulders and held her up. "You've got to get off me."

Suzy pushed off Minnie's chest and tried to find her footing between Minnie's legs inside the tub. Minnie grabbed the sides of the tub and tried to work herself out.

"I've got to pee now." Minnie shook a stern finger at Suzy.

"Pee in the sink!" Suzy pleaded.

Minnie stretched her arms upward and shook her legs.

Suzy held her hands up in prayer.

Minnie opened the toilet lid.

Suzy's eyes got big. She shuddered then slipped into a cold faint, her face whiter than the aged porcelain.

Minnie flashed her light in the toilet. "All clear."

# CHAPTER 10

Ginny awoke to the sounds of branches slapping against her window. "Suzy?" She called out and struggled to sit up. The room spun. She couldn't seem to get the walls to stop moving. She blinked her eyes. The lines were crossing and bouncing. The curtains were unfamiliar. She felt her leg moving and saw vertical lines crossing over each other. She had a gray plunger in her hand. She wondered if its tube was attached to her body. She wasn't sure where it was coming from. Was it an umbilical cord? The strobing fluorescent lights were stabbing in her eyes. She raised her other arm over her eyes.

"Suzy." Ginny needed someone to stop the room from moving. It was making her sick.

She took several deep breaths and tried to think. The tree scrubbing against the window was timed with a swooshing sound in her ears. She lifted her arm off her forehead and squinted. Her eyes fluttered back and forth as she tried to blink them straight.

It was no use.

# CHAPTER 11

Minnie grabbed a rake and handed it to Suzy. The two houses had lost shingles but kept their roofs. Branches, Spanish moss, and palm fronds were scattered in heaps around their homes. Fragments of debris from miles away were strewn in the road and stuck to the boarded windows. Standing water filled the low spots in their yards. Thankfully, both homes were constructed on built-up foundations and had no flooding in their interiors. The road leading into their tract of land was slightly elevated and gave portions of the collected water a place to run off. If another rain came soon, they would have to stack their furniture to make sure things stayed dry.

The skies were azure. Not a cloud was in sight.

Suzy moaned. Her car had been under some water during the storm. A ponding stain was up over the doors, and she hoped the interior was sealed tight. The engine would take a day or two before she would endeavor to start it. They had no power. Her cellphone was at 10% battery, enough to call the power company, but there was no signal. No bars registered. Cell signals were sparse on a good day. She shut the phone off.

"What do we do?" Suzy turned to Minnie.

"We'll clear the yard a bit, hopefully disperse more water." Minnie pointed to the dammed-up spots. "You could make us lunch after you clear Ginny's drive."

Suzy stared at Ginny's small cracker cottage. At least it didn't look like Dorothy's home when it had fallen back to earth in the *Wizard of Oz*.

"I'll check them after a while." Minnie sprayed repellent on her arms and legs. "Spray good. The mosquitoes are swarming." She tossed the can to Suzy.

Suzy wondered how Ginny was doing. Who was looking out for her? Would she understand what was going on?

"I never called The Valley to tell them I'd be away." Suzy suddenly felt her shoulders pitch forward. "What if they tie her down again or God knows what?"

Minnie kept raking.

"What should I do?"

"The whole state has power issues and storm damage, Suzy." Minnie slapped at a mosquito buzzing around her face. "Hopefully, they're concerned for your safety."

Wisner stopped in Ginny's room. "How are you?"

Ginny was in the middle of lunch. Her bed was elevated, with a full tray placed in front of her. She hadn't touched a thing. Her eye mask was pushed up to her forehead, and she continued to look straight ahead. "Where's Suzy?"

Wisner looked at the clock. "Late lunch?"

It was nearing 2 p.m.

"I feel sick to my stomach." Ginny reached for the can of ginger ale on the tray. Her hand shook less once she had a grip on the can.

"That's the best stuff. I'm sure your daughter is on her way back from Romeo."

"We're not in Romeo?" Ginny stared at a spot on the wall.

"You are in The Lily of the Valley Rehabilitation Center." Wisner wondered exactly where Suzy might be and how she was doing.

"This isn't Romeo?"

"You are in Palm Breeze." The doctor crossed his arms and assessed Ginny's disposition.

Ginny struggled to put her can on the tray using both shaking hands. "Could you put my bed down?"

Wisner showed Ginny the bed controls, the call bell, and television remote. He positioned her down. It was obvious she couldn't manage it on her own.

"Do you have children?" Ginny pulled the eye mask back over her eyes.

"I do not. I am caring for my parents. I have…" He stopped short of sharing his ownership in the assisted living facility.

Ginny smiled. "You could still have children. You're very handsome."

"Thank you, Ginny. I'm past that point." Wisner smiled.

"Men can always change their mind. Women are on the clock from birth."

"I suppose."

"You sound like Suzy. She's always certain of things."

Wisner touched Ginny's shoulder. "I'm sure Suzy will be here in the next day or so. It was nice seeing you."

"Will you call her and tell her to bring some hard candies?" Ginny motioned.

Wisner thought a moment. *A reason to call.* "I'll make sure she gets the message, and if she can't get here soon enough…some butterscotch candies?"

"And peppermints, too."

"My mother enjoys both."

"You're a good doctor." Ginny smiled. "Tell your mother I said so."

Wisner nodded. "I'll do that."

Minnie pulled the boards off Ginny's front door. "You know storm season's not over. I'd just as soon keep the boards on the windows unless Ginny's coming home soon. I can put these on the door next storm warning."

Suzy stepped in and turned on the vintage milk glass lamp on the end table next to the door. "Suppose I'll have to turn on every light in the house then," Suzy muttered. "It's like a cave in here."

Minnie nodded. "A cool dark room is good sleeping."

Suzy began flipping the overhead lights on. "Except that I'm not sleeping."

Minnie stepped out to the front porch and let the screen door close behind her. She left Suzy to her business. "Let me know when you want to get into the attic."

"Let's take a look now," Suzy called out.

Minnie stepped back in and pulled open the laddered door in the hallway ceiling. A light came on when the ladder came down. Minnie climbed up a few steps and could see boxes. "Some things here."

Suzy climbed up. It was stuffy, dusty, and dotted with rodent feces. "Noted. It's too hot up here to do this now." She trudged down the ladder. "Maybe another time."

She moved on to Ginny's bedroom, a treasure trove of costume jewelry, linens, and figurines. Suzy opened the closet and saw piles of QVC boxes.

Her mother had an old secretary desk in the corner. It was cluttered with Norman Rockwell figurines, mostly scenes from small town life. Kids fishing. Going to school. Halloween. And more. She opened the glass doors at the top of the cabinet. There were some antique books and a tarnished souvenir spoon. The books were classics.

The spoon intrigued her. The souvenir-handled spoon had a resort pictured on the front. The reverse side displayed the word "Sterling," some faded numbers, and "Tampa Bay Hotel, Tampa, Florida." At first Suzy thought it was the Taj Mahal. She put the demitasse spoon in her pocket.

She opened the desk compartment and found letters in bundles. Some were tied with ribbons; others were in rubber bands scattered with old bills and drawings Chloe had made for her grandmother. There were also some old fountain pens that had dried up and a cloth sachet that had lost its scent. The ribbon bundle was yellowed and tightly tied vertically and horizontally. It looked untouched by anyone but the person who had packaged it. Suzy turned it over to see both sides. The top envelope was addressed to "American Soldier" and had an Ocala, FL postmark.

Suzy saw some silverfish moving around under the papers. She pulled the stack out and shook it over a trash can. A heavy key landed in the can with a thud. She retrieved the ornate metal key. It was tarnished brass with an intricately cut quadrangular bit. The bow had a flat round head with intersecting hearts connected by a barrel to the bit. She put it in her pocket, then grabbed a tissue to sweep out the bottom of the secretary. She returned all the other papers except the ribboned bundle. She shook the bundle over the can.

Silverfish crawled around in the bottom of the trash liner. She grabbed the can and promptly walked it outside, tossing the can on the lawn.

Minnie was smoking a clove cigarette on her front porch. "Spiders?"

"Silverfish." Suzy squirmed. "I hope we're not infested. Should I have the place fumigated while Ginny's away?"

Minnie shrugged. "Get a couple of bug bombs and set them off when you leave. It usually does the trick. That's what I use."

"I've been meaning to have this place termited. That would probably take care of the hidden areas," Suzy heard herself say. *The hidden areas.* She remembered a place Grandmother Woodson had showed her when she was four or five. It was in Ginny's closet.

Suzy took the letter bundle into the living room. She went into the bedroom and tossed a sheet over Ginny's pink chenille bedspread. She began piling up the unopened QVC boxes that had been stashed away for Christmas gifts. Once the boxes were stacked on the bed, Suzy rummaged through Ginny's clothing and selected a few extra items to bring back for her mother. She picked the good outfits, the ones Ginny had been saving for a special occasion.

The top shelf of the closet was lined with shoeboxes. Some had shoes, others held tissue-wrapped knick-knacks from garage sales, church rummage sales, or the occasional trip to the antique mall. Ginny was convinced she'd never go broke, because she was in possession of a priceless treasure that would save her from ruin. She just didn't know which item was priceless.

Suzy got down on her hands and knees and parted the longer clothing items so she could get to the closet's back wall. She felt around. It was solid. She got up and went to the kitchen and found a flashlight, determined to find the concealed plank her grandmother had shown her. *I know it's there.* She sat on her butt. The beam of the flashlight shone on the closet's ceiling. She looked up at the faint stars she'd drawn so long ago in old crayon. Then she brushed her hands on the floor.

"This is linoleum. Who covered the hardwood?"

She crawled out and onto the carpeted bedroom floor and looked around. She closed her eyes and tried to remember the room when it belonged to her grandparents. It was a cream yellow then with sheer ivory curtains. They had a rocking chair in the corner, a vanity with lotions and a silver hand mirror and brush set, a chest of drawers, and some war medals in a small curio cabinet that hung on the wall.

Suzy remembered. "The roof leak!"

She reminisced. The walls had been stripped before the drywall went up. She never thought about the secret place during the construction. She was too excited that her grandparents let her roller skate in the house and draw on their closet ceiling. Suzy wanted to make puffy clouds, but her feeble grandmother insisted on blue, gray, and gold stars.

Her grandfather Edward brought in a ladder and crayons and gave Suzy the freedom to make it whatever she desired. The secret place had vanished.

Suzy put all the home shopping packages back where she found them. She returned to the front room, took a seat in her mother's corner, and untied the first ribbon on the letter stack.

"Let's see what this is about."

# CHAPTER 12

A small herd of five displaced Longhorn cattle and a large cedar tree were among the storm debris blocking the two-lane stretch of US 41. People were out of their cars, discussing options. It was nearly impossible to turn around. It would require a coordinated effort of backing up and executing three-point-turns.

Suzy recognized many of the people from neighboring communities. They weren't people she knew well or actually knew, but people she identified by their job. Betty Martin, the unpolished nail tech; Sheila Ramler, "The best damn tow truck driver in Central Florida." No one could dispute this because it was lettered right on her truck. Jeff Nguyen, veterinarian to the Ocala horse stars; Dixie Sherman, grandma and dive instructor from Homosassa Springs; Jimmy Succup, the owner of Succup Auto Sales; Marilyn Cartwright, the know-it-all mobile librarian; and Jack Tyler, the uncool air conditioning guy. They were among the growing throng of motorists.

Junior monster trucks, swamp buggies, and mudders bounced along the shoulder and ditches, toward the roadblock.

*Who would Sheila be towing?* Suzy tried to get a look. She had nothing to discuss with her fellow motorists. She put her phone on the charger, settled in, reclined her seat, and rolled her windows down. It was going to be awhile. She turned to face the passenger door and look at the green grass and bent trees. *May as well nap.*

"Hey," a very happy young woman stuck her head in Suzy's window. Suzy jumped.

"Do you have a tampon?"

Suzy rolled over, startled to have a human head in her personal space. She nudged her sunglasses down to look at the face behind the optimistic voice. She couldn't figure out why this woman was so happy. Her own period always made her angry. "Sorry."

"No problem. Hope I can get to a restroom before..." The bubbly woman rolled her glassy green eyes that were partially covered by a waterfall ponytail. She stepped back and moved down the road to the next car.

Suzy looked in her rearview mirror.

The younger woman had a bounce in her step. She was thin, freckled, in cutoff shorts and a tank top.

Suzy stuck her head out of the window. "Look for an RV or camper."

The woman jogged back quickly.

*Slow down.*

"Say what?"

Suzy couldn't figure out how the woman moved with ease under the circumstances. "Look for an RV or camper."

"Old people don't have tampons?" The younger woman puzzled.

"You said you wanted a restroom." Suzy was convinced this was going to be a lot of unnecessary explaining.

The cheerful menstruator tapped Suzy's door. "Right! My name is Juliet."

"Welcome to Romeo. I'm Suzy. There once was a town of Juliette south of here. Doesn't exist anymore. Do you live here?"

"I'm from Gibsonton."

"Sideshow town." Suzy nodded and raised her seat.

100

"Isn't it great?" Juliet beamed.

Suzy was immediately confused. *Are sideshow towns great or Gibsonton?*

"My great grandpa was a candy butcher."

"What's that?"

Juliet smiled big through clenched teeth. "Grandpa looked like a jack o 'lantern. Said no child or grandchild of his was going to be a candy clown. He hawked candy at the circus."

Suzy lifted her sunglasses and marveled at the younger woman's perfect teeth. "You could do dental commercials."

"Thank you. Do you live here?"

"I did. Now I visit."

They heard a helicopter in the background.

Juliet looked upward. "Oh my god. Everyone on Facebook says Michael Ryan is on his way to scare the cattle off the highway."

"The action star who lives in Ocala? Never watched any of his movies." Suzy opened her car door and tried to look. "I think it's an air ambulance."

Juliet squinted. "Maybe one of the Longhorn got hit."

"I don't think they come for animals."

Juliet slapped Suzy's arm. "That's hilarious!"

Suzy got out and stretched.

Juliet turned and skipped off. "Thanks Suzy," she shouted and never looked back.

Suzy couldn't imagine skipping at any age.

The helicopter drowned out her thoughts. She closed her eyes. Twigs, dust, and rubble blew about. She got back in her car and rolled up the windows. The copter set down in an adjacent field. It was an airlift.

She wondered which hospital the accident victim(s) would be sent to. *How was Ginny?*

Arnold opened his laptop and typed: *Lennox Legacy*. He had a meeting later in the day and needed to catch up on his commitments to Suzy.

His home office was a walk-in closet conversion. Gone were the racks and shelves. He had a couple of small flat screens on the walls, A/C vents in the ceiling, a mahogany desk, an office chair, and credentials on the wall behind him. The talking heads on the television were muted. He glanced at the stock market news running on the bottom of the screen. He was clean shaven, in a charcoal Tom Ford suit, black Ferragamo moccasins, and his hair was trimmed, combed in a side part. He looked younger and refined.

Arnold's cell rang. He noted the caller ID was private. He continued to type and answered, "Arnold Welch."

He chuckled, pulled a Post-it, and made some notes. "I was really hoping you were calling about my car's extended warranty." He continued to type.

"I'm on it," Arnold added pressure to his keystrokes, clickity-clacking louder as the conversation heated. "Correct. Move... Yes, move... out of aircraft holdings. If the current administration stays the course, we need to pivot."

He mouthed, "Fuck you," as he rolled back in his chair.

"Couldn't agree more." He shook his head, *no*.

"Our asset IS moving toward us." Arnold closed his eyes and sighed.

He had an incoming call from Shedevil.

"Can you hold?" Arnold didn't wait for the private caller to respond.

"Suzy, I'll call you back." He hung up on her.

He returned to the original caller. Dial tone.

"Fuck you, too."

He redialed Shedevil. It went straight to voicemail.

He hung up again.

"You're both fucking ungrateful." Arnold opened the Suzy note-book.

*You hung up on me!* he scribbled on the empty page.

Suzy stopped at a Palm Breeze grocery to grab a sub, some wine, fruit, and bottled water, hoping her refrigerator and trailer had power. The weather was back to a humid 80+ and her car's air conditioning needed recharging. She wondered if Juliet had ever found a restroom or a tampon. All she wanted to do was get to her mobile home, crank the air to 69 degrees, and sleep.

The temperature in the store chilled her dry, sunburnt skin. It felt good, but also made her skin feel like a layer of parchment paper. She needed aloe.

Her phone dinged.

Arnold had texted: `Why did you hang up?`

She started to redial but snubbed him. She hated hearing other people's one-sided calls in groceries, doctor's offices, and in general. She'd get to him when she could. At least he was aware now she had survived the storm.

Suzy pushed her shopping cart to the bottled water aisle and heard squi, squi, squi behind her. Her head ached. It sounded familiar. *Nurse Larsen?* She turned slowly and saw an older man in Crocs. He nodded to her. *Thank God!* She did not need a Nurse Larsen encounter. Not now, not as a mosquito-bitten, red-skinned, greasy-haired freak, in a faded Pink Floyd t-shirt and Minnie's cut-off farmer jeans. Nope. *How could she and Minnie wear the same size? Damn it!*

Suzy stared at the man way longer than she should.

He became uncomfortable and moved away from her.

There wasn't much on the shelves but overpriced water in small containers. Suzy grabbed several.

Essential supplies were still sparse, even though their city hadn't experienced the wrath other Floridians had.

She moved to the snack aisle, looking for inspiration. She saw a bag of pork rinds. Ginny loved them. Suzy grabbed a bag for her mother and a bag of Cheetos for herself.

As she moved into the next aisle, she saw a tiny woman in a parked electric grocery cart trying to reach a jar of pickles. "Can I help you?"

The woman jumped, obviously startled. "Shh! Glass jars." The older woman in a floral print house dress hugged herself, breathing hard.

"Sorry." Suzy grabbed the jar and handed it to the petite, painfully thin senior citizen in thick, black-heeled shoes with laces. *Do they still make those shoes?* Suzy remembered Grandmother Woodson had worn similar ones.

The woman placed the jar in her basket. "You're a little loud."

Suzy investigated the woman's cart. She saw several cans of cheap cat food, a loaf of white bread, orange marmalade, and a quart of whole milk. "You're right." *I hope you have a cat.*

"I've been eating these pickles since I was pregnant with my first." The woman's sapphire blue eyes belied her age.

Suzy continued to stare into her eyes. "The old wives' tale is true."

The woman smiled softly, the folds of her cheeks making parentheses on either side of her mouth. "Do you have children?"

"One in college."

"When I was young, women had ambitions to go to college, but the war changed that. We made planes and ran businesses so our men could fight."

"Rural women didn't." Suzy thought about her grandparents and Ginny. "Where are you from?"

"California."

"What made you come to Florida?"

The woman sighed. "My husband transferred to MacDill. I was busy having babies and raising them once we got to Tampa."

Suzy nodded. She started to reply, but the woman backed up her cart with the precision of a race car driver and swiveled around Suzy. *Okay. Thanks for the chat.*

Suzy finished shopping and returned to her car. *Time to call Wisner back.*

He picked up. She could hear the wind in the background.

"How are you?" he shouted.

*I'm just returning your call.* She sat in the shade with the car door open. "Is this a good time?"

A woman laughed in Wisner's background. The phone suddenly sounded muffled. "I told Ginny you would be back soon. Everything okay?"

Suzy started her car and shut the door. "Thank you. How is she?"

"Confused and missing you."

"I appreciate your help. Sounds like you are on the beach."

"A friend's boat. How are things in Romeo?"

"Ever seen a rat come up through a toilet?" She pushed her sunglasses up. "Or Longhorn Cattle holding motorist's hostage? That's Romeo."

"When are you going to The Valley?"

"Tomorrow. Could I ask a favor? Could you get Ginny's med list? I really don't want to wrestle with the nurses."

"I'll bring the med list if you meet me at the Pink Pelican tomorrow for dinner. 6 p.m.?"

*A date?* "Thank you! See you there." Suzy glanced at herself in the rearview mirror. She pulled the sunglasses off. Her eyes were red and puffy. *Dr. Creepy, your date needs a good night's sleep.*

# CHAPTER 13

Suzy entered Ginny's room to find her mother asleep, slightly ele-vated, wearing a hospital gown and slip-resistant socks. She only had a sheet covering her and was having difficulty breathing, her hair an oily gray. Suzy debated whether to wake her mother or just sit qui-etly until she woke up. She pulled a chair over and placed her bag on the floor. The roommate's curtain was open, the bed unkempt. No roommate was present.

It was all too quiet. The televisions were off, but the lights were all on. It felt like an operating room. Suzy got up and turned off some of the lights. She left the soft backlight behind Ginny's bed illuminated.

Ginny's eyelids fluttered.

Suzy put a hand on her Ginny's shoulder. "Mom."

"I'm losing my mind, Suzy. It's the snake pit."

*How?* Suzy leaned in and gave her mother a hug.

Ginny kept her arms to her sides. Tears streamed down the sides of her face. "I want to go home. I'm having nightmares."

"I'm working on it." Suzy kissed her mother's forehead. "Do you want to talk about the nightmares?"

Ginny shook her head. "They're horrible."

"I went to your house, to board up for the hurricane." Suzy waited to see if Ginny understood.

Ginny's face was expressionless, distracted.

"What happened while I was gone?" Suzy held Ginny's hand.

"I need to go home."

"I need you well."

"They made fun of me. Called me lazy." Ginny coughed. Her eyes brimmed with fresh tears.

Suzy handed her mother the plastic tumbler on her bed tray. "Take a sip. This thing is full. You're not drinking enough water."

"They are trying to make me walk to the toilet, and I can't." Ginny's lips twitched as she tried to form her next sentence. She whispered, "I'm burning."

"You're hot?"

"Down there." Ginny couldn't catch her breath.

Suzy's eyes filled with tears. "Mom, is that why you're not drinking, to avoid urinating?" She gave her mother another sip.

"They belittled me."

Suzy felt her brain heating up. She hit her mother's call bell. She remained calm for Ginny's sake. "Mom, there are nice people and mean people. It's likely someone had a bad day. But we're going to get this taken care of."

Suzy looked at the clock while Ginny wringed her hands.

Suzy went out into the hall and saw no one. She didn't see anyone in the adjacent rooms. She continued to walk. It was 3 p.m. Most of the staff were on break. *Where are the aides?* She moved to the next wing and found numerous folks gathered in the television room having visits and the staff managing a variety of activities.

"Excuse me"—Suzy's brows furrowed—"my mother rang her bell. Is anyone working in her section?"

A few nurses gave her a blank stare. "Who is your mother? What room?"

Suzy gave them Ginny's room and explained her concerns regarding Ginny's hygiene and wanting to know the days and times for showering and exercise. That she needed to use the toilet.

The nurses muttered. Suzy went back to Ginny's room to wait it out.

"They're on their way, Mom. Did you exercise today?"

"I couldn't." Ginny turned away. "Dr. Smith's son said I wasn't ready. That I should rest." Ginny was slurring the S in her words. She took deep breaths as she spoke.

"Where is your eye mask?"

"They took it. Said I was pretending."

A petite older aide entered. "Are you Ginny's daughter?' She looked about Ginny's age.

"I am"—Suzy read the name tag—"Sonya."

Sonya turned to Ginny. "Do you want the bedpan?"

*Bedpan?*

"Mom, wouldn't you like to go into the bathroom and wash up?"

"I've already gone," Ginny whispered.

"Could you step out of the room? I'll change Ginny," Sonya directed Suzy. "Does she wear diapers at home?"

*I don't think so.*

Sonya was no-nonsense. "She should be using the toilet and exercising her legs."

*What am I supposed to say to that?*

Suzy looked at Ginny, who was pointing accusingly at Sonya.

Suzy and Ginny gave each other the "look who is listening" big eyes.

Suzy hated how people spoke in front of the elderly like they weren't even there. "Ginny said she's burning from the urine."

Ginny nodded.

"Mom, speak up," Suzy encouraged.

Sonya turned in time to see Ginny nod the second time.

"I need ointment." Ginny looked over the woman's head.

Her mother wasn't easily intimidated or shy. The fact that she wouldn't make eye contact with Sonya gave Suzy a better understanding of her mother's fear. "I'd like to stay in the room."

"Please shut the door." Sonya pulled the curtain around Ginny, shutting Suzy out.

"Does Ginny have a roommate?" Suzy asked.

The aide gave a sharp, firm response, "I prefer to concentrate on the task at hand. That's why the family is asked to wait in the hallway."

*Fair enough.*

Sonya continued, "If you must have a reply while I'm working… her roommate's visiting her family in the common area, where you and Ginny could be."

Once the curtain was open, and Ginny looked satisfied, Suzy asked Sonya, "Has Ginny exercised or seen Dr. Smithson?"

Sonya peeled her gloves off and tossed them in the trash. "What do you know?"

Ginny shook her head, *no*, to Suzy.

"What should I know?" Suzy glanced from one older woman to the next.

"Ginny refuses to get up. Do anything. She's not dressed, as you can see. She said she prefers the hospital gown."

Suzy considered the aide's tone. She wanted to understand Ginny's side of the story. "Mom, I apologize. You do need a few more things to wear." Suzy pulled up a chair next to Ginny and sat. "Thank you, Sonya. I'll bring more suitable exercise clothes."

Sonya rolled her eyes, which was not missed by Suzy.

With Sonya out of the room, Ginny chirped, "She's the mean one. She does that in front of my roommate and Dr. Smith's son."

Suzy patted her mother's hand. "I see that. But Mom, people like Sonya are not going to change. Don't let her upset you. You need to exercise." She handed her mother the insulated plastic water jug. "You've got to stay hydrated. Don't stop drinking water."

A knock followed, and a new voice came into the room. It was Dr. Smithson.

"Am I glad to see you!" Suzy stood. "Ginny's having some confusion. She believes you would like her to stay in bed."

The shorter, heavyset, bespectacled doctor hugged his clipboard and chuckled. "Ms. Compton, do you believe I want you to stay in bed?"

Ginny perked up. "Dr. Smith's son told me."

Suzy did a doubletake. "This is Dr. Smithson."

"No, it isn't," Ginny criticized.

Dr. Smithson held up a hand to Suzy. He addressed Ginny, "Do you have me confused with my P.A., a tall younger man, red hair?"

Suzy waited for it.

"Yes, your son." Ginny acted like they were both crazy.

Smithson nodded to Suzy. "He introduces himself as Dr. Smithson's P.A., Paul Rivera." He turned to Ginny. "You probably missed his name."

Suzy took a cleansing breath.

Smithson added, "He's very thorough. Ginny's not the first patient to mix up our obvious likeness." He held a hand over his growing smile.

*You're a regular comedian.* Suzy gave him an obligatory smile. "Did your P.A. ask Mom to stay in bed?"

The doctor turned to Ginny. "You believe he said that?"

"I was dizzy and sick to my stomach."

The doctor flipped through his notes. "You had dizziness." He then turned to Suzy. "I'm sure he would have advised against her being up for exercise that day. For her safety."

Ginny gave Suzy a vindicated expression.

"What day was that, Mom?"

Smithson clasped his clipboard, awaiting Ginny's answer.

"He knows." Ginny pointed to Smithson.

Suzy inhaled deeply. "Will one of you tell me?"

"It was a few days ago," Smithson nodded. "Are you dizzy now, Ginny?"

Suzy watched Ginny.

"I have good days and bad days." Ginny clasped her hands together.

*Your witness, Smithson.* Suzy wasn't sure where this was headed.

Smithson snapped his fingers. "Reminds me. You are scheduled to come into my office for a follow-up, Ginny. At that point we'll determine your progress. Will you be bringing her in?" Smithson turned to Suzy.

"How?" Suzy couldn't fathom getting Ginny out of the bed, much less to his office. "Are you releasing her?"

"No. You'll just bring her to my office across the street." Smithson smiled and squeezed Ginny's shoulder.

"Can't you examine her here? You're here now." Suzy had other questions, but now she couldn't think of one. *What the fuck!?*

"The follow-up is part of the post-surgery evaluation."

Ginny nodded, "I remember that."

Suzy stared at her mother. "Doesn't surprise me."

"Great. Are there any questions?" Smithson looked at the two women.

Suzy managed, "What does the evaluation entail? And you can hear Ginny's breathing now. It's mild Darth Vader."

He smiled. "Let's have a listen."

"Suzy, I'm fine." Ginny never wanted to appear sick in front of a doctor.

Suzy couldn't convince her mother that this paradox created even more confusion; however, Ginny was sounding more coherent by the minute.

Smithson nodded. "Insurance requires a follow-up in the office." He placed his clipboard on the bed and put his stethoscope to his ears. He listened to Ginny's chest. "It is a bit labored. I'll prescribe something to clear that up." He touched the sheet over Ginny's knee. "I need to take a look." He waited for Ginny's approval and then pulled the sheet back. The knee was still bandaged. He picked up her ankle and moved her leg back to bend the knee.

Ginny made a face but stopped short of a guttural moan.

Suzy knew her mother would pass out before admitting pain to a bonafide doctor.

"You're doing well." Smithson covered her. "I'll see you both in the office." He smiled at Ginny and Suzy. He waited.

*What just happened?*

Smithson left.

"He…" Ginny could barely say a word before Suzy spoke over her.

"He is Dr. Smithson, Mom. The other doctor is Rivera." Suzy wasn't about to explain what a physician's assistant was.

"Is his son adopted?"

"Mom. Who just left?"

"Dr. Smith." Ginny gave Suzy a concerned look.

"Works for me." Suzy bit her lip. *And I missed another fucking opportunity to get information.*

Suzy walked into the hallway, but she didn't see him. She looked in a few adjacent rooms. Nothing. She came back into Ginny's room. "Mom, what just happened?"

"Weren't you listening?"

"Yes. I'm just trying to understand how you process information." Suzy sat.

"We're going to the doctor's appointment." Ginny was clear and confident.

"What else?"

"I'm not breathing well." Ginny put her hand on her chest.

"Correct. AND you can still exercise, even though your breathing is not perfect."

Ginny stared, remembering.

"What is it?" Suzy asked.

"I had a nightmare, Suzy." Ginny reached for her daughter's hand.

"Dreams are not prophecy. They are subconscious messages."

Ginny squeezed Suzy's hand. "I was an assassin. And you were my assignment."

"Were you watching *Bourne Identity* before you fell asleep?"

"It wasn't funny, Suzy."

Suzy pulled out her phone and did a search. "According to a dream interpretation site, this means you have issues to confront. Which reminds me… I found some letters, an old key and a spoon from the Tampa Bay Hotel in your secretary."

"Are you trying to distract me? The dream was awful. I was going to shoot you."

"Did you kill me?" Suzy put her phone away.

"No. I woke up. I was worried about you."

Suzy kissed her mother on the head. "I'm fine. You got it off your chest. What about the letters and stuff? Does that have anything to do with you being tied down?"

"What did the letters say?" Ginny looked baffled.

"They were love letters. *Darling* was the salutation." Suzy looked at the clock. "I've got to go."

"Those were my mother's. Her treasure." Ginny's expression was troubled.

"I could bring them here."

"No, I don't want to see them. I loved her. But she was very secretive. I wanted to understand her, I truly did." Ginny wringed her hands obsessively.

Suzy hurt for her mother. She could see how unhappy this revelation was. "You must exercise. Promise me you'll try."

"If I'm not dizzy, Suzy."

"You won't be."

"We'll see if you're right." Ginny blew her daughter a kiss.

Suzy blew one back. *I swear to God.*

Arnold paced the airside at Tampa International Airport, awaiting his boarding announcement. He texted Suzy.

Arnold: `Going to DC looksee`

Shedevil text: `Washington or Comics?`

He beamed. Arnold: `You know me well.`

Shedevil: `Comic con`

Arnold: `An Op. May be one for us or I'll solo.`

Shedevil: `Govt. or private? When will you be back?`

Arnold: `Couple days. Priv. How's Ginny?`

Shedevil: `Better. What's the Op?`

Arnold: `Peace project`

Shedevil: `Doesn't sound like DC?`

Arnold: `LOL`

Shedevil: `Peace & Love`

Arnold: `Tell Ginny hello`

Shedevil: `Travel safe`

Arnold answered his other cellphone, "Arnold Welch."

He paused to glance at an airport bar's television. A financial show displayed breaking news. He walked over and read the closed caption text running on the screen as he listened to the caller.

"I'm aware we're in production." Arnold continued to read the caption. "A troop withdraw doesn't equal a cancellation."

Arnold heard his flight's boarding call. "Why the fuck am I flying commercial?"

He listened, his face turning bright pink against his white oxford button down. He closed the call and strode to the gate, briefcase in hand. An air marshal he knew gave him a nod. Arnold returned the nod and continued to the first-class call.

Wisner reserved a gulf view. Informal at sunset, the Pink Pelican still maintained white cloth standards for the occasional celebrity athlete, tourist, or local who sought fine dining in all dayparts. Pink, as the locals called it, didn't dip into the cheap norms of the local early bird. The restaurant offered a light menu with small, overpriced pairings. Wisner didn't need to save money. He preferred coastal ambience and formal linens.

He placed a letter sized envelope under Suzy's napkin. He wore a favorite white golf shirt, khaki shorts, and sandals. He removed his sunglasses and hung them inside the V of his shirt.

The waiter came by and asked for his drink order.

"Iced tea… with half and half and Stevia."

"I like it." The waiter smiled. "I'll be right back."

Wisner crossed his arms and sat back. He watched the walkway leading from the parking lot to the porch dining. The salt breeze and outdoor misters made the temps tolerable in the worst of Florida summers. Large patio windows opened wide for alfresco dining and closed during inclement weather.

Suzy waved to Wisner. She wore a fitted black calf-length knit dress with a light denim shirt-dress coverup.

He stood as she approached the table, giving her a hug and light kiss on the cheek. "How was your day?"

She turned beet red. "Eh."

Wisner grinned. "Then let's hope the evening is better."

The waiter came over and placed the iced tea, half and half, and sweetener on the table. "Can I start a beverage?" he addressed Suzy.

*Okay. We're not drinking alcohol.* "I'll have an unsweet iced tea and a water."

He placed menus in front of them. "We have a few appetizers that aren't on the menu." He went on to explain the offerings.

Suzy watched Wisner prepare his iced tea while he intently listened to the waiter.

"Thai iced tea?" She puzzled.

Wisner laughed. "God forbid. They're good, don't get me wrong. I do have a sweet tooth. But sweetened condensed milk is over the top. How about you?"

"I'm a bitter person." Suzy heard what she had said and looked up at the waiter. "That didn't sound right. I like bitter flavors. But I do enjoy the occasional Thai iced tea. Dark chocolate is my super food."

The waiter smiled. "You'll need to consider our flourless chocolate cake." He left to attend to another table.

"Have a sip." Wisner handed her his tea.

She took the glass and sipped approvingly. "Pretty good."

His smile was comforting.

*God you're cute.*

His hair had grown a little longer and had a pronounced wave. His brown eyes were searching hers. "I like to take things slow."

*What does that mean?* She felt the elevator drop from her heart down to her pelvic floor. *Lord, have mercy.* She looked out at the sunset. "We're missing the main show."

He observed the sun dropping. "Hungry?" He touched her hand.

*Breathe.* "Kind of."

"Do you like fish spread?' He glanced at the menu.

"Sounds good." She picked up the envelope and opened it. She was a little baffled at the number of pages. Wisner motioned the waiter and ordered the appetizer.

She looked up and saw the CPA guy from the Lizard enter alone and move across the dining room. He nodded to her.

Her eyes followed him. *What are you doing here?*

Wisner distractedly stirred his tea. "That's more info than you need, but it provides the complete daily meds for Ginny's stay thus far."

"More than I need." Suzy focused on Frank. "You're talking to a data analyst," she laughed. "This might not be enough."

"That's frightening." Wisner took another sip. "What does a data analyst do?" He turned his chair toward her and crossed his legs. He placed one hand on the table and focused solely on her.

"It's not that interesting. We mostly do diagnostic analytics. We look at patterns and identify what appears to be working well and the factors that contribute and the opposite." *Hmm. What's Ginny's opposite? Me!* Suzy went on, "I have a business partner, Arnold Welch." She fanned herself. "Their family attended the same church as my grandparents. I worked on a study with Bart Welch, Arnold's father. That's how I met Arnold and we formed our own business."

Wisner nodded. "Did you two ever date?"

"God, no," Suzy shuddered. "We're strictly business. He's a funny guy. Weird. He needs a girlfriend who enjoys crude humor and comic books."

"So comic books are a turn off?" Wisner caressed the linen tablecloth. "Not that I'm a geek, but I do like the Marvel franchise."

"Arnold is all about DC. Batman and Wonder Woman predominately."

"Really, because he sounds more like a Deadpool guy." He tapped the table.

Suzy shook her head. "Anyway, Arnold's still involved with his father's firm. We teamed up on the down low. It's an Arnold thing. Everything's on a need-to-know basis, cause Bart's a driver personality." *Hmm. I just heard myself say that. Need-to-know.*

Wisner's brows knit together. "Arnold's father doesn't know about your partnership. And your families know each other?"

"Well, when you say it like that, it sounds clandestine. But it's just Arnold. My grandmother Woodson, Ginny's mom, dated Harlan Welch, I think, Arnold's grandfather back in the day. Not that anyone has said that. Arnold just gave me the wink, wink, nod, nod when he said our families go way back. All of the elders have passed."

"Harlan Welch is a great comic book name. Is there a flow chart?" Wisner laughed. "Easier question: what do you analyze?"

*Thank God! I thought we were just talking comics.* Suzy sat up straight and tried to square her shoulders. "A lot of market research. But we work on government projects, too. Climate data, education, grants, gun law."

Their eyes met.

*How's my posture?*

"You're independent contractors."

"We formed HIPS Data Solutions. Long story. Arnold wanted a cool acronym, and it was down to HIPS 'hidden in plain sight' or DOPE 'data, obvious, proof in evidence.' I didn't want anything to do with dope."

"It's not as boring as Wayne Enterprises or LexCorp, so I'm getting the vibe. So, is weed out?"

"Do you?"

Wisner smiled.

"I don't." *Doctors!*

The appetizer arrived. He placed his hand on hers while addressing the waiter. "We're going to take this slowly. Once we've finished the app, we'll give you our dinner order."

*That's what he meant by slowly.*

Wisner made her a cracker with fish spread, squeezing a little lemon on before he handed it to her.

She stared at it.

"Too much?" Wisner asked.

*I'm not used to anyone putting me first.* She took it. It tasted wonderful.

"I have a tendency to heap." He made a cracker for himself with tabasco.

"You don't think I'm hot?" She finished the cracker.

"Sure." He smiled.

She picked up the tabasco. "Ok to sprinkle it on? It's annoying to manage each cracker."

He nodded. "Go for it."

Suzy peppered the tabasco on.

Wisner kept his eyes on her.

The waiter placed Suzy's tea in front of her.

"How's the fish spread?" The waiter paused.

"Excellent." Wisner looked to Suzy.

"Do you have celery?" Suzy pushed the crackers in front of Frank. *Otherwise, I'll double in size.*

Wisner nodded. The waiter left.

Suzy took her coverup off, exposing the healing sunburn, mosquito bites, and scratches from yard work. She let it rest on the chair next to her.

Wisner touched her arm. "That looks painful."

"Oatmeal baths help." She made herself another cracker. "It was awful." Suzy moved the envelope into her bag.

"That reminds me, what about the Longhorn and the toilet?" Wisner munched.

"Where to begin?" Suzy entertained him the duration of the evening all the way up to the flourless chocolate cake.

She felt guilty. *How can I enjoy myself when Ginny is not well?* Suzy ran the fingers of both hands into her hair. "I don't understand how my mother is suddenly talking nonsense about being tied down, not caring for her bodily functions, forgetful and depressed, and then almost normal."

Wisner sat back.

"I'm supposed to take her to Smithson for a follow up. She's not exercising. How does this work?"

Wisner touched her hand. "One day at a time. Listen, I'm a caregiver for both of my parents. I own a small, assisted living facility where we all live."

*That sounds confining.* Suzy realized, "Your Dad left The Valley?"

"Not yet. Listen, my parents have good and bad days, too. They aren't always the most cooperative either. But Smithson is the best knee guy in Central Florida. The follow-up is your opportunity to discuss any concerns."

"The stalker van is for your parents."

Wisner laughed, "Did you think it was a ruse?"

"Like you don't watch *Dateline*?"

"How do you know I'm telling you the truth?"

*I don't.* "Now I need to overthink my overthinking." She pointed her fork at him. "Did you want to look at the meds?"

"I already did. Ginny is being treated for depression as well as pain and inflammation. I didn't see any conflict."

"Mom never took more than a blood pressure pill, an aspirin, and a multi-vitamin her entire life. She's never been depressed, depressed. Meaning, no medication."

"Do you want to go over it in detail?" he asked.

"I'm not sure," she sighed. "This has been relaxing."

"Let's take a walk on the beach."

It was dark, and the moon was full. They could see the restaurant in the distance and lamplit beach homes accentuated by waving palms. He carried their shoes. Suzy wore her backpack purse. Others walked ahead of them. The moon cast a luminous swath of yellow on the dark gulf waters that crested in ribbons of seafoam. Their clothing billowed, and her hair flew wildly.

"How old is your daughter? You just have one?" Wisner asked.

*I don't recall mentioning my daughter to you.* "Chloe's in college."

Wisner stretched. "What's she studying?"

"General ed at this point."

"I did the same. Took me a bit to decide on medicine."

Suzy stopped. "Can we sit down?"

He laughed. "Sure."

Suzy sat on the sand just far enough from the incoming tide so she wouldn't get wet.

He sat beside her. "Perhaps when things settle down for you, we can do this again."

"Let's be clear," Suzy sighed. "I'm fine being an acquaintance, a fellow caregiver you see at The Valley or The Lizard. We can do drinks, dinner, and laugh. But I'm not looking for love or sex." *I am. But I'm not. Damn it.*

"Friends." He gave her a fist bump. "So, we can Cosplay?"

"Hell, no," she laughed.

"I could use a plus one every now and then."

"Doable."

# CHAPTER 14

Suzy got to her office early. Jamal wasn't covering the security desk. A thin, no-nonsense woman of about 40 asked for her credentials.

"Jamal's day off?" Suzy gave her ID.

"He's taking a leave of absence." The woman looked at Suzy's ID and the computer listings. "Thank you, Ms. Lennox."

"Suzy is fine."

"Ms. Lennox." The woman nodded.

*Taking ourselves a little too seriously.* Suzy spotted her name tag: Anita Bauer. "Ms. Bauer, is Jamal okay?"

"Let's hope so, because it's not my job to know." Bauer waited for Suzy's next question.

*Okay. But now I'm worried about Jamal.* "Could you let him know I inquired?"

"Leave any correspondence with me and we'll make sure he gets it." Bauer's walkie talkie began to squawk. "Excuse me." She moved away from Suzy.

Suzy nodded and went to her office, surprised to find Arnold asleep on the couch. "You okay? Because it's my job to know." She shook him.

He opened his bloodshot eyes and squinted. "Suzy?"

"Did you stay here during the hurricane?" Suzy looked around. There was no evidence of Arnold's usual litter.

"I just got in." He sat up and stretched. He was still in his business shirt, suit slacks, and dress shoes.

"Oh, the DC meeting. That's right." She stared at his attire. "Did we take the job?" Suzy set her things down and pulled her office chair out.

Arnold smacked his face and stood and did a long cat stretch. "No. Want to go to breakfast?"

"No?" Suzy sat and put her feet on her desk. "As in nothing for us?"

"Usual bullshit, the military industrial complex." Arnold laid back down on the couch. "Bart's taking it."

"Shouldn't we discuss it before you give it to Bart?" Suzy sorted a stack of mail. "That reminds me, does your dad really not know about HIPS Data?"

Arnold slapped his face a few times. "Where did that come from?"

"Have you looked at the bills?" She waved the mail at him. "Maybe we should take the gig?"

"Why are you asking about Bart?"

Suzy grabbed a letter opener on her desk. "It came up when I was on a date with the doctor."

"I want a nurse." Arnold clapped his hands together. "Pretty please."

"Oh, there's a nurse there for you. Purple hair, cat eyeglasses…"

"Nice." Arnold rolled to his back and put both his hands behind his head. "What about Bart?"

"We were doing the usual first date tell me what you do… I mentioned the business and you and your dad."

Arnold sat up. "Is he a gyno?"

"No! Perv. And we're just friends."

"What's his name?"

"Frank Wisner. The one who showed up at Ginny's room—remember, she did the masked introduction."

Arnold scratched his head. "Let's talk at breakfast."

Suzy snapped her fingers. "Answer me."

"What was the question?"

"Does Bart know about our business?"

"It's never come up, Suzy."

"Seriously! Are you doing the eye thing because I'm not in the mood."

"You're never in the mood…" Arnold sat up. He looked at her with a solemn and serious expression. "Could you refrain from sharing our business arrangement?"

*Seriously.*

Arnold rubbed his face again. "What's the Ginny connection?"

"Wisner walked in when I was aggravated that Ginny was tied down." Suzy turned on her computer. "Do you listen to anything?"

"Right." Arnold sat back and stretched both arms across the back of the couch and closed his eyes. "I need coffee."

"Go home. Sleep."

"I'm trying to make sense of what you just said," Arnold snapped. His face got red. "Sometimes I just want a straight answer and a little java."

"I'm sorry. You dish it out, but you just can't take it. We've been partners long enough that Bart shouldn't be clueless."

"He's not!" Arnold got up and paced. "I'm not telling you my personal business or why I need privacy. But I'm going to make one thing perfectly clear." He bent over her desk and got into her face. "Don't fucking discuss this with anyone, not even me! And by the way, your fucking notebook over there. Updated." He pointed to bookends that held several binders on her credenza.

Suzy had never seen this Arnold. She didn't like him. He seemed dangerous. She pulled the list Dr. Wisner had given her from her purse. "I'm going to look up some of Ginny's meds." She remained unruffled. Defuse the heat. Let him calm down.

"How's her life story going?" Arnold yawned loudly. He sat down and resumed his position. He rubbed his face. "How did the most skeptical woman in the world agree to date a wise guy?"

"Wise guy. Haha." Suzy rolled her eyes.

Arnold's tone was even now, borderline serious. "Why did you accept a date with him?"

"It felt right. We're just friends."

"Does he know that?"

"Yeah."

Arnold crossed his legs. "Last question."

"Go on."

"What made you trust him?"

*Do you care?* "I find him easygoing." Suzy stayed put.

Arnold contemplated. "No further questions. Dun. Dun." His best *Law & Order* imitation. He lay down on the couch and turned away from Suzy.

She went back to her internet search. She found a website that allowed her to list all Ginny's prescriptions on a given day. It provided her a color code of mild to serious interactions.

She got out a set of highlighters and gave each medication a color so she could easily see how many times Ginny received each dose, looking for patterns.

She thumbed through the pages.

Arnold snored.

Wisner grabbed the newspaper bag off his lawn. He waved to a neighbor.

A large, black pickup truck with dark-tinted windows was parked a block away. He noticed exhaust vapors coming from the tailpipe.

He tucked the paper under his arm and watched the truck. He wondered why they were waiting there. He placed the paper in his right hand and followed the sidewalk toward the truck. It was positioned perfectly near the corner, not necessarily in front of a particular house. He couldn't see the driver, but he could hear music coming from the vehicle. It sounded like the movie score for *The Good, the Bad and the Ugly*.

He waved at the truck with his empty hand, moving toward it into the street on the driver's side. The truck moved into gear and accelerated backward, reversing away from Wisner. Wisner raised his hand to stop. The truck continued until it came to a cross street and turned around to speed away.

A tall, elderly woman who was walking her poodle heard the truck's tires squeal. "Better stick to the sidewalk, Frank."

"Ever seen that truck before?" He approached the woman. "I'm sorry, I've forgotten your name."

"Betty and Boop." Boop did his business on a neighbor's lawn as Betty studied his movement.

"Couldn't see the tag," Wisner talked to himself.

Betty dug into her pocket for a bag.

Wisner squinted. The sun was exceptionally bright. "My mother will get a kick out of your names." He shaded his eyes with his right hand.

Betty picked up her dog's poop and tied the bag. "Truck was there last night."

"Overnight?"

"Couldn't say. Loud music on. I could see a computer was on."

"Maybe a sheriff?" Wisner bent down and let the poodle sniff his hand. He scratched the dog's head. "Good, Boop."

Betty let the retractable leash out. The dog moved from Wisner further up the yard.

"How's your father?" Boop pulled at Betty. "Lana said he's still in rehab." She steadied herself.

Wisner nodded. "He's improving. He'll be home soon. Have you met my parents?"

"No. Lana has nice things to say."

Wisner crossed his arms and nodded. "You know Lana. Come by some time. Mom would like Boop."

Betty pressed her leash and reeled the poodle in. "If I see your Mom out." Betty followed Boop. "We're off." She continued along the sidewalk.

"Have a good day." Wisner watched the two until they were out of view. He glanced at the houses and cars parked in the driveways close by. There were no other people outside.

He checked his watch. Most people were at work or school, so who was the driver looking for?

Suzy opened a bag of Cheetos. It was getting late, and she needed to get home. She went over the drug interactions again. She had created a list and spreadsheet from the hospital and rehab daily records. Some meds were given on different days at different times, some multiple times a day, others PRN.

She made notes:

PRN = prescription as needed

Effexor—antidepressant and nerve pain medication twice daily

Enoxaparin—for clotting—10 days

Glipizide—for diabetes—twice daily

Lisinopril—for blood pressure—once daily

Meclizine—treats motion sickness—3 times daily

Norco—prn for pain

Norvasc—for blood pressure—once daily

Temazepam—sleep aid—bedtime

Xanax—prn anxiety

Polyethylene Glycol—once daily for constipation

Colace—prn—constipation

Haldol—prn for severe agitation

Suzy called Wisner's cell. He didn't answer. "Hey, I'm looking at the med list. Call me." Suzy plugged the doses into an app that indicated which were mild, moderate, or dangerous interactions.

She called Chloe. She needed to talk to someone, anyone, to keep her from screaming.

Chloe picked up.

"Hey daughter, what are you doing?"

Chloe yawned, "You woke me."

"I could use a nap." Suzy drew circles around the drug names. Then put a diagonal line through each. "Do you want to call me back?"

"No, I am going to work out." Chloe perked up. "I'm thinking of joining R.O.T.C."

Suzy drew a question mark and wrote ROTC. "You just got a scholarship." Suzy munched on a Cheeto. "Isn't that the point of ROTC, to get an education through a military opportunity?"

"Damien's in ROTC and he thinks I would like it. The workouts are great."

Suzy tapped her Cheeto-orange fingertips on the desktop. *You don't like being told what to do, Chloe, and you're not a team player. How's this going to work?* "Are you alone?"

"Damien is on his way over, why?"

"Come home this weekend. We'll do a spa day, and you can visit grandma." Suzy licked her fingers, then grabbed for a tissue.

"Can I bring Damien?"

*No!* "Sure." *Otherwise, you'll avoid me.* "We should get to know each other." *And find out why Damien wants you to join the ROTC!*

"We'll stay on the sleeper sofa."

Suzy took a deep breath. *Am I going to like him?* "Stay in Grandma's room. She's still in rehab."

"Let's take her out to lunch."

"I'll see what's possible. Otherwise, we'll bring her lunch and visit in the common area." Suzy threw her Cheetos bag in the trash.

"She'd do a cartwheel for Popeye's Chicken," Chloe laughed.

"Good point. So, what does Damien like to eat?" Suzy closed her tablet. "I'll get some snacks."

"He's keto. All about fitness."

*What the hell is keto?* "What do I get?"

"He's calling. Just Google it. Love you, bye." Chloe was gone.

"So much for talking about Grandma's meds."

Arnold texted: `I'm in the parking lot. Why are you still here?`

Suzy: `Working.`

Arnold: `Did I leave a jacket there?`

Suzy got up to look around Arnold's desk and saw a navy blazer on the floor next to the couch.

Suzy: `Found it on the floor next to the couch. I'll bring it out.`

Suzy picked it up. The suit was heavy. She noticed the label, then felt in the pocket. *A gun?*

Arnold walked in and caught her expression. "I can explain."

She held the jacket out.

"I have a concealed carry permit." Arnold grabbed the jacket. "Don't look at me like that."

"I'm mostly shocked you wear Tom Ford. The gun doesn't surprise me." Suzy went back to her desk to pack up.

"He's no Alexander McQueen." Arnold did the eye dart.

"Why a gun?" Suzy closed her backpack.

"Lions, tigers, and bears…"

"I hate guns." She put her pack on.

"I'll add it to the notebook."

"Seriously! After all the studies we've done? I want nothing to do with guns."

"Why?"

Suzy didn't need to justify herself. "I'd abolish them if I had my way. You know, since Ginny's been behaving weirdly, it feels like everyone is. Is there something you need to tell me?"

Arnold's face turned beet red. "Is there something you should ask?"

"I just did."

Suzy's cell dinged. It showed Wisner.

She texted him: `I've got to drive. Talk later?`

Arnold put the jacket on. "My personal demons do not pertain to you. Anyway, there'll come a time when I'm ready to talk."

*What does that mean?*

Suzy got home to find an Amazon package by her door. She grabbed it and tossed it on the kitchen counter. She put her pack down, poured herself a Chablis, and examined the small envelope. She couldn't remember if she had ordered anything. She took a gulp of wine, then opened the package and found the movie, *The Snake Pit*. "We finally meet."

She grabbed her glass and the DVD and headed to her bedroom. She needed a night off. Something to take her mind off... *Wait. This is going to make me obsess about Ginny even more.*

She decided to stall by showering, then she started the movie and got in bed.

*Insanity as entertainment? Horror, more like it.*

The trailer indicated that the production was based on Mary Jane Ward's 1946 semi-autobiographical novel of the same name. The black and white movie gave Suzy some perspective of the time when her mother would have seen it. Suzy did a quick calculation. Ginny would have been in elementary school when the film came out, which means her Grandmother Woodson would have taken Ginny to see the movie. She remembered stories of their going on adventures to Ocala. *Childhood memories. That's why it made an impression!* Or did Ginny see this on a classic movie channel later in life?

The movie played.

"Seriously! The lead character is Virginia! Oh Mom, I'm sure that made an impression on you. Why does everything come back to Virginia?"

Suzy paused the movie to Google the meaning of some names. Virginia—Virgin. Pure. *That's a subconscious pressure.* She Googled the movie. She saw warnings that it was not recommended for children. *That's long before movie ratings.* She scrolled through comments from famous people who had seen the movie as children and a medical professional's opinion from the era. The snake pit title had a connotation that if a person were to be thrown in a pit of snakes, it could scare them into insanity or possibly an insane person into sanity. *So, an asylum would be a scare tactic in this reference vs. a place to get well? Or is scaring the crap out of someone a wellness strategy?*

Suzy hit play. She watched. This Virginia ends up in a mental hospital and doesn't know why. She has no memory... *I'm beginning to understand.*

Ginny stood for Nurse Larsen. She swiveled her hips to get into the wheelchair.

"Is Suzy coming?"

The nurse brushed Ginny's hair. "Your daughter is taking you to see Dr. Smithson."

"Am I going home?"

"Depends on what the doctor says." Larsen handed Ginny a damp washcloth. "You should wash your face."

Ginny took the cloth and stared at it.

Larsen made motions for Ginny to imitate. "Wipe your face, Ginny."

Ginny wiped a bit and put the damp cloth in her lap.

"Do you need to go to the bathroom?" The nurse put the footrests down on the wheelchair.

"I should." Ginny put her feet on the metal rests.

The nurse put the brush down and grabbed the cloth. She scrubbed Ginny's face pink. "That should wake you up." She wheeled her into the bathroom. "You're transferring well. Your daughter's not seen you out of the bed in a while."

"I walked for Suzy." Ginny pulled her sweater closed.

"That was several weeks ago." Larsen unlocked the wheelchair's wheels and looked up to see Suzy enter. "Ginny is using the toilet."

Suzy's eyes got big. "That's great, Mom."

"You saw me walk," Ginny mumbled.

Larsen handed Suzy a folder. "This is for Dr. Smithson."

"Where are we going?" Suzy opened the folder and looked at the stapled forms.

Larsen called out from the bathroom door, "You and Ginny are going across the street. Six story building. He's on the third floor."

Suzy noted the address on the outside of the file.

Ginny dried her hands on a brown paper towel as Larsen rolled her to Suzy.

"Have a good visit." Larsen snapped a seatbelt around Ginny's waist.

Suzy gave the file to Ginny. "That reminds me, Chloe and her new boyfriend want to take you to lunch." Then Suzy looked to Larsen. "Is there any place we could do lunch that's in walking distance or is there a courtesy van that can drop Ginny off?"

"You can't take her off campus. It's a liability issue." Larsen turned to leave.

"Whoa"—Suzy moved to the doorway, blocking Larsen—"I'm taking her off campus now."

Larsen pushed her glasses up the bridge of her nose. "Technically, you are taking her *on* campus."

"So, a Valley employee could take Ginny to the Smithson appointment?" *How did I not challenge this earlier?*

"Yes. But as Healthcare Surrogate, you want to know how Ginny's doing…" Larsen smiled down at Ginny and turned a stone-cold stare at Suzy.

*Bitch!* "If it's a liability's issue, wouldn't The Valley take her over and I meet them for the appointment?"

"But you're here," Larsen grinned. "Problem solved."

Larsen pulled disposable sunglasses from her pocket. She put the dark rimless film with paper temples on Ginny. "It's bright out there."

Suzy threw up her hands. "Why didn't we use those instead of the mask?"

Larsen cleared her throat. "A patient checked out earlier and left them. You're welcome."

"Wait. Is there a cafeteria on campus?"

Larsen looked at the clock. "You're going to be late."

"Suzy, I'm not hungry." Ginny was annoyed.

"The hospital cafeteria is an option." Larsen expelled a deep breath.

*That's not even on THIS campus!* "We'll plan lunch with Chloe when we get back." Suzy pushed Ginny out of the room.

The small transport wheelchair took every bump in the pavement like a wheelbarrow on a cobblestone road.

"Good thing you're strapped in, Mom." The noon heat sent a trickle of sweat down the back of Suzy's head to the crack of her ass. "Are you hot? I'm thermal combusting." The pitted pavement caught the wheels of the transport chair creating unexpected stops. "God, I hope I don't fly over you."

Ginny crooked her head to look up at Suzy. "You're breathing heavy. You should exercise with me."

"*You* should exercise with you, Mom!" Suzy stopped in the shade of a large oak and locked the chair's wheels.

"I'm under a doctor's care, Suzy. Don't sass me."

*Don't sass me.* "My shoulders are killing me." Suzy took her backpack off and placed it on Ginny's lap. She rolled her shoulders, then her neck.

"Hang it on the back of the chair." Ginny faced forward. "You really should walk more."

Suzy took the folder from Ginny and fanned herself.

"Funny, we're on our way to discuss *your* walking." *How's the ride?*

"We're going to be late, Suzy."

A four-seater golf cart passed them. It had The Valley logo on it, two smoking nurses, an elderly patient, and an obese uniformed driver.

"That's bullshit!" Suzy called out.

The elderly male patient waved at Ginny.

"Shh!" Ginny said. "He can hear you." Ginny waved back.

Smithson's waiting room temperature and patient base were both 80 plus.

Ginny pulled her sweater tight around her waist. "Why's your face so red, Suzy?"

Suzy fanned herself with a magazine. "My internal organs are boiling."

"Go to the restroom and wash your face."

*Brilliant idea!* "Thank you, Mom." Suzy got up at the same time a nurse came out and called "Ginny Compton."

Suzy moved with Ginny out of the waiting room to the coolness of a hallway leading to the patient rooms.

Once they were settled, Suzy used the room's sink to towel her face. They were both lulled into a forty-five-minute heat sleep while they waited for the doctor.

Smithson knocked, then came in. "Afternoon ladies."

He had Ginny stand and hold onto a walker. He moved her leg.

She couldn't get on the table, and he determined her follow-up x-ray would need to be rescheduled.

Suzy asked about the anti-depressants.

"I don't prescribe those," Smithson said. "The shift physician at The Valley and any specialist they consult with can answer those questions."

*Of course.*

Smithson went on about how well he performed the surgery and Ginny's exemplary behavior in her patient role.

*Exemplary.* Suzy felt her heartbeat fast. It came on suddenly, and she felt lightheaded. Maybe it was a lack of sleep or food. Or maybe it was the stress of listening to this doctor pat himself on the back while also trying to convince her mother to cooperate with him and other dizzying facts. *Don't pass out.*

"Some patients take longer than others to recuperate." Smithson wanted Ginny back in four weeks.

"Four weeks?" Suzy said in almost a whisper. Her throat was dry.

Ginny promised to do her exercises.

"I'd like to get the x-ray then."

"Do it now." Suzy's tone was demanding and hoarse, her frustration flooding in. She didn't need Smithson's nonsense. "This *is* the follow-up!"

Smithson nodded. "Ginny…"

"We can come back," Ginny offered.

*No. We can't!* Suzy clapped her hands rapidly. "Mom, if you don't get your x-ray today, your next visit will be with Nurse Larsen accompanying you."

Ginny looked stung.

Suzy continued, "Do the x-ray now. The next visit can be by Teledoc."

Smithson looked to Ginny with a comforting smile.

Ginny smiled at him. "Aren't we coming back in four weeks?"

Smithson wrote some notes. "It would be helpful to get the x-rays today," he said softly.

Ginny looked at Suzy. "Are you going to help me?"

Suzy took a long inhale. "I'm not an x-ray tech."

Smithson went back to hugging the clipboard. To Suzy, "Do you have any other questions?"

"Yeah, why is this room an inferno? Your hallway is like a vegetable crisper. Shouldn't there be warning labels about keeping hydrated?" She rubbed her eyes.

"We'll get you a bottle of water." Smithson reached over and gave Ginny's shoulder a squeeze. "Keep up the good work, Ginny."

*What work?* "Hold please," Suzy addressed the two of them. She calmed down. "Mom's getting an x-ray now and then we're going to see if she's improving. Right? Because, sorry Mom, you're not doing your exercises, so he can't say good work." Suzy held her hand up to her mother. "And it's not your fault from what I have observed. Something's not right. You're confused."

"Your mother had a major surgery," Smithson reminded Suzy.

"And what percent of your major surgery patients are not exercising or rehabbing as planned?"

"Suzy, have some respect for the doctor."

"Your mother, like a small percent of my patients, is progressing at a slower pace."

An hour later, the x-rays showed what Smithson confirmed, a knee that was healing beautifully. When they got back to The Valley, Ginny wanted to rest.

Suzy went to the bathroom, washed her face again, added lipstick, and tossed her sweaty locks. She was starving, but equally tired. She sat next to her mother. "I'd get in bed with you, Mom, if we were at home."

Ginny chuckled, "This bed's too small."

Her roommate had been discharged. Suzy turned her chair and propped her feet on the bed.

Ginny grabbed her television remote and turned the TV on. Suzy was impressed. This felt like old Ginny.

"Can we discuss the government conspiracy?"

Ginny didn't follow. "What conspiracy?" She found a home shopping show.

137

Suzy closed her eyes. "The one that tied you down. You said people were watching you and me."

"I didn't say that." Ginny turned up the volume.

"Turn it down, please," Suzy sighed. "Could you take a minute to focus?"

Ginny muted the television.

"Mom, you were tied down the first time I came to visit you."

Ginny gave Suzy a concerned gawk.

"You wanted me to write your story. You said you were part of a government program." Suzy motioned for Ginny to hand her the remote. She turned the television off. "Focus, please."

"Are you sure it was me?"

*You seriously don't remember?* "Maybe government was the wrong choice of words?" Suzy exhaled.

Ginny played along. "What kind of program?"

"You brought it up, Mom." Suzy rubbed her eyes.

Ginny grew quiet.

Suzy handed Ginny the remote. "You've had a busy day. Relax."

# CHAPTER 15

"Nice surprise hearing from you." Wisner's voice was soothing to Suzy's ears. She could almost smell his cologne.

"Hey, want to grab a sunset?" Suzy said, as she walked to her car. "I could meet you somewhere." She stopped in her tracks. She saw his van as she stepped under the parking garage canopy. *Where are you?*

"Where are you?"

Wisner let his window down. "Watching you."

She heard an echo in her phone and saw him wave.

She shut her cell off and walked over. "Are you coming or going?"

"Going."

Suzy stuck her head in the window. She could smell him now. "Any dead bodies back there?"

He laughed. "We could drive over to Main Street. There's still time. Get in."

"Are you trying to abduct me?" She couldn't believe how he brought out her playful side. Her confidence.

"Yes."

Suzy walked around to the passenger side. "She was last seen getting into the good doctor's van."

Wisner started the engine, then put the van in reverse.

Suzy buckled up and watched him drive. He was still in doctor attire: a white dress shirt with a few buttons undone, khaki slacks, and brown wingtip shoes. Heavy cologne. His hair was unruly.

He smiled at her, giving her heart a hit of arrythmia. "What are you thinking?"

"How do you get away with wearing cologne when most doctor offices have signs that discourage it?"

"No one has complained."

*I'm not.* She took a deep breath. "A few days ago, Mom and I had lunch with Chloe. Her boyfriend couldn't make it. It was a picnic in The Valley's courtyard with Larsen being super-nosy. Anyway, Chloe and Ginny spent time spitting into a DNA test tube after we had our meal. Made me want to gag. But surprisingly, Ginny is starting to act kind of normal, which makes me wonder, how?"

"That's great. She's recovering." He drove the back streets to a nearby marina.

"What are you thinking about?"

"Grabbing a pizza and a beer." He focused on finding the perfect parking spot. "And sharing a sunset with you." He backed the van up.

Suzy looked out the windshield to see a gorgeous tangerine pink sky. The marina was bustling with boaters returning from a day on the gulf. Some had been fishing as a business, others for leisure, and a few had been on tourist ferries. They got out.

"Cabin, mansion, or mountain chalet?" She posed.

"Well, why not all three?"

"That was not a selection."

"Expand your thinking."

"I should."

"Well, given we live in Florida, I'll go with mountain chalet." He paused momentarily as a skateboarder crossed in front of them.

"Interesting… cold."

He squinted as they faced the sun. "What about you? Which would you choose?"

"Cabin, hands down. A mansion is too much to manage, and while I might enjoy a chalet, a cabin seems cozy."

"Cozy. Noted."

When they had reached a quiet spot, they sat on the short end of the pier and put their feet in the water. They stayed that way for a while, just listening to the seagulls and watching the sky fall into sunset.

The sun's yoke dipped below the horizon as Frank put his arm around Suzy. "This is the friend shoulder move."

Suzy closed her eyes. She bent her head on his shoulder. "I accept."

Both were content.

"Frank"—she turned to look at him—"you're an appropriate guy."

"I've been called better." He smiled.

# CHAPTER 16

Larsen checked Ginny's vitals. "Time to go exercise." The nurse made her notes.

Ginny grabbed the rail of her bed. "I don't think I can. I'll fall."

"Come on, Ginny. This isn't a hotel. You have to exercise or go home." Larsen pulled an outfit from the narrow closet next to her bed. "You need to get dressed."

Ginny began hyperventilating. "Tom..tomor...ow."

"Breathe through your nose." Larsen put the clothes back into the closet. "I'll get something to calm you." Larsen closed Ginny's gaping mouth and encouraged her to breathe.

"I want to go home," Ginny whimpered.

Minnie grabbed her mail from the seat of her truck. Her cellphone rang. She put the call on speaker and stuck her phone in her open shirt. "What's up, Suzy?"

The towering woman slammed the truck door and sorted the mail.

"Ginny's being discharged."

"That's great." Minnie opened her power bill. "I just came from the P.O. Boxes."

"It's not." Suzy was agitated. "Mom's not walking. I can't bring her to my house because I'm not home all day."

"How can I help?" Minnie proceeded to her front porch and sat on the step. "You want to bring her here? FYI, Ginny just has junk mail."

"Can you keep her for a week, until I can figure out what her insurance will take care of? And her bills are all forwarded to me."

Minnie placed the bills together. "I can do a week. So, she's in a wheelchair?"

"She will be."

"I'm going to have to build a small ramp up her porch. I'm sure I have enough scrap board to cover the stairs. It'll be easier than trying to lift her if she has to come and go."

"I didn't think of that." Suzy's voice trailed off. "She does have a walker she's supposed to use."

"When will you be here?"

"Tonight. She's being discharged around 4 p.m. and that means we will be in 'going home' traffic on U.S. 19."

"I don't envy you. Okay, I will open the house. It's going to be dark when you get here, so drive up beside the house as close as you can, depending on how much I get done." Minnie swat a mosquito that landed on her arm.

"Good idea, we won't have to juggle her," Suzy agreed.

"I'll get Ginny some chicken and potato salad. She's a lot more cooperative when there is bait."

*Cooperative?* "When was Mom uncooperative?"

"Suzy, you and your mother, hell Chloe, too, are the most obstinate humans on the planet. Ginny will hate the ramp. I could barely get Ginny to come to the front door when she was walking. She always insisted on the back door. Said if she allowed anyone in the front, it would trigger those watching to send traveling salesmen or government census people to pester her."

*Watching?* "Did she say *who* was watching? Has anyone come to her house?"

Minnie laughed. "Not lately. Google Earth doesn't know we exist. We're hidden. Actual census takers miss us thanks to the Jennings farm. When Romeo's post office closed in the 1950s, we got mixed into the Dunnellon addresses. Your family and mine always got mail from the postmaster at Romeo and later a box in Dunnellon."

"True," Suzy mused. "Jennings kept the place closed off with warning signs. The old man never had television. Radio was it."

"Oh my God, his CB radio would blast through my favorite shows or record player. I still don't understand how." Minnie fanned herself. "Ginny and I were watching the local news about a prisoner who escaped Starke and as soon as they were to give his last location, Jennings connected with someone and his 'Big 10-4' drowned out everything. I never heard Ginny cuss until that day. We were grateful when a storm took his tower... Hey, I've got to go if I'm building that ramp."

"Thank you, Minnie! See you tonight."

## 1920 Tampa Bay Hotel

Monica woke to unfamiliar furnishings. She glanced around: a vanity, a dressing mirror, a tall potted plant, a wicker chair. Where was she? Her stomach gurgled and her head ached. She pulled the sheets back and noticed she was wearing her white cotton slip and pink stained underpants. She spied her tapestry bag on the white dresser.

The room's drapes veiled the outline of a large keyhole-shaped window. It looked like something from a fairytale, arched round at the top and angled down to a flat bottom.

She held her stomach, sure she was going to vomit. Was she in a tower? Was this her Rapunzel confinement?

"What have I done?" she whispered to herself.

She then noticed a tray of assorted empty dishes, silverware, a demi-tasse spoon, glassware, and two bottles of wine on the bedside table.

There was a knock at the door.

She jumped. She could hear laughing, then a series of knocks.

"Sleeping Beauty, Lou and Joe here. Are you ready to have some lunch and play a little shuffleboard?"

"No, thank you." She pulled the sheets up around her shoulders. Her mother was expecting her home to work today. Where was Deacon Welch? How would she get home?

The theatre! She couldn't remember much after that.

"You okay, Monk?"

"How did I get here?" she called out.

She could hear the men chattering. Why did he call her Monk?

"Could we come in? We're quite the spectacle talking through your door if you know what I mean?"

She got up and looked for her dress. She found it in an armoire. She slipped it over her head, stopped, and looked at her long hair in the mirror. It needed brushing. She tied it in a loose knot. She padded across the floor, wondering where her shoes and stockings were.

She opened the room's door and two handsome faces greeted her. They looked fetching, better than she felt. Both were grinning happily. She could smell their cologne and shave soap.

"You were quite the bearcat." Joe lightly tweaked her nose and growled. He handed her a small bouquet of flowers.

Lou took off his tweed cap and tucked it under his arm. "You surprised us all, Monk."

She looked into their fresh eyes. Hers were burning and tired. "All? How?"

"Permission to be frank?" Lou stepped toward her. His scent delivered a sharp spike to her nasal passages and then her brain.

Monica investigated the hallway and saw no one, so she let the men in. She stepped back. Lou stared into her eyes.

She shuddered. "Why are you calling me Monk?"

He pushed her aside, strode to the window, and looked out. "It's your nickname. You picked it out yourself. See those wine bottles there."

Monica's brows drew up. She sniffed the flowers, felt queasy. She whispered, "Prohibition."

Joe plopped onto the wicker chair in the corner. "It's legal." He crossed his leg over his knee and put his hands behind his head. "Catholic monks made it."

Monica picked up one of the bottles and saw the monk image on the label. "It's sacramental wine?"

"It's not exactly legal for general purposes but was acquired as a gift to Deacon Welch. He's receiving a couple of cases." Lou continued to look out the window. "This place was once a palace. It's too bad old man Plant died."

Monica sat on the edge of the bed. "How do I get home?"

Joe moved toward her and got down on one knee. "Do you remember anything?"

She shook her head.

Lou turned around. "We'll take you in my Studebaker. Right after lunch." He grabbed the wicker chair and moved next to Joe. "Monk, you're embarrassed 'cause you're a good girl. It was your first-time drinking and gambling."

"I'm no longer a good girl," she whispered. She thought about her mother, Catherine Hibbitt Woodson, and father, Joseph. Monica was their perimenopause baby, their only. They ran their own grove stand along Florida State Road No. 5. They cherished her, worried about her. Her father was unwell, never having quite recovered from a rattlesnake bite that nearly took his life.

Lou touched her knee. "You did us proud. You could hold your own with any New York girl."

"I'm not a flapper." She felt ashamed.

"Could have fooled us last night." Lou winked to Joe. "You're now a modern woman."

Joe shook his head at Lou. To Monica, "It's a long drive to Romeo. You'll feel better if you settle your stomach and eat."

Her abdomen burbled on cue. "I couldn't. I need to go home." She held her belly. Her eyes welled up.

Lou was now firm and displeased. "Freshen up. We'll have a light lunch and drive you home. Even check in on the deacon and make sure his wine was delivered."

"We drink grape juice for communion." Monica felt flushed.

"Wine's just old grape juice," Joe laughed.

"Could I lie down?" She curled up on the bed. "Come back for me after you've had lunch?"

"Sure, Monk." Lou took Joe's hand and pulled him up from the floor. "We'll bring you some soup, crackers, and a ginger ale. You nap."

Joe bent over Monica and gave her a kiss on the cheek. "Sleep tight, Snow White."

Monica kept her eyes closed. "I feel I've eaten a poisoned apple."

"I'm your Prince Charming, baby. You're in good hands."

"That was Sleeping Beauty. You'd be the Handsome Prince if it was Snow White. But I woke up thinking I was in Rapunzel's tower."

Joe tweaked her nose softly. "That wine must have been made by the Brothers Grimm."

Ginny slept the entire drive home from The Valley. When Suzy arrived at Ginny's, Minnie had the front porch swept with a basket of flowers on either side of the posts next to the new ramp. The storm panels were gone. Lamp light glowed a soft ivory through the tied back curtains and opened screen door.

Ginny barely stirred as Minnie picked her up and placed her in the wheelchair.

"The house looks amazing." Suzy grabbed her mother's things from the back seat.

Minnie sniffed. "She's damp. Your car smells like urine."

"I was hoping they would give me some supplies, but I couldn't stop with Ginny like this." Suzy's eyes welled. "I'll run and get some things in the morning. I just need to load some towels under her and clean her up."

Minnie pushed the wheelchair up the ramp and into the screened door. "Suzy, I don't know if I'm the right person to care for Ginny."

*Don't panic.* "It's just one week." Suzy rummaged through the bag Larsen had given her. "There's only a small batch of medications to hold her over until I can get Ginny's physician to prescribe them locally."

Minnie pushed Ginny into the house. "I'll grab some towels so we can clean her up."

"Don't worry. I'll call a nursing agency to see about some home visits."

Ginny woke. She looked at the living room. "Home?"

Minnie stood in front of Ginny. "You are, Miss Ginny. Can I get you some of your favorite chicken and potato salad? We want to shower you first."

Ginny nodded.

"That sounds so good." Suzy plopped onto the sofa. "Give me a few, Minnie." Suzy stretched out on the sofa and closed her eyes. "I can barely keep my eyes open."

Suzy woke to the smell of fried chicken on the table beside her. She glanced over to see Minnie assisting Ginny's shaking hands with a spoonful of potato salad. Ginny was in a fresh nightgown and propped up on her recliner. "Did you shower her?"

Minnie nodded. "I got in with her. It was that or lift her in and out of a bath. Shower was easier."

Suzy laughed. "I'm sorry I missed that." She grabbed a piece of chicken and took a bite. "Oh my God, this tastes so good. Right, Mom?"

Ginny looked to Suzy. "It's okay."

Minnie shook her head in disbelief. "Miss Ginny, how's the potato salad?"

"Salty." Ginny pushed it away.

The next morning Suzy said goodbye to Ginny. "Minnie's right here with you. I'm going to come back in a few days. But Minnie can call me at any point. Just work on getting well. Okay?" She kissed her mother's forehead.

Ginny was disoriented. She ignored Suzy and called for Minnie to throw her clothes away. She didn't need them.

Suzy met Minnie in the kitchen. They talked in whispers. Ginny had better hearing than the younger women.

Suzy got close to Minnie. "Why would she want to throw her clothes away?"

"It's definitely a chemical issue." Minnie looked at all the meds on the counter that Suzy had brought back. "I wish we knew which one turned *on* her thinking."

Suzy made a bowl of cereal for Ginny and started toward Ginny's room when Minnie stopped her.

"I thought you were leaving. How's she supposed to get back to normal if we treat her like a patient in a hospital?" Minnie took the cereal and sat it on the table. "I'll bring her in once her tea is ready. Just go. I'll let you know how she's doing."

Suzy nodded. "I'll call you later, once I'm at the office. I need to pay bills and check on some deposits. If you need anything, just text or call."

Minnie gave Suzy a hug.

"Mom, I'm leaving," Suzy called as she was heading for the door. She went back to Ginny's room and saw her mother sitting on the edge of the bed and looking into her bedside drawer.

"Throw these away." Ginny pointed to a bible and some tissues, mints, and aspirin.

"Why throw them away?" Suzy walked over and took the aspirin, not certain if Ginny would take them by accident. "You may need them at some point."

"I don't want them."

"Want and need are different things. You could regret getting rid of something you don't want today, but in fact may need later."

Ginny grabbed the bible. "Take it." The elderly woman tossed it at Suzy. "It's never done this family any good."

Minnie stuck her head in. "Are you ready for breakfast, Ginny?" Minnie took the bible and aspirin from Suzy. "I'll keep it."

Ginny stared at Minnie.

"Let's use the walker." Minnie tried to coax Ginny up.

"Dr. Smith's son says I am not ready." Ginny stayed put.

Suzy kissed Ginny's forehead, then turned and said, "Thank you, Minnie."

Minnie placed the walker in front of Ginny. "He said you're ready to take some small steps. I'll catch you if you stumble."

Ginny stood and grabbed the walker. "Get behind me." Ginny wore her slip resistant socks and shuffled a baby step forward.

Suzy marveled at the simplicity of their interaction. *Note to self: Be more like Minnie.*

Suzy and Arnold reviewed their outstanding commitments. He sat across the small boardroom table in their inner office.

Suzy had the bills organized by accounts payable and receivable. "We'll split up the calls. It's obvious we've let too many slide the past 90 days."

Arnold cleared his throat. "Notmydepartment," he muttered under his breath.

Suzy handed him three. "You call these. See if you can get a credit card payment or something. I'll whittle these." She moved a stack in front of herself.

"We could hire a collection agency to do this." Arnold gave her a gameshow host wink. "I like earning and spending better." He added another wink.

Suzy grimaced. "Part of earning is collecting. And since when do you wink?"

He gave her a big toothy smile. "I'm trying to be delightful, in hopes you'll take over all collections." He winked again. "Is it working?"

"No and stop doing that." She dialed the conference speaker phone.

Arnold put a finger to his lips and watched the master.

The line picked up. "Betty Hicks Charitable Foundation. How may I help you?"

Suzy leaned in. "This is Suzy Lennox from HIPS Data Solutions, and I would like to speak with your accounts payable."

"Oh Suzy, this is Renata. Have we not paid you?"

Suzy pointed at Arnold.

Arnold walked his hands across the table to make mock footsteps sounds. "Hey Renata, what's up?" He gave Suzy the gameshow host grin.

"Was that you in D.C. recently? We were waiting in the cab line, and I waved. You didn't see me. You got into that black Rolls limo. I swear there was Secret Service with you."

Arnold shook his head, no. "Now Renata, if there were Secret Service, which there wasn't, I'd have to say there wasn't, because you could be a foreign spy trying to gather intelligence on Suzy and we all know... Shh!" He whispered, "Suzy has no intelligence." He gave Suzy a wink.

Renata cackled. "Sorry Suzy. So, it was you, Arnold?"

Arnold gave Suzy a wide, exaggerated smile. "Renata, the secret to our service is you must feel you got a deal when you hired us?"

"He must be a hoot to work with," Renata concluded. "We'll get that check out today."

"One of a kind." Suzy gave Arnold a thumbs up.

They closed the call.

"Now that you're over collection anxiety…"

He wiped his brow. "Let's hope the next client also saw me in D.C."

Suzy tapped a pen on the desk. "A Rolls limo?"

Arnold gave her a straight face. "It wasn't the pentagon, Suzy. It was a government contractor who had tentacles in Bart's wheelhouse."

"And why didn't we want that job?" Suzy made a note on the Hicks invoice regarding the day and time of their conversation.

Arnold got serious. "What do you want to know?"

"Why did you turn it down? Did we miss a big payday?" Suzy grabbed the next invoice.

Arnold closed his eyes. He threw his head back. "Be more specific."

Suzy grabbed another invoice. "What or who was the study for?"

"The contractor wanted data on protestors, their background, and allegiances to understand influencers." He gave her the eye dart.

*Whatever.* "Listen, from now on, we discuss it before you turn something down." She moved the speaker phone. "That doesn't sound like something we would turn down."

"Actually, it's to promote war." Arnold was serious. "And I'll answer anything. Just ask."

"Well, I'd like a chance to consider it. I mean, I'd actually like to have a savings account and maybe an I.R.A. someday."

Arnold saluted her. "You will. Ask. Me. Anything."

"Why do you keep saying that? Tell me anything. I don't need your jokes every day." She dialed the next number. "Shoo. Go make your calls."

"I can be a dick, I know. But really." He did a mime wipe from smile to serious.

The caller picked up, and Suzy went into her collection spiel. She waved Arnold off.

# CHAPTER 17

The 168-hour week moved excruciatingly slow. Minnie followed the instructions The Valley had given Suzy, but it seemed Ginny was getting progressively worse. The older woman couldn't focus on simple tasks, barely ate, wheeled herself aimlessly from one corner of the small house to the other, and was satisfied only when Minnie parked her on her small front porch each day to wait for her mother, Monica. A woman who had died long ago. Ginny watched intently for her mother, sometimes pointing to the distance.

Minnie called Suzy.

Suzy was due to pick up Ginny in the next few days to bring her to her Palm Breeze mobile home or take her to another rehab. Suzy's phone went to voicemail.

"Hey, when are you coming to get Ginny? Where are you taking her? She's not well. Call me." Minnie hung up after she left the voicemail.

Ginny scooted up to Minnie and gave her several scraps of paper.

Minnie held out both hands and took the paper fragments. "What is this?"

"The doctor said." Ginny stared at Minnie, then a moment later, rolled away.

Minnie grabbed the arm of the wheelchair. "What did the doctor say, Ginny?" Minnie looked at the hand torn pieces of a magazine.

"I stay here." Ginny continued to move her feet though Minnie held the chair in place.

Minnie's phone rang.

"Suzy is coming for you, Ginny. She'll take care of you." Minnie let go of the chair and answered the call.

"Hi Minnie," Suzy sounded distant, vague. "I called her social worker, Rosa. I'm also having a difficult time trying to place her back in a rehab. Rosa said I have to take her to the emergency room and once they see her confusion and know what's happening, they'll get her placed." *If I can even get her in the car?*

"I'm sorry you have to do this." Minnie was upset.

Suzy had never heard her friend sound defeated. "I'll be there in the morning. I'm going to get up early so I'm able to deal with the five-hour round trip from here to Romeo and back. Thank you, Minnie. You have been good to Ginny." She hung up.

Frank Wisner took a long pull of his beer. "You can bring Ginny to my assisted living."

"Thank you, Frank. You are a good friend and very considerate."

Wisner guzzled the rest of his Lone Star, awaiting the lecture to follow.

"But Lana can't manage her and your parents," Suzy shredded the damp napkin under her drink. "She might cause your parents stress. And I know you are probably thinking, they could possibly defuse hers. Who knows?" She waved to Gretchen. She wanted another Chablis. "Why isn't she getting better?" Suzy could not move her mother to Wisner's place. They barely knew each other.

"Did you say she wasn't eating properly and experiencing confusion?" Frank put some cash on the table. "It's a possible UTI."

"I'm getting sick of the urinary tract infection excuse!" She pushed his money back to him. "It's the only thing you medical people fall back on, and it has not been the issue. The tests don't lie...I'll buy."

Frank held his hands up. "I'm trying to help. You ask my advice, then you insult me. I'll stay out of Ginny's care." He stood.

"Kiss and make up." Gretchen placed fresh drinks in front of them.

"I'm going home. I need to sleep." Suzy handed Gretchen a fifty-dollar bill. "Keep the change."

"Sit, Suzy." Wisner touched her hand. "Let me drive you to Romeo tomorrow. I'll get someone to cover my patients."

She closed her eyes. "I'm not mad at you. And no, take care of your patients. I'm frustrated that no one knows why Ginny's getting worse."

Gretchen gave Suzy her money back. She held her hand out to Wisner. "She can't afford this."

He handed her his credit card. "Give yourself a big tip. Maybe you can convince her." He was brooding.

"Please, dear God. Don't let it be." Chloe peed on the test stick.

She pulled her underwear up and sat on the toilet lid.

Damien knocked on the bathroom door. "Are you okay?"

"I hope so," Chloe shouted back. "I'll be out in a few."

# CHAPTER 18

Suzy pulled up to the emergency room of Gulf Terrace Hospital. Ginny looked at the entrance. She pushed the button to lock her car door.

*How do you know to lock the door?* "Mom, we have to let them examine you."

Ginny crossed her arms. "No."

Ginny was triaged and they started an I.V. They determined she was dehydrated and didn't have a UTI. Minnie had made sure she took all her daily medications, and Suzy did not fault Minnie for Ginny's condition. She knew her friend did her best to feed and care for her mother.

"Mom, they want to keep you tonight and continue to evaluate you. I want to make sure you don't hurt your knee."

Ginny was becoming increasingly agitated. "You lied."

Suzy touched her mother's arm. "I'm sorry, Mom, I did lie. I said we were going to my place, but your social worker said I should bring you here."

Ginny's eyes got big as cue balls. She stared through Suzy, even though she was facing her.

"Mom, are you okay?" Suzy tried to hold her mother's hand.

Ginny slapped her daughter's hand, then felt the tubing going into her arm and looked at the I.V. bag. She grabbed the I.V. tube in her arm.

Suzy screamed, "Need help!" Suzy caught Ginny's hand and tried to stop her from pulling the I.V. out of her arm.

A security guard stuck his head in. "What's going on?"

"Get a nurse or someone. I can't control her." Suzy wrestled with Ginny.

The guard left.

Ginny scratched at Suzy's hand. "Go!"

"That hurts." Suzy slapped at her mother's hands. "Stop. This isn't helping!"

Ginny reached around and pulled the I.V. bag off the post, the needle out of her arm, and lobbed the whole contraption into the hallway outside of the treatment room just as the E.R. doctor was entering.

"Whoa." He dodged it.

Ginny screamed manically at the doctor, "GO!"

Suzy's hand was clawed but no blood had been drawn, just deep red surface tears. "I don't know what's happening." Suzy continued to shake. *I can't breathe. I want to die. What's wrong with her?*

Two nurses came in to see what was going on.

The doctor pulled Suzy out of the room. "I'm going to make this easy on you. We're going to Baker Act her. She needs a psychiatric evaluation. She'll be transferred to the geriatric unit."

"What does Baker Act mean?"

"It means we can hold her for 72 hours for a mental health evaluation. We don't need your consent or hers. She's a danger to herself and others. It's the law."

Suzy continued to shake her head and rub her face. "I can't do that to her." *The Snake Pit!*

"Listen, you can't manage her like this, and we can't either. We have to get her safely to a place that can." He looked Suzy in the eyes and tried to gain her agreement.

Suzy felt her throat constrict. "I…"

The doctor touched her shoulder. "You don't have to do anything. I've got the paperwork. She's in a situation."

Suzy wanted to go back in the room when she saw a couple of people going in to restrain Ginny.

Ginny screamed, "Get A-way!"

The doctor stopped Suzy in the hallway. "She needs help."

Suzy buried her face in her hands. It felt like an electrical current was running through her brain. She wanted to cry. Her head hurt.

A nurse approached the doctor. "Geriatric is full. She's going to Coastal Bay."

"What does that mean?" Suzy tried to breathe through her nose.

The ER doctor rubbed his neck. "She's going to our sister hospital. They do not have beds here. Coastal Bay does. They treat geriatric in the general population."

Ginny screamed, "Suzy!"

She jumped. *Why is he rubbing his neck?*

"She had a knee surgery recently. Will they know …" Suzy paused as the doctor nodded.

"I'll be sure they have the details. Go home. Have a glass of wine. See her tomorrow at Coastal Bay, okay?"

*I'll see her tomorrow. That's just a few hours.* Suzy nodded. "Okay."

The security guard escorted Suzy around the opposite direction of Ginny. "Here's the address for Coastal Bay." He handed her a yellow Post-it Note.

Suzy took it. She had exchanged her mother for a yellow square of paper.

# CHAPTER 19

Suzy stood at the thick metal door with a three-inch by five-inch double-paned glass window. The window had wires running through it in a checkered pattern. It was large enough to frame the face of someone looking out or in but nothing more.

A man Suzy knew from professional circles stood next to her. He had a large package of adult diapers in his hands. They pretended not to know one another. This wasn't a networking event and certainly was not something either of them would discuss at future events.

Her heart was racing from the jog across the parking lot. She hadn't eaten but a few almonds and a cup of coffee. She wasn't certain a noon visit was even possible. She didn't know the protocol. It appeared the guy next to her had the same idea or knew something she didn't. He pushed the call button.

Suzy heard a woman's voice come on.

The man announced his name into the speaker panel and motioned to Suzy.

She stepped up to the panel. "Suzy Lennox to see Ginny Compton." *What did he say his name was?* Her mind was blank. What was she attempting to do? She couldn't think. She heard him talk. What did he say?

They were asked to wait.

The visitor's hallway in front of the secured door was just a worn beige leather couch next to the stairwell and elevator. Faded mental health posters hung over the couch for visitors to educate themselves. On either side of the white cinderblock walls framing the metal door were handwritten visitation rules, the most obvious being no handbags, backpacks, briefcases, or suitcases of any kind. Anything incoming had to be in a clear plastic bag for inspection. Suzy had her car keys and driver's license in her pocket. Her bag was locked in the car. It seemed obvious she'd be forced to return things to her car if she had too much. She saw a woman's face look through the barred window.

Suzy looked at her fellow visitor. She tried to rack her brain for his name. *I should at least remember your industry. Seems weird for both of us to just stare at the door and not...*

A buzzer went off. Suzy jumped. It sounded like something from a horror film where people needed to evacuate from radiation poisoning or run from the Blob. *Is he deaf?* Suzy couldn't understand how the guy next to her didn't jump.

A light strobed in the stairwell window to the same frequency of buzz. EH. EH. EH. EH. EH.

Suzy put her hands over her ears. *What the fuck!?*

He continued to hug the diaper package.

A code was announced on the intercom that Suzy couldn't decipher from all the buzzing. Her ears were now ringing loudly. She could barely hear or think. She read his lips. Someone had escaped. The code was a hopper or some such term.

He continued to hug the package of adult diapers as the EH, EH, EH assaulted them.

Suzy's heart and ears followed the pace of the EH. *Did I take my blood pressure medicine?*

The alarm stopped suddenly, followed by the click of metal locks. A woman in scrubs motioned for them to come through the metal door.

*Jesus! What's next?*

They were motioned into the holding section as the door behind them closed. Ahead was another door that had the same locking system. The nurses inspected them and gave them instructions. They passed through two sets of locked doors and were now in the psych ward.

*We're locked in!* Suzy felt a little faint. *Don't you fucking pass out! Oh my God. What am I doing here?*

Networking guy left and went into a patient room.

Suzy stood paralyzed. *Now what?*

The patient rooms had no doors. They surrounded a central medical office that had wired security glass on three sides, a waist-high cinderblock wall, door, and passthrough window, as well as a circle hole for patients and staff to talk to each other if the door was closed.

*How did someone escape?* Suzy looked around for Ginny. Lunch was not a visiting hour, but if you knew the floor routine you were accepted into the ward. They bent the rules for working people. But Suzy did not know the routine.

*How the hell do I get into these situations?* She wanted to spy into each room but also not appear to be unfamiliar. *Who am I kidding? They know I've never been here!*

A nurse with a rolling computer cart made her entries. She calmly asked a patient standing next to her to wait until she finished her work. She and Suzy made eye contact. "Most everyone is in the television room or the lunchroom." She pointed to two rooms behind Suzy.

*Thank you!* Suzy nodded. She found Ginny hunched over in a wheelchair. Her hospital gown exposed her back. Suzy tried the close the gown. When she and Ginny made eye contact, her mother tried to wheel away. "Mom." Suzy stopped her.

Ginny wouldn't look at Suzy. She turned her head away each time Suzy tried.

"Go." Ginny wheeled herself.

165

Suzy held onto the chair, then locked the wheels. "Mom, I'm here. I love you. I'm trying to figure out what happened." She could feel her shoulders tightening. She tried to kneel next to Ginny but knew better. The few chairs in the television room were taken by younger patients, all dressed in regular clothing. Ginny was the only one in a hospital gown.

Suzy overheard the man who had brought the diapers in address the older patients he was visiting as, "Mom and Dad."

*Both parents? Why? How?*

Suzy watched Ginny tug at the wheels, not realizing she was locked in place. Suzy unlocked the chair's wheels. *How does anyone get better in this place?* Suzy followed Ginny. She watched the staff work their booth. A few younger patients walked around.

A goth girl with black pixie cut and black clothing, pale as a vampire, smiled sweetly at Suzy. "Ginny's a nice lady," she said. "We watched The Golden Girls." The girl had markings that indicated she had harmed herself or had a harmful encounter.

*Breathe.* "Golden Girls…" A lumped formed in Suzy's throat. She turned away as a tear spilled.

"I'll look out for her." The girl tugged at a hang nail.

Suzy nodded. *Ginny warned me. Don't leave her here.*

Her mother wheeled to the end of the hall and sat there, her back exposed again. Suzy couldn't imagine how she wasn't shivering.

"Are you cold, Mom?" She kissed the top of Ginny's head. She tied the gown closed.

"Go." Ginny turned to face a wall.

Suzy's nose ran. She tried not to look at anyone. How were the staff and patients so calm? Is everyone medicated? She wiped the back of her hand under her nose.

She saw networking guy. He was headed toward the doors.

*How do I get out of here?* "Mom"- she hated to sound panicky, but she didn't want to miss the opportunity for her own escape—"I'll be back tonight at regular visiting hours." She jogged over and got behind him as they were lead through the double set of secure doors.

She paused in the hallway. She didn't want to be on the same elevator and have the awkward silence.

"See you later," he said as he pushed the elevator's down button.

Suzy wiped her eyes. "Right." She got in with him anyway and rode the elevator down. She followed him through the hospital lobby and into the parking lot. They split off to go to their own cars.

*Why can't we talk about this? We clearly have elderly parents in the psych ward. We're adults. Adult children of elderly people in the same God damn ward. Why can't we look at each other? We know each other! From fucking networking events! NETWORKING! We're opportunistic assholes. We're knowledgeable in fucking chamber of commerce meetings, but we cannot accept that we come from broken people.*

Suzy got in her car and laid on her horn. "I'm a fucking asshole!" she screamed. She looked at herself in the rearview mirror. Her eyes were red. She grabbed her sunglasses and pushed them on. "My mother is not a mental patient, God damn it!" She punched the horn again; grateful she could not see anyone in the parking garage.

She started her car. "I am figuring this out! And when I do, the whole fucking world will know!"

She returned five hours later to join eight other people who were visiting family at the psychiatric ward. One of the eight was networking guy. They nodded to each other in silent solidarity.

Ginny was despondent. She wheeled herself away from Suzy again and avoided eye contact.

Suzy moved to the nurse's station. She talked through the glass hole, "Hi, can someone tell me what Ginny's treatment plan is?"

"She's being observed," a petite nurse said dryly.

"Can I see the med list, please?" Suzy looked at two female and one male nurse working the shift. They all stared at her.

"We're just observing her."

"What does that mean?" Suzy puzzled. "Is she not getting meds?"

"Doc wants her observed."

"For how long? She just had a surgery, you know. She's still rehabbing." *What doc are they talking about?*

Ginny maneuvered her wheelchair like a battery-operated toy that didn't have the ability to know it was stuck.

*What exactly are you observing?*

"Doc will make a recommendation," the nurse reiterated.

"What doctor?" Suzy left the booth before she heard the answer and went to Ginny. She tried to kneel but couldn't do so comfortably. "Mom, come back to the sitting room."

"They decide," her mother mumbled.

"Who?"

"Go home." Ginny tried to wheel herself again but couldn't seem to navigate backwards. Her gown opened again in the back and Suzy tried to close it.

Suzy marched back to the booth. "Can I have a blanket or something to put over her?"

"You could bring her some clothes," the male nurse who was farthest from the hole chimed in. "I'll get a blanket."

*Fuck! How did I not think of this?* Suzy looked at everyone in the ward. Even networking guy's parents were in regular clothes and sweaters! *Fuck me! Does my brain not work? Am I totally ignorant? Why are Ginny and I the only two that seem out of place in this place?*

Goth girl cozied up beside Suzy. She was a little too close, like a purring kitten looking for someone to scratch her head.

"Ginny's not doing well," the girl said.

*I shouldn't ask your name. You're young. You have a chance. No one should know you are here. Should they?* Suzy stared at Ginny. *Should anyone know Ginny's here?* "Can you help her?" Suzy looked into the eyes of the alabaster girl.

Goth's eyes lit up. Her mouth didn't quite form a smile. "I'm helping her eat."

*Thank God!* Suzy felt her knees give. *Would they just observe while she was not eating?* "Thank you." Suzy wanted to hug the girl. She looked at the glass booth and they all seemed to be observing *her*.

Suzy called Frank, Chloe, and Arnold. All their lines went to voicemail. *I need to talk to somebody.*

Suzy drove to the Lizard. She needed a drink and some perspective. When she got there, it was happy hour and only one empty seat was open at the bar. The jukebox jammed Bon Jovi's *Livin' On A Prayer*.

Suzy gave her drink order to a guy she'd never seen before. "Chablis. Is Gretchen off tonight?" She felt her neck tighten. She needed to unwind.

The guy looked over Suzy's shoulder and tossed a napkin in front of her. "You don't know?" He poured her wine.

"Know what?" Suzy took a deep breath.

"We were robbed two weeks ago."

Suzy took a huge gulp of her wine. "Where's Gretchen?" *Don't say it. Don't say it.*

The bartender shook his head.

"What!?"

Gretchen snuck up behind Suzy and goosed her.

Suzy jumped and screamed, "The fuck!"

Gretchen and the other bartender laughed hysterically.

Suzy grabbed her glass and threw the wine in the guy's face. The room went dead silent, and she turned to yell, "What fuck are you looking at!?" Her face went from red to near purple. She screamed a blood curdling wail that stunned the place. "I don't need this shit!" She charged out the door and chucked her glass with such force that shattered it into a million diamond-sized fragments.

Gretchen followed her. "I'm sorry. What's the matter? Come back. We really were robbed."

Suzy paused, then shot Gretchen the bird. "Bitch!"

"It was a joke." Gretchen grabbed Suzy's hand and pulled her toward the bar. "Come on in. You obviously need another drink. Tell me what's going on."

A few patrons came out.

Suzy began hyperventilating.

"She needs a paper bag." A random patron suggested.

Gretchen motioned for someone to bring a broom and a bag.

"Breath in and out." A regular handed Suzy the bag.

Suzy complied.

"Breathe twelve times and then breathe without it."

More patrons were filing out. The CPA guy came out, too.

"Someone called an ambulance," Suzy heard among the chatter.

"Gretch…" Suzy tried to talk.

A woman helped her down to the curb. "Try the bag again."

Another patron brought her a glass of water. She gulped it. Choked.

A siren approached. Suzy saw the ambulance pull in.

"I've got to go," she coughed. She started to cry again.

The EMS workers approached. One squat down next to her.

*I'm not going. I'm not answering any questions.*

A debate took place over her head. The EMS told patrons they couldn't help Suzy if she refused. A small fight broke out when two drunks shoved each other arguing over Suzy's rights.

Her phone rang. It was Frank. She handed it to Gretchen. She continued to cry. She had no clue what was being said.

"Frank's coming over." Gretchen dismissed the EMS.

One of the drunks tumbled onto the gravel and skinned his arm. "Hey!" He called out the EMS.

Suzy continued breathing into the bag again.

The remaining bar patrons wandered back into The Lizard, mumbling encouragement to Suzy as they left.

Suzy looked to Frank for a shred of hope or reasoning as she got into his car. "I saw Ginny. She's rejecting me. She's stuck in a loop of … I don't know…" Suzy hesitated to say more when she saw Frank wince when she explained going to the hospital twice.

He drove the backstreets toward her place. He wanted to take his time and give her a chance to talk things out. "Do you hear yourself, Suzy? You know Ginny's not well. You need to deal with it. Gretchen was just joking with you, and you created a spectacle. I'm beginning to think you love the drama."

*Seriously!* "Stop the car!"

"You act like only you can solve Ginny's problems and that all of her doctors are corrupt." He laughed bitterly. His tone was like the crack of a tree ready to drop. "You insult me, Suzy. And you're not even aware."

*You're mad! At me?*

"You won't listen," he went on. "You won't accept help. You expect everyone to fall in step with you …." He pulled the car into a supercenter parking lot. "You need to get a grip!"

*I've insulted you? That's rich!* Suzy grabbed her bag and got out of the car. "I'll get my car and get a fucking grip."

It was dark and they were now closer to his place than The Hungry Lizard. She began to walk.

"Let me drive you there." Wisner got out and started to walk with her.

"Sorry for upsetting you. Sorry for offending your EMS brethren. Sorry for not wanting to end up in a fucking hospital like Ginny." She walked faster. "Sorry for fucking bothering you about medical shit that is killing my mother." Suzy stopped while he caught up to her.

"No one is killing Ginny." Wisner raised his voice, "That's your arrogance! That's the insult, Suzy. No one is superior to *you*."

"Oh! You need to feel superior? I am supposed to apologize?" She shoved him. "Clearly, I am superior! So, go fuck yourself."

He started to say something, then stopped short.

Suzy looked back at his van, saw the warmth of the exhaust hitting the night air. "You know your car is still running."

He dug his hands in his pockets.

She marched off.

"I'm coming back." He jogged off to his van.

*You better. I'm seriously not walking the whole way.*

He drove slowly beside her. "Get in."

"Okay." She let him take her back to her car.

# CHAPTER 20

Coastal Bay called Suzy. A male nurse said Ginny had fallen, and they had to tie her down to do an x-ray of her bruised butt and knee. "She's in bed next to the nurse's station so we can watch her, but she is still tied down. It's the only way to keep her safe."

*You mean, observe her falling? Bruised! Tied down! Again?!* "Do you tie people down regularly? Is she hydrated?" Suzy was sick to her stomach. "Is there a doctor I can talk to?"

The nurse put her on hold. "Actually, the doctor's in."

*More bees with honey.*

"This is Dr. Lopez. Are you Miss Ginny's daughter?" She sounded young and upbeat. "Poor baby, Miss Ginny's so confused."

*God, help us.* "Dr. Lopez, I am freaking out. This all started when Mom had a colonoscopy before her knee surgery and dizziness. The hospital put on Effexor for depression, and she never had depression. Then she had the knee surgery. She went from clarity to confusion to ... you're looking at her now. And I don't know why everyone keeps giving her more and more antidepressants and then a multitude of other things to offset other side effects. It's clearly not working. Now she's bruised and tied down?"

"Are you coming to visit today?" Dr. Lopez had the voice of a hug and mug of hot chocolate.

"Of course. I'm afraid for her." Though Suzy wanted to be upset, this woman's confident tone stripped her of worry. "Will you be there?"

Dr. Lopez had a smile in her voice. "I won't. But I think I know what it is. It's anesthesia related. I'm going to give her an anti-psychotic, Olanzapine. I think you'll see a difference. We'll get the Olanzapine started, and I'm sorry I'll miss seeing you."

*God, I hope you're right.*

Four hours later, Suzy was back at the psych door. She hit the buzzer with the confidence of networking guy and nodded at the nurse opening the door. They were peers now.

Suzy was unafraid, ready to take on anyone who messed with Ginny. When she got in, Ginny was on a gurney, drinking a grape soda. She waved at Suzy. "They promised me a grape soda if I took my medicine."

Suzy was astonished. "Mom!"

Another nurse came up and handed Ginny an inflated paper bag. "And popcorn."

Suzy wept.

Ginny smiled. "Are you okay?"

Suzy hugged her mother. "This is a miracle."

A male nurse approached Suzy. "Ginny's being discharged tomorrow. I think her social worker will call you about arrangements."

Suzy nodded. She grabbed a few kernels of her mother's popcorn and ate them. "I love you, Mom."

She kissed Ginny's head.

It had been three months since Ginny had surgery; 72 hours since she entered Coastal Bay; and only four hours since the Olanzapine stars had somehow aligned.

The sun moved nimbly down the pink skyline. "Ginny's almost normal."

Suzy and Frank strolled to a dune that provided them with a front-row view of the sunset. It was warm and breezy. An obese man with a metal detector stood in their line of vision. Seagulls dove near a boy tossing potato chips.

"There's a picture." Suzy rolled her eyes. "He's stopped right in front of us." She pointed at the guy with the metal detector.

Frank squinted. "I believe he was here first."

Others were camped on towels or ambled along the coastline.

He watched her profile, her hair flowing in the breeze.

He wrapped his hands around his knees and leaned into the view. "Where are we headed?"

"As a couple?" Suzy asked.

He sat up and dusted his hands off. He searched her eyes. "What are we doing?"

"We're friends watching the sun set. I'm a big jerk. I have control issues and you're a damn nice guy."

He nodded. "I apologize for missing the postoperative cognitive dysfunction. You were right to fight for Ginny and she's lucky to have you as her health care surrogate and daughter."

"What do you want me to say?" She dug her toes in the sand.

"I really don't know. I'm torn between wanting to know you intimately or just walking away."

"Can we please ride out this friendship thing a while? I still have a conspiracy to debunk."

Suzy's phone lit up.

Chloe: FaceTime.

Suzy toweled her hair and glanced at herself in the bathroom mirror. Her white terry robe was cinched tightly around her body. She accepted the call.

Chloe's face beamed. She looked like a younger version of Ginny: small and lively, with a wide grin and natural auburn tresses with silver-blonde highlights. "What are you doing, Mom?"

"Well, I just got out of the shower, so I'm frighteningly clean. You might want to dim your settings."

Chloe put her eye up to her phone's camera. Suzy saw a close-up of one of Chloe's hazel eyes.

"I see what you mean." Chloe pulled the phone away, laughing. "You look fine."

"Glad I passed inspection." Suzy sat on her bed holding the robe tight with one hand and the phone with the other. "What are you doing?"

"I got mine and grandma's genealogy back!" Chloe smiled then pouted. "Grandma's didn't take. Mine doesn't tell me much. We're all German, Irish and English. Boring! And it has some people listed that are DNA cousins. Maybe the names will make sense to you? It doesn't show a father type. Or it could be I don't know what I'm looking at. Maybe you'll figure out who our fathers are? I don't get why you don't want to know."

They had had the same discussion since Chloe was ten.

- Who was grandpa?
- Where's my dad?
- Why don't you get married?

Suzy took a deep breath. "I am not personally familiar with the tests, other than some studies that showed people who migrated from other countries and the impact their culture had on certain communities."

"That's boring." Chloe stuck out her tongue.

Suzy glanced from Chloe to the tiny thumbnail on the top corner of her phone's screen. She was glad her un-makeup-ed face was obscured. "I'd like to see it."

"I'll send you my log in. Let me know if any of the people are familiar."

Chloe heard a ping on her phone. "Hold on."

Suzy watched Chloe read a message and laugh. "Mom, you need to do the DNA, too. I'm listening to a true crime podcast where they found a killer through a genealogy test like this." Chloe's eyes lit up. "Was my father a serial killer?"

*Maybe?* "He spared me. I don't think so." Suzy sighed.

They both laughed.

Chloe perked up. "When grandma gets better, we have to get her hooked on these podcasts. She'd love it."

*She was tied down.* "Grandma's old-school Sherlock Holmes." Suzy flopped back on her pillow. "I'm trying to get her off all the prescribed drugs."

Suzy heard another ping on Chloe's phone.

"Hey, didn't Sherlock Holmes use morphine, or was he a cocaine addict? That's why he was such a super sleuth, right?! Or something? I have to go. I'm meeting Damien." Chloe blew a kiss to Suzy. "I'll send the DNA stuff later."

*A mystery detective addict?* "Love you." Suzy blew a kiss back. Her phone's screen went dark. "Thanks for calling." Suzy tossed the phone onto the middle of the bed. "Mystery, drugs and crime, and DNA cousins."

# CHAPTER 21

Arnold circled the newspaper listing. "Are you fucking kidding me? This is perfect!" He called Suzy. "Hey, there's a movie at Tampa Theatre. You have to go!" He threw his head back as he listened to her complain and give him excuses. "Suzy, Suzy, Suzy… stop, you need to hear me out." He mouthed, *Oh my God!* He pulled at his hair. "Meet me." He bitch slapped the air. "It's a chance to get away from Ginny. And Frank's likely sick of hearing you complain. We can dish and gossip." He drew devil horns on his newspaper. "I agree," he replied to her mumbling. He banged his head on the table. "This is important. You've got to do this." He nodded. "You love history. The theatre is a landmark." He made a sign of the cross. "I love you, Suzy! Thank you! I'll text the details. See you there."

Suzy and Maxine, The Circle of Life Senior Care's administrator, had battled each other in the weeks since Ginny had moved there from the psychiatric facility. Her new doctors had insisted Ginny was not willing to work on solutions. Now she was lucid, on an anti-depressant and antipsychotic blend of medications, but she still experienced extreme highs and lows. Suzy could not seem to convince anyone that the

Ginny they were dealing with was the product of their own chemical voodoo. It was now becoming apparent that too much change had also an environmental effect on her mother's anxiety. They argued regularly.

Frank wanted to treat Ginny and have her live with his parents. Suzy worried she would have to move Ginny again later. She and Frank were friends, not a couple.

The Circle of Life Assisted Living had a warm cottage ambience that won adult children on the setting for their elders. The facility rotated their employees to mirror the demographics of the touring family. This front-facing inclusion sold the available beds instantly. Yet it became evident after the resident moved in that the age divide among the personnel kept each side in check. The younger staff wanted to handle the meds and light duty, while the older staff wanted the younger staff to handle the heavy lifting and get out of the meds room. The night crew had the same dynamic as the day crew, only they slept or watched television after tucking everyone in with a sleep aid. It seemed every employee tried to keep the residents out of their way.

No one wanted to do laundry, so a midnight shift came in and worked until dawn twice a week, bleaching everything, and frying all the resident's elastic waist bands to a crackly crunch. Names that had been Sharpied into clothing browned and often became so unreadable that the nurses' aides distributed garments by size. Often, this brought echoes of, "Where did grandma's new sweater go?" when the family visited, sending the staff rummaging through closets.

The Circle sent all prescriptions to a local pharmacy for distribution into blister packs that were supplied in a 30-day cycle by daily daypart. All a nurse or aid had to do was pop the foil on the back of the blister pack and dump the pills into a paper or pudding cup and watch the patient take them at the prescribed time.

Ginny was on an upswing from her last battle with depression. Her mood swings changed with each pharmaceutical blend, though the doctors and staff had no consistent method of documenting their effectiveness. A medication change meant that all the blister packs for a given patient had to be sent back to the pharmacy for redistribution into a new set of blister packs, guaranteeing dosages were missed or doubled depending on the shift receiving them.

Do Well Drugs local pharmacy had Circle's account. Do Well was only open until 9 p.m. and delivery to nursing facilities stopped at 7 p.m. Monday to Saturday. Sunday the pharmacy was closed, so patients who were not admitted to the emergency room were dosed Sunday by the E.R. doctors, returned to the facility with a new prescription that would not be filled until Tuesday at the earliest. The new medication would be added once the blister packs were sent back to the pharmacy Monday for an update. Depending on the Tuesday delivery, meds ordered Sunday may not be administered until late Tuesday or possibly Wednesday.

There was always a debate about a med change. Did the doctor agree to stop cold turkey or wean the patient off? Often, a small dose of a new med was added to the changed med to balance out any potential side effects. Reduction of the number of medicines was never part of the equation.

Ginny sat at one of the assisted living's long dining tables with a group of stoic residents. Each occupant focused on their plate. Some had special utensils to aid in their self-feeding routine: odd-shaped plasticware for arthritic fingers, bowls for scooping, and handled tumblers for some, lidded sippy cups for others, alongside traditional Melmac table settings. Very few breakables were used. The residents knew their own paraphernalia well enough to trod, wheel, or scoot to their designated spot.

Suzy waved to Ginny. Ginny didn't notice. She made her way over to her mother and pulled up an empty chair.

"Mom, how's your dinner?"

"Horrible." Ginny continued to look down and eat, her neck slumped into a rigid hump position.

"Well, you're eating it. It can't be that horrible." Suzy looked at the turkey and dressing meal her mother was eating. It looked good to her, especially since she had not eaten much that day.

"Taste it." Ginny barely moved her head.

"Okay." Suzy took a bite. It was bland, with an odd gel texture and no flavor. "Maybe add some salt?"

Suzy looked around the table. There were no saltshakers. Pepper shakers were on every table. *Okay, salt restrictions are a thing.* Suzy peppered the food.

Ginny pushed the plate away without another bite. "I can't eat anymore."

Suzy took another bite. "That didn't help."

Ginny got up and shuffled her walker toward her room. "I want to go home."

"Mom, you are making progress. You're walking. But you're not able to cook or care for yourself." Suzy followed Ginny.

No one noticed their departure.

"Minnie can help me." Ginny's small room had a twin bed, a television, nightstand, chest of drawers, closet, and hamper.

"I have to pay Minnie." Suzy inspected the bathroom and closet. "She won't let you sit alone. Your last trip home scared her."

"Minnie is brave." Ginny propped herself up in bed. She grabbed the television remote and turned the television on. "I have nothing to do."

"This is all you did at home. You want to play cards? I'll play cards with you."

August, a nurse's aide, stuck his head in the door. "After dinner, we have a sing-along, if you ladies want to join in?"

Suzy's phone dinged. It was Frank.

"I don't want to play cards." Ginny changed the channel and did not look at the older aide.

Suzy shook her head *no* to August. "Thanks for asking."

"Next time, Ginny." He winked at Suzy and left.

Frank: `Dinner tonight?`

Suzy: `I'll get back to you. I'm visiting Ginny.`

Frank: `Tell her hello.`

"Frank says hello, Mom."

Ginny gave her a puzzled look. "Who?"

"The doctor you met at the rehab. We're friends."

"I don't know him." Ginny yawned. "I'm tired."

*Yes, you do.* "You introduced us, when you had the eye mask on."

Suzy: `Got to go.`

Frank: `Never mind.`

Suzy: `Sorry.`

"What do you remember about your knee surgery?" Suzy took a few photos of Ginny.

"My knee hurts." Ginny pointed to the knee that had not been operated on.

Suzy sighed. "That knee wasn't replaced and I'm not thinking it ever will be." *Not if I can help it!* "Do you remember the emergency room, Mom?"

"No."

*That's a good thing.* "Do you remember the hospital… the psychiatric hospital?"

Ginny shook her head, *no.*

"Okay, I'm going to see what's going on here." She kissed Ginny on the head and left. Suzy made her way to the medication dispensary. Wheelchairs surrounded the door in half-circle, baby birds awaiting the momma bird.

"Excuse me," Suzy called.

A dispensary nurse gave her a smile. "Does Ginny need something?"

*I need something.* "Could I get Ginny's med list before I head out?"

"It's going to be a bit."

Another nurse popped up. "I'll get it."

A few moments later, Suzy had photocopied sheets of Ginny's daily meds. She moved to the television room and sat in an overstuffed blue gingham chair and propped the list on a *Good Housekeeping* magazine. She circled each and looked up the usage.

Zoloft—Treats PTSD, anxiety

Ativan—Sedative for anxiety

Trazodone—Antidepressant

Remeron—Antidepressant

Lorazepam—Sedative

Lexapro—For generalized anxiety disorder

Citalopram—Serotonin Reuptake Inhibitor

*Serotonin helps regulate mood, memory, sleep, sex, bone health…

Naloxone—Treats narcotic overdose

Hydromorphone—Narcotic for moderate to severe pain, high risk for addiction

Olanzapine—Antipsychotic

Suzy sent Maxine an email requesting the phone number of all of Ginny's prescribing physicians as well as an evaluation by a licensed therapist.

Suzy returned to the attending nurse. "Can I request they cut back her meds?" *How have I not thought of this before?*

The nurse nodded. "You most certainly can. Nobody does. Half of these folks don't see anyone. Their families live in another state. They're lucky if anyone calls on the phone. It's sad. Only a few people even talk to us."

*I'm a shit.* "I'm sorry." Suzy looked into the woman's eyes and then looked at her nametag. "Dacia."

"Your mom's really sweet." Dacia smiled. "Talk to the doctor when he's in. Ginny's taking a lot! I just don't understand it. They're all on too many drugs if you ask me." She motioned to the flock that was beginning to move on to their rooms.

Suzy felt her shoulders stiffen. "Yeah. Somehow, she's better than she was."

"Tell the doctor not to add another medication 'til they consult you. It's the only way."

"Thank you, Dacia. And I'm sorry it has taken me this long to introduce myself. I'm Suzy Lennox, Ginny's daughter." Suzy extended her hand.

Dacia shook her head. "You don't have to shake my hand. I'm here for Ginny." She smiled. A call bell sounded, and Dacia looked around. "We're here for Ginny. You can call at any time. I need to check on Mr. Wilson." She excused herself.

Suzy looked around. It seemed the whole floor had cleared out. Televisions were playing loudly, and room doors were open, but not a soul was visible.

# CHAPTER 22

Arnold waited for Suzy outside the Tampa Theatre. The marquee read *Silent Classics*.

The historic theatre was near the on-ramp to interstate 275 and its I-4 connection. It was west of the Hillsborough County Courthouse and located on Franklin Street, where artists regularly set up impromptu exhibits for weekday office complex and city employees to appreciate.

Opened in 1926, the Tampa Theatre was a streetcar destination from Sulphur Springs and Ybor City, as well as wealthy neighborhoods along Bayshore Boulevard in Hyde Park in its heyday.

Tampa's heritage dates back to the Spanish explorers Ponce de Leon in 1513, Hernando de Soto in the 1520s, and the indigenous Tocobaga, Mocoso, Pohoy, Creek, and Seminole Indian tribes from the pre-1700s to the 1830s.

By 1824, Florida was acquired from Spain. The establishment of Fort Brooke on the mouth of the Hillsborough River was instrumental to the development of Tampa and operated as a key outpost during the three Seminole Indian Wars and the Civil War.

The late 1800s to 1890s brought wealth and a diverse mix of jobs and labor from industrialist Henry B. Plant's railroad lines and luxurious entertainment center at the Tampa Bay Hotel and Casino, to the Cuban entrepreneurial cigar factories, and Ferlita Bakery.

A city within a city, Ybor City was a growing cultural amalgam of Afro-Cubans, Italians, the Cuban resistance movement led by poet José Martí, African Americans looking to build their own communities, and northerners joining the manual labor force in the fisheries and port.

As the city entered the 1900s, Tampa grew to 15,000+ residents and was considered one of Florida's largest cities and a destination for tourists. From its Sulphur Springs water park and one-of-a-kind alligator farm; to the Columbia Restaurant founded in 1905; to The Victory Theatre opened in 1920, and the Tampa Theatre that followed in 1926, Tampa was an entertainment paradise. As the nation entered Prohibition, crime and crime bosses were plentiful in Ybor and Tampa.

At the city's southernmost point, MacDill Air Force Base opened in 1947 and was designated the United States military Central Command in 1983.

Tampa is Hillsborough County's urban center, connected by coastal waterways and suburban communities bordering Pasco, Pinellas, and Polk counties.

Arnold waved to Suzy. He stood under the vertical sign, *TAMPA*, above the theater.

Suzy jogged across Zack Street to the larger-than-life historic marquee. "I don't get your excitement. The movies are silent," she huffed, taking the ticket from him.

Suzy had seen random Charlie Chaplin and Buster Keaton clips growing up, but knew nothing of the silent film star Lillian Gish, nor anything about silent movies per se. She and Ginny watched television but did not go to the movies very often. They were ABC *Movie of the Week*, *America's Most Wanted*, and annual telecasts of *The Wizard of Oz*, *Sound of Music*, *Gone With The Wind*, and *The Ten Commandments* kind of viewers.

"They have a killer Wurlitzer organ." Arnold bounced on his toes. "It's part of the show."

Suzy glanced at his feet. "What you were like on Christmas morning?"

They passed smokers on the sidewalk. "My mother made Christmas magical for what little I remember. Bart was a dick! Don't distract me."

Suzy glanced over her shoulder as they passed the free-standing ticket booth. "Now that's cool."

"I know." Arnold opened the door for her. "You ain't seen nothing yet."

The lobby was adorned in colorful tiles of red and green, with ornate embellishments. The concession stand was the most modern fixture in the vintage structure. Others were in line ahead of them. Suzy looked around. "It's like a museum."

"There are ghosts in the balcony… but don't worry, we're sitting in the lower section. There's limited paranormal activity there." Arnold squealed softly.

"And you know this how?"

"The ghost tour, duh!"

"Duh," Suzy agreed.

"I can't wait for you to see the Wurlitzer!" He clapped.

She pointed for Arnold to move ahead. "You could just go to a church. It's an organ."

He sighed. "I only wish we were seeing *The Phantom of the Opera*."

Suzy scrunched up her face. "Not a fan. Creepy how some women find the Phantom romantic… Eck."

"I was referring to the classic Lon Chaney, Sr. silent film. The phantom is quite misunderstood."

Suzy ordered them each a popcorn and soda. "Well, I'm glad we're not seeing that."

"The Phantom tries to help the woman he loves, but things…" he concluded softly, "go badly."

"So, is this a light-hearted movie?" Suzy was hopeful.

"*Way Down East…*" He bent his head side to side, thinking. "There are moments. But no."

"Is Florida the Way Down East?"

"Nothing to do with the story."

Suzy handed Arnold a bag and a plastic cup. "What's it about?"

Arnold stuck his tongue into the popcorn bag and grabbed a kernel. Chewing and talking, "It's a woman's story for sure, a real departure from the director's first film that spawned all kinds of hate crimes."

*I don't want to know.* "I have a bad feeling about this." Suzy sipped her soda.

"Well, it isn't about who made it."

"So, the Wurlitzer is like your John Williams *Star Wars* fixation?"

"No." Arnold found seats under the balcony in the middle of the theater. "Glean what you will from the experience." He moved into the row of seats.

"This isn't ancient porn?"

Arnold's eyes lit up. "That's what you can get me for Christmas!" He arched his eyebrows enthusiastically. "But no, it was originally a play written by a woman, Lottie Blair Parker."

"Which reminds me: can you cut the sexual harassment bullshit? It's getting old."

He sulked. "If you'll cut the serial killer bullshit?"

"It's not acceptable to subject me or anyone else to nonstop dirty jokes and innuendos."

"Nonstop. That's a compliment I have not earned."

She gave him a dry stare.

Arnold sucked on his straw. "Then it's not acceptable to constantly subject me to mur-der." He crossed in front of her and sat to her right.

*Asshole!* "Fine." She put her purse on the seat to her left.

Arnold turned to her. He tongued several kernels of popcorn and chewed heartily, staring at her. "We need to turn off our phones."

They juggled their snacks and turned off their phones.

"Any last words before the Wurlitzer?" Suzy threw popcorn at him.

He tried to catch it with his mouth. In his best English accent, "Did you know that your grandmother and church friends, of which my grandfather Harlan Welch was one, saw this very movie at the Victory Theater a few blocks from here? It doesn't exist anymore. So, this is a close as it gets to being in the same place."

"You're making that up."

He gave her a two-finger salute. "The group went to Sulphur Springs from Romeo, had a grand weekend which included seeing this movie."

*Right.* "And how do you know this?" Suzy munched.

"My grandfather's diary." Arnold heard the stage floor opening. The Wurlitzer began. "Look!"

The sound billowed from below. The organist and platform ascended, flush with the elevated stage. Arnold gave a fist pump into the air. "Love it."

Suzy shook her head. She looked to Arnold, then the stage. She could not relate. It sounded like the music at baseball games or on the *Lawrence Welk Show* her grandmother had watched.

Arnold swayed back and forth with "Everything's Coming Up Roses."

*You belong in a nursing home.*

The older female organist worked the keys and foot pedals in exaggerated form.

Suzy looked away.

The theater's elaborate 90+ year old atmospheric interior was something she could appreciate. Its statuary, inset floral columns, sconces of golden, colorful flowered plaster motif, gargoyles, tapestries, stained glass, and oriental lamp lighting amid an intricate opera house stage was the real experience. The ceiling's night blue color had inset lights that added a spiritual courtyard feel of twinkling stars, while the heavy curtain covering the screen yielded a Shakespearean vibe. She could easily imagine the cast of *King Lear* or *Hamlet* awaiting their curtain call.

As the pre-movie concert concluded, the hefty drape curtsied for the feature.

Arnold turned to Suzy. He was very serious, almost edgy. "Watch carefully. I'll explain."

*Watch what?* She knew his idiosyncrasies. *If this is porn, I will kill you.*

The film's title *Way Down East* and director D.W. Griffith were scored with the words: "A Simple Story of Plain People." The film's narrative filled the big screen, separate from the acting. Suzy saw these words: "The dashing Lennox Sanderson, who depends for his living upon a rich father."

Suzy elbowed Arnold. "Lennox, Simple Story of Plain People?"

She continued to munch her popcorn. The actress Lillian Gish has a sweet, round porcelain doll face. Her opaque complexion and tiny mouth are framed by a wispy bird's nest hairdo. Her impoverished character, Anna Moore, is encouraged by her mother to seek financial help from their snobbishly wealthy Tremont cousins.

Suzy was glued the story, barely noticing the lack of speaking. The music carried the emotion of the action.

Anna chickens out of the ask and finds herself a Cinderella of sorts to her pretentious kin.

*Dang it, Anna.*

An eccentric aunt, who looks like the inspiration for the Planter's Peanut character, dresses Anna in sexier attire for a party. Anna's new dress attracts the pasty-faced, shifty-eyed opportunist, Lennox Sanderson. Sanderson eyes all the women, not just the easy roaring twenties dancer types, but the good girls, too.

*Wow Arnold, you brought me to a movie about a womanizer named Lennox. Thanks!* She glanced at Arnold who watched her watch the movie. "Stop!" she whispered.

He turned back to the screen, then back at Suzy when she wasn't paying attention.

*What the hell?*

Suzy began to feel queasy when Lennox Sanderson dupes Anna into a fake marriage so he can have sex with her.

*My great grandmother saw this?!* Suzy sipped her soda.

Lennox Sanderson tells Anna they have to hide their marriage a while. Then the unspeakable happens. Anna discovers she's not legally married, and now she's pregnant.

*Fucking hell! I don't need this.*

Fast forward, Lennox Sanderson leaves her. Anna's mother dies. She has the baby. The baby is sick. Anna baptizes the newborn to saves its soul.

*Seriously!* Suzy is glued.

The rooming house learns Anna has no husband. The baby dies. Anna is penniless and scandalous and must be kicked out of the rooming house.

*Oh my God!* Suzy feels an unnerving déjà vu.

A hero emerges to save Anna, but not before she gets thrown out on a snowy night.

When the lights came up, Arnold was snoring.

"At what point did you fall asleep?" Suzy shoved him.

Arnold jumped. "Damn it, I missed the ice floats." He yawned big. "Lillian Gish did her own stunts."

*Somehow, I don't give a shit.* "Explain." Suzy grit her teeth.

"It was a real snowstorm…"

"Not that. You said you'd explain why we're here."

"I said glean what you will." Arnold rolled his shoulder and yawned again.

"You said our grandparents saw this risqué film. And oddly, I have the last name Lennox. And the women in my family had kids…" She suddenly felt nauseous. "Out of wedlock." *Two Virginias. One died.* Suzy elbowed him. "What the fuck do you know, Arnold?"

His face turned from pale to red and splotchy.

She couldn't tell if he was sick or ready to throw a punchline. "Don't fucking joke with me!"

He started to say something and looked around.

Suzy gave him a stone-cold stare. "You said, I had to see it." *Your father has something to do with this, doesn't he?* "Get on with it." She felt her face heating up.

Arnold watched other theater patrons walk past them. He nodded. "Suzy, remember when you worked with Bart?"

"The Gulf War Study," she acknowledged.

Suzy was back at the Econo Motel now, remembering the stains on the hallway carpet leading up to the room. The faceless man, Chloe's father, had said he was in Desert Storm. The Econo's room was registered to Mr. Lennox. *In the movie, Anna lied to the rooming house and said she was Mrs. Lennox.* "Arnold, I never told you what Ginny wanted me to write. But with her brain fog and whatever the fuck this is, it feels like I'm being set up!"

He held his hands up. "Calm down. Bart was required to reach out to you."

*Ginny was telling the truth!* "What the fuck are you talking about?"

"Remember when you turned 45?"

"Not really."

"It was also the 5th anniversary of HIPS Data."

"How does any of that relate to seeing this movie?"

"Everything." He stopped talking.

"You're not telling me anything. Is this another one of your jokes?" Suzy felt her blood pressure rising. She stood and shoved her drink cup and popcorn bag into Arnold's chest. "Take care of the trash... the poor white trash. That's it?" She shoved him.

"Hang on, Suzy." Arnold grabbed her arm. "I'm not the enemy."

Suzy pulled away from him. "Odd choice of words. The enemy. Gulf War study. This wasn't a war movie?"

An usher came by and offered to take Arnold's garbage.

Suzy jabbed Arnold in the chest. "Metaphors are everywhere. You and your father, hell, your grandfather, are all groomers of some kind." She crossed her arms.

Arnold kept quiet.

"Our business is a ruse?" Suzy's eyes welled as she began to hyperventilate.

Arnold started to cry. "I love you, Suzy."

She slapped him across the face. "Who are you?"

He shook his head wildly. Tears streamed down his face. "I can't…"

"Is Bart Darth Vader and we're Leia and Luke?! Spit it out!"

Arnold wept uncontrollably and sat down. "I wish." He cradled his head and continued to sob.

"Should I call the police?" The usher asked Suzy.

Arnold sobbed openly. "I'm sssso sorry."

"Sorry about what?" Suzy spat. "What do you mean you love me, you sick fuck!?" She slapped his head. "Why was Bart required to connect with me!?" *You are criminals!*

Arnold continued to weep.

Suzy ran out of the theater.

# CHAPTER 23

Suzy called Chloe. "Send me the Ancestry log in again. I can't think. I haven't looked." She was having trouble breathing. She leaned against her car, grateful that Chloe was home for the weekend.

The two met at a coffee shop not far from the theater. Chloe grabbed an organic vanilla milk, and Suzy ordered a medium roast with cream and raw sugar. She felt dizzy and nervous. She didn't feel like she could handle much more caffeine.

"What's with us?" Suzy looked at the milk. "We're not drinking our usual order?"

Chloe smiled weakly. "I've got a hangover of sorts."

Suzy tried to smile through her misery. "I hope you're not drinking regularly."

"I'm not." Chloe gave Suzy a pouty face. "My tummy hurts."

*Been there. Done that.* "Maybe I should drink milk?" Suzy grabbed a milk. "I barely ate. Good idea."

Chloe wrapped her arms around her mother's waist and put her head on her shoulder. "Let's watch *Dateline* and have Chinese tonight."

Suzy smiled. "That sounds good." Suzy needed a distraction from Arnold. *Why do I feel like we're going to be a* Dateline *episode?* Suzy's face twitched as she began to chuckle. *I can't win.* "I'm worn out." Suzy put one arm around Chloe's shoulder.

They grabbed a table. Suzy pulled her tablet out and logged on. She dabbed at the corner of her eyes, then pushed the tablet to Chloe. "Show me where you found the info. I seriously can't focus."

"What's with Arnold?" Chloe typed while she talked. "You two always have these love-hate situations. You're like an old married couple."

*Bite your tongue!* "Don't make me sick, Chloe. Arnold is a brilliant guy, a perv..."

"Whoa. Did he do something?" Chloe's doe eyes made Suzy wonder if she had even been as good a mother as Anna Moore. After all, Chloe was not baptized. Anna had at least done that.

"I don't know." Suzy now felt like she could vomit.

"What does that mean?"

"I'm going to start my own business soon, because I'm just not putting up with his shit any longer."

"Oh, so it's a business thing." Chloe took the lid off her milk and sipped it slowly. "Why'd you go to the movie?"

*Will I end up in the snake pit?* Suzy held onto her coffee and stared off into the distance.

Chloe waved her hand in front of her mother's face. "Is he stealing from you?"

Suzy took a deep breath. "I don't think so."

"You're acting weird. What are you hiding?"

"It's complicated." Suzy looked down at the tablet. "I'm not even sure how to explain it."

"Say it."

"The movie was about a woman who is duped into a fake marriage, so the guy Lennox could have sex with her."

"Whoa," Chloe said. She held her stomach and looked a little queasy. "Arnold wants you."

"No! Well..." Suzy thought. *He said he loved me. Ew.* "I get why you'd think that, but the movie goes on to show a woman having a baby and it dies and..."

Chloe's eyes teared up. She looked down at the keyboard and signed into the genealogy site. Up came the highlighted regions of the world. "Um," she persisted, "I was hoping we'd have some interesting history. But we're just plain old white people."

Suzy was lost in her own thoughts. She looked at the screen. "Maybe we should take a genealogy class?"

"That would be cool." Chloe pointed to the screen. "Look at that name. Gerald Felps Jenkins."

*No clue.* Suzy turned the tablet to herself, opened another tab, and typed. "Let's check Facebook for Gerald. This report says you have shared DNA across 37 segments and no family tree, whatever that means."

"He's not on Facebook." Suzy was rattled. "Let's do a Google search."

Suzy and Chloe read the results. They looked at each other. "Jenkins!"

"Click that tycoon story." Chloe pointed.

They both read.

"Gerald Felps Jenkins died in an automobile accident near his home late last night. He was believed to be the only blood relation left in ammunition tycoon Luther Felps Walcott's family. Walcott's estate has been in limbo for nearly seventy years. People who work for Walcott's firm called the mogul a vindictive recluse. The estate provisions require his trust managers to strictly adhere to a strange set of secret conditions. Walcott specified on his deathbed that his descendant(s) could only inherit the fortune if they met the mandatory generational lineage and other qualifications sealed with the probate court. The estate is now valued at $1bn."

"That obituary was five years ago," Suzy said. *Cannot be.*

"I'm a billionaire!?" Chloe laughed. "Right?!" She squealed.

*Maybe?* "We both know things are never what they seem." *Is this Ginny's relation or Chloe's?*

Chloe took control of the tablet. She started searching. "Let's Google Walcott."

Suzy took the tablet. "No. I'll look into this."

"Why can't we look now?" Chloe pulled the tablet back and started typing.

"Chloe, stop."

Chloe drove her fists up. "I don't have to go to college!" She pointed to the screen. "Look at that!"

They both looked at string of investment articles.

"Calm down." Suzy was grateful the place was near empty.

"I'll buy grandma a mansion and hire a staff for her. She can shop on QVC all she wants."

Suzy rubbed her forehead. "Arnold said Bart was required to…" She shut up. *Gulf War Study. Ammunition. Oh my GOD!*

Frank stood at The Valley's nurse's station, looking at charts. Nurse Larsen sidled up next to him. "You got company."

He turned to see Suzy marching toward him. She looked miserable, sobbing.

"What happened?" He went to her.

She had a paper bag in her hand and took several deep breaths.

"Thank God, for a minute I thought you were drinking." Frank searched her eyes. "Did something happen to Ginny?"

Suzy took several deep breaths and started to weep. "Chloe, she…" *Chloe had an abortion.* Suzy whispered to Frank as she continued to sob.

Larsen moved behind the desk to watch.

Frank and Suzy started whispering and moved away from the nurse's station.

Frank caught Larsen staring. To Suzy, "Let's go outside."

Suzy wasn't ready to leave. She walked up to Larsen. "You know, I thought I hated you. I don't. I don't know your story. But I'll just say this, don't let him or any man take advantage of you."

Larsen was flabbergasted. "I don't hate you either, Ms. Lennox. But I have a feeling he might." Larsen gave Wisner a smirk.

Frank fumed. He looked at Suzy. "Take advantage?"

Suzy took a few more hits off her empty paper bag. "I mean men in general."

"You said, him." Larsen pointed at Wisner.

"Maybe I do hate you," Suzy spat at Larsen.

A patient room rang. "Saved by the bell." Larsen left the desk.

"You need to leave." Frank was adamant.

"Go ahead, call security. I'm not afraid. What are going to do? Baker Act me?" Suzy shoved him.

"I'm sorry, I truly am." He didn't budge.

Suzy grabbed him. "I think I'm going to pass out."

He held her. "Chloe's a grown woman. She made a choice."

Suzy moaned, "Don't… I really think I'm…" Suzy began to slide down.

Frank held her tight as she began to slump.

Suzy swayed. "Lightheaded…"

"Let's get you to a bed." He picked her up and moved her to an empty patient room.

Suzy panted, "I'm …"

Frank took her pulse. "It's okay. Go ahead and faint. I'll be here. You're exhausted."

Suzy went white and was silent.

A cherry scent filled Suzy's nostrils. The sound of sucking and slurping made her swallow hard. She saw the purple hair first, then Larsen's grin. *Where am I?*

Larsen sucked a Tootsie Pop as she studied Suzy. "Welcome back. Doc had to see an actual patient."

Suzy felt clammy and disoriented.

"What do you want to do?" Larsen took her blood pressure. "You want to go to the ER and through their triage?"

Suzy lifted her head. The room did a half turn before settling down. "I'm leaving."

"Anything you want me to relay to Dr. Wisner?"

Suzy's stomach growled.

Larsen looked bewildered. "Was that me or you?"

Suzy gave her a scowl. "No message."

"So hey, what was that crazy warning about earlier? You and doc fighting?"

"Forget it." Suzy grabbed the bed rail and pulled herself up. "We're just friends. I... never mind."

Larsen stepped back as Suzy scooted to the opening at the end of the bed.

"I'd ask you to put the rail down, but if it's not obvious." Suzy paused. Her vision and her head needed to sync up.

"Oh, of course." The nurse put the rail down as Suzy jumped off the bed. "Silly me."

*Thanks.* Suzy looked for her purse. "Do you know where my bag is?"

"Come with me." Larsen led Suzy to the nurse's station.

Suzy took her backpack from the nurse and put it on. The room bounced a bit and then stopped. She blinked until her head settled. "Cheers."

"I could take you down in a wheelchair." Larsen moved toward Suzy.

Suzy backed toward the elevator. "I'm fine."

She wasn't fine. She was distraught. Sorrowful. Her daughter had had an abortion. And she hadn't the opportunity to be there for Chloe, nor a chance to bury whatever remains there were of her grandchild.

Suzy met Loretta Kempster, Ginny's new psychiatrist at The Circle's entrance. Loretta was semi-retired, worked with a limited number of patients, and was fond of The Circle's relaxed atmosphere. They shook hands and moved toward Ginny's room.

Suzy had to be strong for her mother, and she wanted to comfort Chloe. Everything was too much right now.

Kempster made small talk as they walked. Suzy wasn't up for an ice breaker chat.

Kempster waved to a small group gathering near the piano. "What do you think of their buddy system?"

Suzy turned to look. "No clue."

Kempster smiled. Her sixty-plus complexion was moisturized and polished to fifty-ish. Suzy stared at Kempster's lack of lines.

The doctor let Suzy enter Ginny's room first. Kempster explained, "If the group wants to suggest changes, they gather their buddies for a meeting at the piano. Their foreman shares the verdict with The Circle's administrator."

Suzy gave Ginny a hug. "Mom, do you know about the group meetings by the piano?"

"No." Ginny was curt.

Kempster encouraged Ginny. "It might be nice to join in."

Suzy looked from Ginny to Kempster. "She's a bit of a lone wolf."

"Ginny, maybe you should join the pack?" Kempster smiled at Ginny.

Ginny stared.

Suzy and the doctor looked at each other and sat.

"Ginny," the doctor said. "How do you feel today?"

"Nothing." Ginny mumbled.

"What does that mean?" Suzy asked and then mouthed *sorry* to the doctor.

Ginny looked at both of them. "I feel nothing."

Suzy realized this was her cue to leave. "Mom, Dr. Kempster wants to meet with you regularly."

Kempster nodded. "Ginny, would that be okay?"

"Then can I go home?" Ginny had little to no expression. Her tone was flat.

Kempster looked to Suzy for approval. "That could be part of our goal setting."

Suzy got up. "I'll be on the porch, Mom. I'll see you before I leave." Suzy gave Ginny another hug.

It was twenty minutes before Kempster came out to meet Suzy. They went over the current meds list and discussed Ginny's goals. Suzy wanted to introduce vitamins to her mother's daily routine and reduce the number of pharmaceuticals. The doctor wanted to add more psychotherapy sessions to determine what additional rehabilitation Ginny could pursue.

"So, we're working to get her home?" Dr. Kempster clarified with Suzy.

"Definitely. She has to have some assistance, but yes, home." She looked around the porch. It was becoming less appealing by the minute.

Dr. Kempster put her sunglasses on. The concrete floor was dusty, and the wicker furniture smelled of nicotine and a faint whiff of cat urine. The porch had a nice view of a large fountain, though the scent of reclaimed water bursting at regular intervals from the fountain's jets was nauseating.

The doctor was not fazed by the setting. "Suzy, your mother is guarded. I can see she's experiencing some emotional blunting. We'll lower the dose of a few medications because she's not able to smile."

"What do mean about her smile?"

"She lacks expression."

"That's a medication thing?"

"I need to look at what she's taking." Kempster pulled Ginny's folder from her bag.

"You mean a side effect."

"Yes." Kempster made notes. "Is your mother a reserved and quiet woman?"

"At the moment."

The doctor pulled her sunglasses off and put them on the top of her head. "It seems that this is who she is."

Suzy's wondered, "I beg your pardon?"

"Side effects happen." Dr. Kempster clicked her pen closed. "But sometimes blunting it is caused by an emotional disorder."

"No"—Suzy was riled—"this is not who my mother is!"

Dr. Kempster paused and clipped her pen to the folder.

*You're psychoanalyzing me now.*

"No one wants to see their parent decline or age."

"You don't know my mother." Suzy took her phone out. She showed the doctor a video of Ginny and Chloe arguing over the villain on a *CSI* episode. Ginny's had thorough details. Chloe and Ginny were laughing and joking. Suzy scrolled to photos of her mother happy, laughing, gardening, and opening QVC boxes. Then she showed her photos of Ginny at rehab with a blackout mask and in a bed, despondent.

"We age and change over time." The doctor enjoyed the gardening photos. She smiled at Suzy.

"True, doctor, but look at the date on the video." Suzy held the phone to Dr. Kempster's face. The doctor took out a pair of readers and put them on. The date was small.

"I see," Kempster observed.

Suzy nodded. "That was a month before her surgery. The photos of her with the mask are post-surgery. Not my mother. She became that. The work of professionals, I might add."

Kempster offered no explanation.

"Her knee, if she had the mind to use it, is a medical miracle, a piece of art. But her mind and the rest of her well-being are… how did you say it? The way she is."

Kempster held up her hand. "I haven't known your mother but a few weeks. Let me discuss her progress with the facility's physician. To be very honest, I don't receive a lot of family feedback. We do our best with the information we have."

*That's scary.* "Thank you for being honest"—Suzy was sincere—"but the information you have isn't anything, just notes other doctors put in her chart. How does a patient, a vulnerable patient, ever achieve a decent quality of life? You treat them with no information. You don't ask enough questions of the family. The Ginny you talked to today has no memory of what makes her happy or how she even got to this place. She can't help you. She lost her mind. Literally! I had to watch that. If I hadn't asked more questions, she would still be in a mental hospital or overmedicated in skilled nursing. She's improving, and I'm thankful for that. But she's still not totally back inside her body or her mind."

"You're a good daughter." Kempster nodded sympathetically.

"No, I'm not." Suzy searched for the right words. "I'm *trying* to be a good daughter. She deserves the quality of life she *was promised* when we scheduled her surgery. They warned that she could die, maybe get an infection, or have complications, but nowhere were we told she could lose her mind or have postoperative cognitive dysfunction. No one told us to be concerned with her anesthesia. The anesthesiologist told us there could be temporary confusion, a sore throat, or bruising from the I.V., but not P.O.C.D. I even had to ask Dr. Lopez at Coastal what the Olanzapine was for. Lopez is a saint as far as I'm concerned, but she still didn't educate me. I had to probe. Do my own research online."

Kempster listened quietly.

Suzy hoped she wasn't wasting her breath. She really wanted to open a dialogue, not just for Ginny, but others like her, maybe even someone at The Circle.

"Not even one doctor seemed to think an elderly person's post-surgery confusion was important or treatable. It's like they all skipped that class in med school."

Kempster switched back to her sunglasses and slipped everything into her Coach briefcase.

*Go ahead, hide.*

"We're going to dial back some of her medications, Suzy. I think she's been misdiagnosed as bi-polar." Kempster looked at her Apple watch.

"Bi-polar? Hold the phone. No one told me my mother is bi-polar, considered bi-polar, or being treated for bi-polar disorder."

"Well, I just did"—Kempster stood—"and I'm going to work with you."

Suzy made the sign of the cross. *I actually believe you.*

They both made their way to their parked cars.

"Are you Catholic?" Kempster asked.

"No, but if this works, I could be persuaded."

They both laughed.

*Please don't be a liar. Wait, I must go back in. I promised to say good-bye to Mom.*

Suzy dialed Bart's number. It was 9 p.m. She normally wouldn't call someone after 7 p.m., but it didn't seem time had much meaning these days. As a rule, no one answered their phone anyway.

"Barton Welch."

*Barton.* "Hi, hey, it's Suzy Lennox. Thanks for answering. Don't you have my number in your phone?" She didn't know how to discuss what she and Chloe had found. "Arnold's been weird lately."

He ignored her phone number comment. "How so?" Bart sounded concerned.

"I really don't know how to say this, but Arnold and I saw an old movie and Chloe had a DNA test. Anyway, we did a genealogy search. There's something fishy about our families." Suzy took a swig of Chablis.

Bart's line was quiet.

"Are you there?"

"Has Arnold done something offensive?" Bart asked.

"Not really."

"What does 'not really' mean?" Bart's tone was dull.

"Well, his humor is always offensive, but that's not what I'm referring to."

"What are you referring to? It's rather late in the evening to be calling about my son's behavior. What has he done?"

"We went to see this silent movie. And I know Arnold is a geek …" *Where am I going with this?*

Bart's tone got impatient. "Go on."

"I'm just going to say it." Suzy poured herself another glass of wine. "Chloe and I saw an article about a tycoon. It appears that she is a DNA cousin of some Jenkins, Felps, and Walcotts. The article said there is a will with lots of secrets."

"How is Arnold associated with this revelation?"

"That's why I'm calling. He mentioned that Harlan Welch and my grandmother saw the same movie at an old theater that no longer exists."

Bart's breathing was heavy. "What is your concern?"

"Your tone just changed." Suzy felt the heat of the wine increasing her bravura. "Arnold said you had to engage with me when you hired me for the Gulf Study."

The line went to a dial tone.

*Here we go again.*

Suzy tried to call Bart back. He didn't pick up.

Suzy texted Arnold: I called your dad.

Arnold: I'm aware. He's trying to call me.

Suzy: He hung up on me.

Arnold: Give him a day to process.

Suzy: Process what?

Arnold: Your call.

Suzy: Did he tell you what I said?

Arnold: Would it matter?

Suzy: Would it matter? What's with you people?

Arnold: Anything else?

Suzy: Fuck you.

Arnold: Goodnight

*That's weird.* "Arnold, you suddenly sound like an adult?" Suzy tossed her phone on the bed.

# CHAPTER 24

Ginny smiled as they played rummy. It was surreal. It had been a few weeks since Suzy and Dr. Kempster had implemented a plan. Ginny was increasingly happy, able to process and remember more. They were on their way to weaning Ginny off the antidepressant cocktail that had wrecked her thinking, but she wasn't out of the woods yet. She still needed an antidepressant and antipsychotic blend to keep her stable. This amounted to a couple of pills vs. a cup full of pills.

"Mom, you remember the Welch family?"

"Vaguely."

"Well, we have a meeting with Barton Welch about a trust. I'm not sure exactly how we are related to the people mentioned in the trust, but I want you to come. Okay?"

Ginny placed a few cards down. "Do you really need me?"

Suzy picked up a card. "You might know some of these people. It sounds like Chloe might be related to someone in the estate."

"Related to the Welches?"

"No." Suzy discarded a card.

"I don't understand." Ginny studied the string of cards on the table.

"Well, it's not a Welch, but someone they represent. Do Felps, Jenkins, or Walcott ring a bell?"

Ginny closed her eyes to think. "Maybe."

"Then we need you. I'll come Saturday around 10 a.m."

Ginny nodded. "Is my lavender dress here? I've been saving it for a special occasion." She picked up a card from the deck.

*Finally!* "Perfect, we'll look in your closet." *Let's hope it's not falling apart from dry rot.*

Bart stood. He pointed Suzy, Ginny, and Chloe to a set of couches that faced one another. A coffee table divider, with a sweating pitcher of water, short tumblers, paper napkin squares, a small spoon, and a dish of mints met the expected courtesy.

*Would a few cookies break the bank, Bart?*

Arnold's father wore a white button-down shirt opened at the collar, no tie, a suit vest, and matching slacks with highly polished shoes. His starched sleeves were folded to the elbow. A gold pinky ring was the only jewelry on his left hand. He sported an aging man's hair-loss-hawk: balding, with patches of close-cropped gray hair on each side of his head. Arnold looked nothing like his father. Bart had a roman nose, chiseled jaw, narrow eyes, and thin lips.

The office was devoid of corporate markings, plaques, personal photos, or client information. Instead, it looked almost presidential in its art and furnishings, a high-profile setting with devices hidden in walls, tables, and lighting, to provide clickable access to secured presentation screens, televisions, and recording equipment.

The women sat together on one couch.

Bart sat across from them.

Arnold walked in through a door seamlessly hidden as a wall. He was dressed in a charcoal Armani suit and was clean shaven, his hair trimmed to a tousled textured Caesar.

Suzy did a doubletake. *Arnold?*

Arnold gave her a snapped chin-up nod.

*Son of a Bart!*

Bart poured a glass of water for Ginny.

Suzy took the glass before Ginny could. "You drink it." She handed it back to Bart.

Chloe cracked, "Good one, Mom." She pointed at Bart and Arnold.

Arnold sat next to his father and remained cool, disinterested.

"Absolutely"—he drank the water—"I respect your caution."

Suzy turned to Ginny. "Do you want a glass of water, Mom?"

"No." Ginny sat quietly.

Suzy introduced her family. "Mom, Chloe, Bart is the man I worked for one time. Arnold is his son, and we became business partners, as you know. Grandma Woodson and members of Bart's family went to church together. I'll let him explain the rest because I'd like to know more too."

Chloe nodded. "Word."

Ginny smiled at Bart. "Was Jerome your family?"

*Good probe, Mom.*

"Great place to start." Bart sat back and put his arm along the top of the sofa.

*Opened body language. Tony Robbins 101.*

"Jerome Felps became a friend of my father, through your mother, Monica," Bart acknowledged Ginny. "Our families, the Woodsons and Welchs, attended an upstart church that broke off from the Free Methodists that were, for all intents and purposes, Holy Rollers. The founding members of David's Church were sophisticated people who did not want to worship like charismatics by rolling on the floor or speaking in tongues. They wanted a civilized Christian church.

"The book of Matthew clearly spells out that Jesus is in the royal family line of King David. David's Church was a well-educated community who generously taught their members in open settings. They chose Blue Run. We know it as Rainbow River, but in our parent's day, it was called Blue Run, and that's where David's Church met."

Chloe swung her leg. Suzy and Ginny listened attentively. Suzy gave Chloe a look.

Bart paused until the women gave him the go-ahead. "Was there a question?"

Chloe shook her head.

Ginny spoke up, "The Woodsons left David's Church not long after my sister, the first Virginia died. Was Jerome her father?"

Suzy and Chloe looked at each other.

*She's back!*

Bart shook his head. "I'm not certain."

## 1920 Juliette, Fl

The Studebaker was loud. The car rumbled with Monica's thoughts. She shouted, "Why did you take my church to that scandalous movie?"

Joe raised his hand. "That was my idea." He leaned in from the backseat.

She turned to him. "Why?"

"To get to know a tomato like you." He winked.

Lou had his left arm leaning out the open window, his right hand holding the steering wheel. "The Deacon wasn't letting you out of his sight. So, we took the troops." He reached over with his right and patted her knee.

She pushed his hand off her.

Lou rested his hand on her knee again. "Don't be shy, Monk."

Joe gave Lou a flick to the back of his head. "You can't have all the bees. This one's mine."

"Not the Queen." Lou moved his hand up and squeezed her thigh.

"Stop calling me Monk. And stop that!" She slapped his hand and moved toward the door.

Lou laughed uproariously. "You two." He slapped his cousin. "You're like an old married couple."

"Old married..." Monica suddenly remembered the show at the Victory. "We didn't? You didn't?"

Lou turned back to Joe. "I think she's beginning to thaw out."

They both howled.

Monica felt dirty. "You tricked me, like they tricked that poor woman on the poster!"

"Hey, Monk," Lou hollered, "you think Joe's a Lennox Sanderson?"

The men howled.

"What have you done?" She couldn't remember how she got to the Tampa Bay Hotel or why they were constantly laughing at her. "Why are you laughing?"

Joe stopped. He realized she was truly frightened. "Lou. Lou. Hey. She's upset."

Lou looked at Joe and Monica. "What's the big deal, Monk?"

"Did you trick me?"

Lou grabbed her thigh again. "No trick, Monk. Only treat."

She slapped his hand and grabbed the door handle.

"Tell her, Joe." Lou reached back and gave his cousin a slap on the face. "Tell her."

"Tell me what?" Monica's mind was racing.

Lou grabbed her knee again. "You said you liked fancy things and fancy places. Don't you remember? You begged us to take you to New York."

Joe punched Lou in the arm. "Hands off, Lou."

Lou grasped her inner thigh.

"Tell me what?" she screamed at Joe.

"We made love. I didn't have to pretend to marry you. You said you were Anna Moore. You were toasted, baby. You said you were Mrs. Lennox, and I was your Mr. Lennox. You..."

"No!" Monica screamed. She reached for the steering wheel.

Lou tried to block her. Joe leapt up and hit the floor of car as the Studebaker's right front wheel swerved off the road, making a crunching sound. They bounced and flew off their seats. The vehicle swerved, narrowly missing a tree, and finally dug into a patch of mud.

Lou punched Monica in the jaw. "Bitch!"

Her head went flying. She thought her neck would snap. She blinked her eyes.

"You're crazy! You need a head doctor, Monk! You act like we dropped you a Mickey Finn or raped you. We didn't! You got drunk. Loose. And enjoyed yourself. Why, you and Joe pleasured each other most of night while I watched. I kept my hands off you for Joe. We finally left you to sleep and grabbed a few more girls and went to my room."

Monica opened the door. She struggled to find her belongings. She stumbled. Her vision began to clear up. She swayed as she walked. Where were they? She looked around and recognized a bend in the road. She walked, veering back and forth as she tried to see straight. She could hear the men arguing. She walked faster.

Lou turned to Joe. "I'll give her something to feel God damn sorry about." He removed his shirt and trousers before sinking his shoes into the mud outside his door. He bolted after her in his undershirt and underwear, mud flapping up his legs and shorts.

"No!" Joe bounded over the front seat and out the driver's door, sinking into the sludge. As he got to firm ground, he chased after Lou.

Monica ran faster, dropping her tapestry bag.

Lou ran hard, with the speed of a lion pursuing his prey.

Joe tripped on a tree root that sent him into a freefall. He couldn't catch himself and wrenched his ankle. "Lou, no!"

Joe got up quickly and his right ankle gave. He hopped on his left foot, screaming. "No!" he cried.

Lou tackled Monica.

Bart droned on, "Jerome Felps and Luther Felps Walcott were first cousins. Jerome was a country fellow. Luther was a city slicker, a handsome man who grew up in New York where his father's family was heavily invested in ammunition from as early as the American Revolution, making gunpowder for muskets.

"By World War I, Walcott Cartridges sold hundreds of millions in munitions to the allied forces. They would eventually take control of failed companies in the 1929 Wall Street crash and revive them."

"I hate guns," Suzy mumbled.

"Walcott thrived and became Walcott American, Inc." Bart rubbed the top of the sofa. "Where others went bust, they did not. Walcott went from ammunition as a corporate identity to other lines, of which baby formula was one."

Chloe's face twisted.

"At what point did baby formula come into play?" Suzy grabbed a pillow and hugged it.

Bart nodded. "Let's look."

He opened a drawer from the coffee table and grabbed a remote and clicked. A slice of the ceiling opened, and a large screen descended. He hit play, and a grainy black and white news reel started.

"I remember seeing these." Ginny watched intently.

Bart showed them clips from the 1920s. When he paused the clips, he said, "I apologize if any of this offends you. The Roaring 20s was an uninhibited time. Luther frequented speakeasys, did business with gangsters, and enjoyed the company of women who openly explored their sexual freedom. And to be forthright, he could afford wild orgies. He was also a frequent guest at Polly Adler's house of prostitution, among many in New York." Bart ran the reel that showed the Jazz Age and included clips of Luther shaking hands with dignitaries.

**1920 Romeo, Fl**

Monica introduced her parents to Jerome Felps and Luther Walcott. "The boys go by Joe and Lou. We were in a road accident."

"Dear Lord!" Catherine gasped.

Joseph looked at the trio. Monica's dress was torn and had grass stains on the back. She and Jerome had bruised faces, and Luther's shirt was torn and smudged with greasy handprints and mud. Their shoes were caked with dried dirt.

The three climbed the porch steps and stamped their feet. Each ran their shoes across the welcome mat, leaving clumps of soil over "Welcome."

"The deacon was so worried last night." Catherine dried her hands on her apron.

"Come in." Joseph stepped aside so the young people could enter through the screen door.

Jerome nodded. "Sir, thank you." He entered limping.

Luther put his hand out to shake Joseph's.

The older man hesitated. He gave Luther's filthy hand a firm squeeze and stared him in the eye. "Appears you've only superficial wounds. Mother will grab the iodine. I'll have a look at your car."

Luther addressed Catherine, "Quaint place." The door slammed behind him.

Joseph grabbed his cane and stepped out to have a look at the Studebaker.

Monica followed her father to the yard. "They'll be leaving shortly."

Joseph whispered to Monica, "Is that the war monger?"

Monica cast her head down. "I didn't know."

"He's running guns between the Italians, Cubans, and bootleggers." Her father was unforgiving. "Walcott's in Tampa to see Charlie

Wall or Trafficante, the papers say. He doesn't care who gets killed. He's manufacturing the weapons."

Monica remembered it then. She had caught one of the throws at the gambling parlor. The Bolita game! She had almost dropped it, but Jerome reached out, and together they caught the velvet bag of one hundred numbered lottery balls. Wall laughed. She and Jerome tossed it to the catcher, who held one ball in the sack. Everyone waited in anticipation for the bag to be tied off and the winning numbered ball revealed. Then cheers and boos commenced.

"Deacon Welch came over last night to make sure you arrived safely. He waited for your train." Joseph leaned on his cane. He glanced from Monica to the car.

Guilt engulfed her.

He walked around the car. "Surprised that wheel got you here."

"They had a time getting it on." She felt profound melancholy. "I'm sorry."

He wasn't strong enough to protect her any longer. "Did he do this?" He stopped and placed two fingers under her chin to have a better look at her face.

"It was an accident, Father. I caused the accident. I grabbed at the steering wheel." It was partially true.

"Why'd you grab the wheel?"

She looked down.

"The left side of your face is bruised. Were you driving? Where were you last night?"

"My jaw hit the steering wheel."

"You grabbed the steering wheel and hit the steering wheel?"

Her lips quivered. She glanced up to stop the tears and took a deep breath. "They got me a room at the Tampa Bay Hotel. We... I, missed the train."

"A woman doesn't ..." His voice broke. "Walcott is dangerous."

A tear escaped her bruised left eye.

"If he believes I'd let him disrespect you, he owns us."

"I don't understand." Monica felt queasy. What had she done?

"I wish you had killed him." Joseph was disgusted. "I assume that's why you grabbed the wheel."

"No Father, it was an accident. I was horsing around."

Joseph pointed his cane at the house. "I should kill him with that God damned Walcott shotgun behind the front door. But if I did, his father would probably want to avenge his son's death. That'd put you and Ma in greater danger."

"Greater?" She swallowed hard. "I missed the train. They were kind enough to put me up in the hotel." She could hear the screen door flap closed.

"Mr. Woodson, sir." Jerome hobbled out.

Her father whispered to her, "The deacon failed you."

Jerome looked from Monica to Joseph Woodson, realizing he'd interrupted their conversation.

Monica gave Joe a faint smile.

Her father crouched down and looked at the damaged wheel again. "It will get you out of here."

Bart used his laser pointer to introduce Agnes Felps Walcott to the women. "This is Luther's mother. She visited the tenements and slums of New York and wanted to educate women about hygiene, manners, child rearing, and faith, things she felt could improve the family dynamic of the poor. Agnes died of La Grippe when Luther was a young man in his early 20s. He adored his mother, and the formula line was added in her honor."

Suzy marveled at the similarities between her grandmother Monica and young Agnes. "Do you suppose Luther was attracted to grandmother, because she and Agnes looked alike?"

Bart nodded. "It's assumed." He continued the presentation. "Luther's father, Jacob Perish Walcott, ran in the social circles with the Rockefellers and Roosevelts."

Ginny grew quiet.

Arnold leaned in to tell Suzy, "The trust is a majority shareholder in Walcott stock."

Bart cleared his throat and motioned for Arnold to hold his commentary. "Luther suspected he had illegitimate children all over New York. He had an insatiable appetite for women, and he didn't want to soil his family name by recognizing his bastard children."

Suzy's eyes welled with unexpected tears. *We descend from this monster.*

Bart continued, "Luther wanted the Felps line to inherit his wealth because that would honor his mother. Though being the vengeful fellow that he became, he was not going to make it easy on anyone. Luther knew Monica Woodson because he and Jerome met her and her church group at Sulphur Springs."

Arnold pointed at Suzy.

Suzy shook her head.

Bart resumed, "Luther was obsessed with Monica. We surmise it was her close resemblance to his mother or the romantic notion that she lived in a town named Romeo, which had a neighboring town, Juliette. She was Anna Moore come to life or a Shakespearian damsel. We're not sure."

Chloe raised her hand. "Who is Anna Moore?"

Suzy answered, "She's the movie character who was duped in *Way Down East.*"

"Monica was about your age, Chloe, at the time." Bart added, "She lived a very simple life."

*Plain people.* "Plain people," Suzy recalled. "The movie about Anna said it was a story of Plain People, or something like that."

"Mom," Chloe said frustratedly, "you and grandma are plain people, but you have a business. Grandma had the stand until she retired."

Ginny pointed to Bart. "I remember you." Ginny now had an accusing tone. "We're near the same age."

Chloe and Suzy turned to Ginny.

Bart looked Ginny in the eye. "Remember?"

"You were there." Ginny nodded.

"Where?"

"At the clinic." Ginny pointed at him. Her voice grew volumes. "You didn't want me to see you."

"If I didn't want you to see me, how do you know it was me you saw?" Bart was calm.

"I know who you are." Ginny crossed her arms.

"Who am I?"

"You're the one who stopped the abortion."

Suzy froze. Chloe looked to her mother.

Ginny began to cry. Chloe reached over and hugged the older woman.

"I did it at Monica's request, Ginny." Bart was unapologetic.

## 1922 Romeo, Fl

The day began like most since Virgina Catherine Woodson was born. They were a happy household, focused on every smile or coo of the beautiful baby girl named for Joseph Woodson's mother, Virginia.

Monica drove her father's 1914 Ford Model T pickup down Highway 5, heading home from a shopping trip in Dunnellon. Her father agreed to watch baby Virginia while the women picked up mail, supplies, medicine, and some fabric.

He forbade her from ever communicating with Luther or Jerome. He didn't want the men to know about the baby or have control of their lives. He wanted Monica to raise her daughter at home and inherit the family house, land, and produce business when he and Ma went home to the Lord. He did not want his granddaughter used as a pawn to control Monica or possibly be stolen away.

"Pa's not going to be happy, is he?" Monica kept her eyes on the road, awaiting her mother's response.

"You should have left it at the post office for the church mission," Catherine fretted.

Monica looked at the cases of Walcott Evaporated Milk in the truck bed. "But we need it. It's not like Virginia should be deprived."

"Pa doesn't know you've been talking in letters to Joe," Catherine sighed.

Monica swallowed. "I can bury the cans. Or burn them with the trash!" Monica looked to her mother for agreement.

"We do not lie, Monica."

"Well, that's not true. Pa tells everyone I'm grieving my dead soldier husband who never got to meet his child."

"Shh!"

"Ma, our whole church went to the picture show with Lou and Joe. Pa made Deacon Welch swear on his life to tell people I got home on the next train. That's a lie!"

"We don't talk about these things!" Catherine took her hankie and blew her nose. She looked away from Monica.

"I'm bringing the milk in, and I'm not lying. It's not like anyone permits me to make a single decision. I'm feeding Virginia with the milk her father supplied."

Catherine jeered, "Which one?"

Monica choked down the insult, tears trickling down her cheeks.

Her mother had never been cross or disappointed in her, even when she learned that she was pregnant. Catherine had always been her support and lifeline. "Ma, please."

Catherine wept into the embroidered cloth.

"Okay, now for the uncomfortable part." Bart opened a drawer and placed a photo on the table. It was Monica, Jerome, and Luther on the porch of the Tampa Bay Hotel. They were young, giddy, beautiful, and laughing. Monica's hair was up in a Gibson Girl twist. She wore a modest plain frock that accentuated her curves. The men each had a tight arm around her waist. Their sleeves were rolled up, and you could almost feel the tug of war for Monica in their grip on her tiny waist.

"Ginny, your mother was being wooed by both men. Luther was inspired by Lennox Sanderson, the male lead in *Way Down East*. Monica did not return with the church group but spent the weekend with Luther and Jerome."

"Mother wasn't a loose woman," Ginny said defensively.

Bart spoke directly to Ginny, "My father, Harlan Welch, made a commitment to look out for the first Virginia and you after he failed to protect Monica from Luther."

Ginny crossed her arms. "What about Jerome?"

Bart looked to Arnold, then Suzy. "We're all here because my father, Harlan Welch, became the liaison between Walcott and Monica. Our family has maintained the Lennox Legacy Trust that was first established in 1921."

Chloe gave a time out signal. "You all made money managing this trust. And your name is Welch. Kind of like Bernie Madoff made off with his clients' money. Are you welching on the trust?"

*Good point.*

"We have not." Bart was outraged. "We're not industrialists, or gun people, Chloe. We're here because Monica made sure Ginny had Suzy. And, furthermore, this was the only way my father knew how to make it up to Joseph Woodson. My father was a man of God and felt responsible for one lamb straying. He—we—have kept the trust intact for you ALL!"

Chloe clapped cynically. "Thank you so much. You could have thrown Mom a bone. Paid off her mortgage or something."

Arnold tried to placate Chloe. "That would have cost you. We would have preferred to tell you. You think it's easy to be the shitty guys? It's your family's secret, not ours. My grandfather screwed up, but we've been trying to manage that mistake our whole lives."

Bart spoke to Ginny, "Your sister, Virginia, and your grandfather, Joseph Woodson, both died on the same day. Little Virginia was in her crib. She looked like she was sleeping. Dead. Joseph had a heart attack or stroke and was found in the backyard with the hose gripped in his hand, watering a small ear tree."

"I always hated that tree." Ginny crossed her arms.

*I always loved that tree.*

To Suzy, Arnold continued, "I manage a portion of the trust's assets. Luther formed the Lennox Legacy Trust for the first Virginia as the sole heir in 1921 with shares of Walcott stock, farm property, land purchases, and commodities. When Virginia died, he didn't do anything to change the trust. The wealth that grew stayed in the trust. Closer to his death, Luther consolidated his assets and included the trust into the whole his heir would acquire."

Suzy held the photo of the trio. "Are there more photos?"

Bart rapped on the drawer. He placed more photos on the table. "Jerome and Monica got together after he learned of Virginia's death. Luther left them alone. Catherine never remarried. But to respect her mother, Monica continued to secretly rendezvous in Ocala with Jerome."

Ginny looked perplexed. "Why didn't Jerome marry Monica?"

Bart shook his head. "We don't know. There's no marriage record."

Bart passed several photos to Ginny. "Your mother and Jerome continued a 20-year love affair, meeting in his Ocala home. To her Romeo neighbors, Monica was considered an old maid. To the residents of Ocala, she was the wife of Jerome Felps."

"They pretended to be married?" Suzy poured a glass of water. "Why?"

"When Jerome left for war, Monica continued her trips to Ocala and communicated with Luther regarding Jerome's regiment. Luther, being in the ammunition business, could receive privileged information."

"Edward Compton wasn't my real father?" Ginny was bewildered. "I always thought he was. He was my stepfather?"

"Luther was your father." Bart was honest. "Your mother did not want be alone when her mother would eventually pass. She and Luther had a brief affair during the time they were mourning Jerome's death."

Bart showed the women photos of Monica and Jerome in Ocala, then Luther and baby Ginny. Suzy studied the home. It was a two-story Victorian gingerbread with two distinct domes and minarets.

Chloe looked at the photo. "It looks like that Hershey kiss building in Tampa."

Suzy smiled. "The University of Tampa."

Bart nodded. "The University was the old Tampa Bay Hotel property."

Ginny was confused. "Why was this a secret?"

Bart paused. "Luther loved Jerome and Monica, in his own way."

## 1942 Ocala, FL

Monica retrieved the house key from her black beaded handbag. She traveled light on weekends. She gripped the flat round key head of intersecting hearts, pushed the barrel into the keyhole until the bit connected, and unlocked the decorative blue wooden door of corner inset hearts. This was her happy place, a place to design and sew fine clothing for herself and her husband, and to earn the commissions she received from neighboring dress shops. She kept the designs here for the clothing her mother wanted no part of. In fact, her mother had wanted no part of anything outside of her existence with her husband, Joseph.

"Back here," a male voice called out.

She was startled. "Jerome? Are you back, darling?" She rushed to dining room. "Thank God!"

But it was Luther who sat at the head of the table. His face was ashen, and his eyes were red. He'd gained weight and looked swollen. He poured himself another scotch. "Sit," he said softly.

"How did you get in here?" Monica put her purse down.

"Jerome's dead." He took a swig of his drink.

"Oh, my God." She sat, feeling warm tears fill her eyes. She closed them.

Luther sobbed, "God damn it!" He slammed his glass down. "I could have saved him." His voice broke. "You know how stubborn he could be."

Monica couldn't speak or think. It was Pa and Virginia again.

Luther reached his hand to Monica. "I'm going to bury him in New York with the rest of our family."

"I need him here," Monica pleaded. "I'll tend his grave." Monica reached for Luther, then retrieved her hand. "I can't keep losing people."

Luther took out a handkerchief and blew his nose. "What happened to Virgina?"

Monica's imploring eyes met his painful gaze.

He was in poor health. His debauched lifestyle had finally caught up with him, and he was only forty-four years old.

"We don't know. Ginny and Pa both looked like they went in their sleep. We think Pa smothered her"—her voice seized as her heart raced and she felt a dullness in her thoughts—"… because I brought home the Walcott milk Joe sent. Pa never said a word, but he didn't trust you or Joe."

Luther pounded the table. "The uneducated fool. He didn't trust me! Look at what he did. He killed an innocent."

Monica was mortified by Luther's accusation. "But there's no proof Pa did it."

"I'm willing to say I'm not good person, Monk." He laughed regrettably. "But I never killed a child."

"Pa hated that you disrespected me. He wanted to kill you! He wanted no part of you in his house. He loved Virginia… wanted to forget…" Monica lashed back.

"He should have killed me," Luther spat, "or at least tried."

"Then what?" Monica's lip tremored. "I'd still be a poor woman raising a baby in a rural farm town and never escaping, always being the whisper on everyone's lips!" She grabbed his glass and threw it against the wall. "That's what Pa was trying to avoid!"

"He could have negotiated a deal, like a real man."

Monica was insulted. "Negotiated?! Am I the hostage in this negotiation or was Virginia? What exactly was he to negotiate?"

Luther exhaled. "I set up a trust for Virginia. Did you think I was going to let Jerome's kid…"

"She was yours; he knew that," Monica said bitterly. "We tried for twenty years. We never conceived. I think that's why Jerome wanted to serve. He loved me, but he couldn't give me…" She stifled herself.

Luther dropped his face into his hands and wept, his shoulders trembling. "God damn it!" Luther looked up at her. "I could give you another child."

She was ill, thinking about the attack that had brought her only child. This is what Pa warned her about, Luther's control over her life and her child's.

"Don't look so offended. Think of it, Monk, you'd have part of Joe. The trust was never dissolved. I'm not asking you to marry me unless that's what you want."

Monica shook her head, *no*.

"I'm not likely to live to see fifty, Monk. My liver's failing. I'd like to know Joe and I left the world a better place through you. Consider it."

Ginny turned to Suzy. "I don't understand."

Suzy turned to Bart and Arnold. "What about Grandpa Compton?"

"Edward Compton was Jerome's best friend on Guadalcanal. He brought Jerome's letters to Monica. He married Monica and raised you. He wanted you to have what your sister didn't have: a father."

"Did he know about the trust?" Ginny asked earnestly.

"We believe so."

"So, what happened to Luther?" Suzy wondered.

"Luther felt betrayed for himself and Jerome when Monica married Edward. He didn't care about Jerome's friendship with Edward, nor Monica's happiness at that point. He became vindictive and decided that the trust would be left to his first-born grandchild who lived to be forty-five, which was ironically Luther's age when he died of cirrhosis of the liver," Bart said.

Chloe snapped her fingers. "That's why my great grandmother made sure Ginny's child was born."

Ginny turned to Suzy. "I don't know who your father is. But I think he does."

They turned to Bart.

# CHAPTER 25

**1922 Dunnellon Train Station**

Monica boarded the train for Ocala. She had done this each month since her father and daughter had died. Her mother stayed home with the San Pedro family who bought the next acre over from the Woodsons on the backlot of the Jennings farm. Together they ran the grove stand.

This was Catherine and Monica's agreement. Monica kept her trips secret. Catherine asked no questions if her daughter returned home in three days.

Suzy felt ill. "Who are my father and Chloe's father?"

"They're both military attachés, we believe." Bart was dry. "We don't know who they are. Luther devised a plan to keep tabs on Monica, Virginia, and whoever else from the grave. Think of the stories you've heard about men or women seducing soldiers for government secrets or intelligence gathering."

Chloe exclaimed, "He hired men to rape women!"

Bart looked to Ginny and Suzy. "Were either of you raped?"

Ginny and Suzy grew quiet. Both shook their heads.

"I don't understand," Chloe spat. "He basically said that Luther planned to have you impregnated."

"I did not," Bart snapped.

Arnold massaged his chin.

Chloe got louder, "Let's recap. Monica slept with Jerome or Luther or had a three-way and then produced the dead heir and Luther, ding, ding, ding, ding, produces the living heir. Luther's highly jealous and decides to punish his daughter Ginny in the future and makes sure his gun company keeps making millions and that she won't inherit, but rather, her daughter will. Because he wants to get back at Monica who loved Edward. Right?"

Arnold nodded. "You said it better than I could have."

Suzy turned to her daughter. "Chloe, I could have been Monica at the Tampa Bay Hotel. I loved to drink and dance and … have sex."

Chloe shuddered. "Ew. I don't need to think about that."

"I'm just being honest," Suzy sighed. "I was running around at Ocala bars. That sounds ghostly now that we know about Jerome and Monica's affair. I cannot conjure your father's name or his face because it was a one-night stand. I was an adult, a stupid one. It sure sounds like we're genetically predisposed to repeat the same."

"Mistakes," Ginny said. "We're not mistakes."

"Chloe, I only recently remembered your father was in Desert Storm. I'm not apologizing. I wasn't a slut." *I wanted to be.*

"Sounds like you were drugged, Mom." Chloe was pissed. "And Jerome was a total dick."

Arnold yawned.

"There's no judgement here." Bart was frank. "Women make decisions about their own bodies."

"When it suits you, Bart," Chloe seethed. "Monica was taken advantage of. These are men who knowingly use their dicks as a weapon, shooting sperm bullets to flower babies."

Bart exhaled exasperatedly. "I have no response."

Chloe clapped sarcastically.

Ginny looked at all of them. "I got pregnant with your mom in 1969. My friend Mabel and I were naive. We partied on the river with friends, college kids, whoever."

*That's where I get it!*

Ginny continued, "Until today, I never understood why we didn't talk about things. We just pretended things were normal and moved on, just slowly convinced that life was fine. My mother never told me anything."

"Wait"—Suzy was rattled—"you used Lennox for my last name, but you don't know my father?"

Ginny's face got red. She blew her nose. "Mother convinced me to use Lennox, to give you legitimacy. The only father I've ever known is Edward, who I now know was my stepfather. He was against Mom pushing me to use Lennox, but he gave in. They both told me to put the father's last name as Lennox on your birth certificate, Suzy."

"No father's first name?" Chloe was disbelieving.

"No one would explain anything to me," Ginny sobbed.

The women turned to Bart.

Bart held up his hands. "I was not part of any of that. I was a young man myself. I was working for my father on a need-to-know basis."

Chloe balked, "Everyone was keeping tabs on the golden egg. How much easier can you make it, than to use the last name Lennox?"

"Oh." Ginny was pensive.

*Am I supposed to feel bad for being born?* "Oh my God. Grandmother was brilliant." Suzy looked at everyone. "She wanted to make sure that when she died, she left us a clue!"

Chloe turned to her mother. "Are you going to excuse all this covert patriarchal bullshit?"

"Why are you so angry, Chloe?"

Arnold looked embarrassed. "Dad and I should let you all have some privacy."

Chloe threw her head back. "Really! We're in Dr. Evil's lair and now you want to give us some space?"

Arnold shrugged.

Chloe threw a handful of mints at Arnold. "Fucking Mini-Me here, wants to give us space. Bart, surely this is being taped?"

Arnold pointed at Suzy.

"No," Bart said softly.

Ginny reached for her granddaughter. "Chloe, be respectful. I'm tired. This has been upsetting."

Suzy felt a shiver. "Bart, does Walcott have something to do with Chloe's scholarship?"

Bart was evasive.

"Chloe, do you think this is deliberate?" Suzy suspected. "Damien fits the same profile. He's ROTC, the top of his class…"

Bart held up his hands. "Time out, ladies. This isn't the *Handmaid's Tale*."

Chloe pulled her phone from her bag and texted Damien: Were you hired to date me?

"Let's see what Damien says." Chloe watched her phone.

The room got quiet again.

They waited.

Chloe ate a few mints, mumbled, "We're all part of some fucking experiment! *Wormwood. Borne Identity*."

Her phone dinged.

They watched Chloe.

Damien: Hired? Are you high?

Chloe: Why did you ask me out?

Damien: Are you okay?

Chloe: Yeah. Answer.

Damien: What am I supposed to say?

Chloe: Seriously.

Damien: Where are you? Someone messing with you?

Chloe: I'm with my mom.

Damien: She doesn't like me. That it?

Chloe: Did someone tell you to date me?

Damien: My recruiter thought you were hot. I told you that.

Chloe: Did he tell you to ask me out?

Damien: No. WTF?

Chloe: What's your recruiter's name?

Damien: Joe. You talked to him, Chloe.

Chloe: Right. Ok.

Damien: Are we good?

Chloe: Love you.

Damien: Love you. Later?

Chloe: Yeah.

"Fuck," Chloe yelled. She looked at her mother and grandmother. "Fucking spies are too goddamn smart."

"Watch your language, Chloe." Ginny squeezed her tissue and dabbed her eyes.

"What do you mean?" Suzy asked Chloe.

"I mean they know our algorithms. Bart's right. Fucking Luther, mother fucker knew how to manage Monica. He didn't have to order anyone to rape anyone. He was a genius. He wanted us to all be the product of moles and secret agents. I'm sure Luther's people had to be involved in espionage."

Bart held his fingers to his lips.

Suzy turned to her mother. "Did grandmother ever hint at any of this?"

"I probably didn't listen." Ginny rubbed her forehead.

"To Chloe's point, a lover can infiltrate..." Bart shut up.

"Infiltrate?" Suzy was aghast.

"We're easy marks, Mom. Luther wanted his bloodlines to be Avengers or something."

Arnold put his fist in the air and quickly pulled it back.

Suzy poured herself a glass of water. "Well, that does make me feel a little better."

Arnold cleared his throat. "Justice League."

"What?" Chloe said to Arnold.

"D.C. comics version of the Avengers is Justice League," Arnold clarified.

Everyone stared at Arnold.

"Forget it," he said.

"When do we get to the money?" Chloe groaned.

Bart's jaw pulsed. "There is a twist."

"Fucking hell!" Ginny scowled.

Suzy spewed her water.

Everyone stared at Ginny.

Ginny stared Bart down. "Get it out!"

Bart nodded. "Luther set up perpetual investigators to watch the trust managers. To make sure we didn't assist anyone in discovering the trust. He wanted his heir to find it on their own merit."

Ginny thought a moment. "How did we figure this out?"

Suzy looked at Arnold. "I went to the movie with Arnold."

Bart hit a button and loud music started.

Ginny grabbed her heart.

Arnold mouthed to his father, "Sorry."

Bart put a finger to his lips. Everyone stayed quiet. He turned the music off.

*This place is bugged.*

"Now what?" Chloe rolled her eyes. She turned to her grandmother. "Are you okay?"

Ginny nodded.

"Can't we at least talk about the money?" Chloe persisted.

"Not until the trust transition team contacts us," Bart sighed.

"Unbelievable," Chloe bellyached.

Arnold leaned forward. "If anything happened to Bart, I would continue to manage the trust and I'd have to hire a backup should something happen to me and so on. Or a judge would handle it. There are provisions we must follow."

"Does anyone else feel like they're in a whodunit?" Ginny wondered.

Suzy's jaw dropped. "So there really are people watching us."

Ginny nodded at Suzy.

"Mom, you act like you knew this."

"Somehow, I did." Ginny was blunt.

Bart dug his hands in his pockets. "All of us."

Suzy and Ginny headed back to The Circle Assisted Living. Suzy took her time driving. Ginny was not looking forward to returning. Chloe headed back to school.

"Tell me about Mabel." Suzy pat her mother's hand. "You two sounded like such good friends."

"She moved away when I got pregnant. My memory isn't good."

*I'm sorry.* "You want me to see if I can find Mabel on Facebook?"

"No. When I had you, I settled into being a mommy. If I'm being honest, Mabel and I weren't hanging out with good people. They were a little dangerous. We could have been victims of a serial killer at some point."

*That's beginning to make sense.*

Ginny's eyes searched Suzy's. "I was happy to be reined in. I hated selling vegetables and citrus. But I think about it now. It was a good life. We had fun. We were poor, but we really didn't miss out on anything."

They grew quiet.

"Mom, if this inheritance pans out, maybe we could help other women."

"I want my home."

"How about a better place? A new home with two stories, an elevator and a cook…"

"I want *my* home."

*Then, I'll build guest cottages for your staff.*

Ginny stared out the window. "I'm not feeling well." She was shaking.

Suzy found a place to pull off. "Do you want to talk about it?"

Suzy looked in her rearview mirror and saw a black Escalade with dark tinted windows slowing to the shoulder behind them. She couldn't see the driver.

"Mom, there's an SUV behind us."

Ginny had trouble turning her head. "Do you have your flashers on?"

"No."

"Someone wants to help you."

Suzy continued to stare in the rearview mirror as she talked to her mother. "Are you okay?" She didn't want to put words in her mother's mouth. *God knows you've been through enough.*

"I remember things now that I blocked out before. That photo Bart showed us. Luther was very loving. And I don't understand why he punished me? Why he created a will that cut me out?"

Suzy felt a lump form in her throat. She leaned over and hugged her mother.

There was a knock at her window. Suzy turned to see a very handsome man in his thirties, with a crew cut, clean-shaven face, and a brilliant smile. He waved.

Sheila Ramler's tow truck honked and pulled in front of Suzy's car.

Suzy rolled her window down. "We're fine. I just…"

The man handed her a business card. She read it and handed it to Ginny.

Ginny's mouth dropped. "The eagle has landed."

They both turned to look at Reginald Perish.

"Welcome to Walcott American. Your driver, Michael, is here. We've asked Ms. Ramler to take your vehicle to a garage of your choosing for any necessary vehicle maintenance. However, we encourage you to use your Walcott driver."

Suzy looked in the rearview mirror and saw a man in uniform standing next to the black Escalade.

*How do I know you are not trying to abduct us?* "Excuse me," Suzy pulled out her phone and texted Arnold.

Suzy: `A black SUV pulled up and said I have a driver?`

Arnold: `Take a photo of the guy and send it to me.`

Suzy asked Reginald to pose for a photo. She sent it to Arnold.

Arnold: `Never seen him before.`

Suzy: `?`

Another black Escalade pulled up behind Michael's. Sheila introduced herself to Reginald and waved to Suzy and Ginny.

Suzy watched in her rearview mirror as she saw Arnold and Gretchen exit from the second car. *What the fuck!?* Suzy got out of the car.

Sheila started getting her truck prepped to take Suzy's vehicle. "Did you win the lotto, Suzy?" Sheila shouted. "I've never seen so many important-looking people."

Suzy saw Arnold and Gretchen grinning as they approached. *Maybe.* "What's going on?" She watched Gretchen shake Michael's, then Reginald's hand. She was dressed in a seductive black suit, diamond necklace, and stiletto heels.

Gretchen waved to Ginny. "Hello Ms. Compton."

Michael helped Ginny out of the Hyundai and into the back of the Escalade.

Gretchen approached Suzy. "Frank's at The Lizard if you want to go. He's fully vetted."

Suzy's mouth dropped. "Chloe was right!"

"CPA guy, too." Gretchen nodded. "In case you were looking for options. It's your choice."

"I don't even know you." Suzy wanted to be mad at Gretchen, but somehow, she couldn't.

"You really don't," Gretchen laughed.

"We need to talk!"

Suzy looked to Arnold. "Do you and Gretchen know each other?"

"We're becoming familiar." He made the eye dart to Suzy behind Gretchen's back. "Turns out, she's part of the transition team, aka the watchers."

Gretchen laughed. "The watchers! I'm glad we made it to the next phase."

Ginny let her window down to listen.

Suzy threw her hands up. "So, all of you were just going to go on with this covert shit until I was Ginny's age?"

Gretchen crossed her arms and gave Suzy the familiar warm smile she trusted. "We couldn't do anything, Suzy. You and Ginny have interacted with people who were instructed to give you space, let you live your life, not interfere, standdown, be ready when you turned 45. You've been working with Arnold in a capacity that was not in the plan. He's been trying to help you learn about the business without telling you why."

"This seems so far-fetched," Suzy mocked. "I'm waiting for Ashton Kutcher to say I've been Punked." She looked around.

Gretchen stayed poised and strong. "Think about it another way. A president has a playboy son who gets off course and possibly tangled with the wrong people. There are people keeping tabs on the playboy. You're the extreme opposite. You're a nobody, no disrespect, who is a major somebody, who needed eyeballs and protection, but no interference. That's the way Luther F. Walcott set this up. He had history with your family. He had loss. He fell for Monica. He couldn't have her, but he wanted their blood to have meaning in the future." Gretchen put her hands in her suit pockets. "Monica was technically a one-night stand for Joe, but she persisted. You can't buy that. He didn't want to and neither did Luther. He was willing to give you his wealth in the future if you discovered it. Plain and simple."

Suzy slapped a mosquito that landed on her arm. "Plain. There it is again. Not simple. How long have you been with Walcott?"

"Give or take fifteen years. I move around. And seriously, Suzy," Gretchen reasoned, "think about it. Jewish and Catholic grandmothers have been influencing relationships for years. You're thinking about this like its completely foreign, and it's not. You and Ginny slept with a guy you didn't know. People do that all the time. You don't need to keep beating yourself up."

"I heard that," Ginny shouted. "You're a regular Mata Hari."

Gretchen walked over to the car. "I mean all of this with the utmost respect."

Ginny nodded. "I understand. You're quite convincing."

Suzy joined Gretchen. "But none of this would have come to fruition if Ginny had not had knee surgery."

"Then, I'd still be serving you at The Lizard," Gretchen agreed. "And having breakfast talks at 3 a.m., until I was reassigned. Reminder, I'm not the only one on your detail. You'll learn."

"Gretch, Mom's anesthesia brought back the repressed memories that she's still not totally sure about, but I doubt I'd have ever come to any conclusion working with Arnold."

Sheila interrupted Gretchen, "Where am I towing her?"

Suzy suddenly realized Sheila had been there the whole time. "Sheila, do you need my triple A card?" She handled Sheila the keys.

Reginald addressed Sheila, "Ms. Lennox's Walcott account will pay any expenses."

"I'm taking this over to Dodge's Garage." Sheila swung Suzy's keys.

Gretchen nodded to Sheila. To Suzy, "Whenever you discovered the trust, as long as it wasn't through the trust managers or anyone they hired to assist you, or leak it to you, is the only thing that matters."

Suzy pointed to Ginny. "To be continued, Mom. You good?"

"As long as you don't leave me," her mother called out.

*In the Snake Pit. No chance.* "We're good," Suzy shouted back. "I'm at a loss for words." She turned to Arnold. "What do we do now?"

"HIPS Data Solutions will be dissolved. You have a lot of decisions to make."

"Good." She punched his arm. "Let's get out of this mosquito-infested place and grab some empanadas."

Arnold's eyes lit up.

Suzy slid into the Escalade next to Ginny and shut the door.

"You're taking me home." Ginny made eye contact with Michael.

Suzy looked to Michael. "Could someone call The Circle Assisted Living and let them know Ginny's moving?"

"Consider it done." Michael pointed out some beverages and snacks in a picnic hamper in the back console.

Suzy was starving.

Ginny pat Suzy on her knee. "They'll take good care of us."

Arnold opened Suzy's door. "Mind if I ride with you?"

Suzy and Ginny moved over. "Do you want anything?" Suzy pointed at the snacks.

"No. I'm not going to spoil the empanada-fest."

She nodded. "By the way, I really liked the pitch you left in the notebook."

"Killercane!" Arnold leaned over and tapped Ginny. "Serial killers caught up in a hurricane."

Ginny thought. "Tossed in the ocean with the sharks, I hope."

Arnold and Suzy said in unison, "Sharknado vs. Killercane!"

Suzy elbowed Arnold. "What percentage of the portfolio are guns?"

"There are roughly seven major shareholders, and you are the majority shareholder." Arnold said.

"Hmm." Suzy shook her head. She turned to her mother. "Maybe the government conspiracy you were referring to after the surgery was prophecy. Cause I don't know how I'm going to follow in grandfather's footsteps." *Ohmygod, I called Luther grandfather! Yikes.*

Ginny cleared her throat and gave a head click toward Michael. "You don't know what you don't know. Give Arnold and the Walcotts a chance to educate you."

"You're right, Mom." Suzy patted her mother's knee. They both gave each other the "look who is listening" big eyes.

Michael started the Escalade and began to move forward. Sheila was the lead, towing Suzy's old Honda Civic. Gretchen and Reginald followed in the other Escalade.

Michael continued to make eye contact with Suzy in the mirror. "Can I turn on some music?"

"Sure," Suzy said. "Surprise me."

Michael put on Mozart's Sonata No. 17 in C.

Suzy had not listened to classical music much. "Interesting."

"My pleasure." Michael focused on his driving.

"That would sound great on a Wurlitzer," Arnold said.

"Does someone need Wurlitzer lessons?" Suzy snapped her fingers. "That's what I'll get you for Christmas."

Arnold clapped. "Yes!"

Suzy's phone dinged. It was Frank.

Frank: `Gretchen quit The Lizard.`

Suzy: `She did.`

Frank: `Any reason?`

Suzy: `She's going to work with me.`

Frank: `You land a big account?`

Suzy: I did.

Frank: Congrats! Sunset dinner at Pink Pelican tomorrow?

Suzy: Yeah. 6 p.m.

Ginny listened to the music. Her eyes closed. "I've heard this somewhere before."

*I don't want to know.*

## THE END.

# SPOILER ALERT

*What's True—Spoiler Alert—Read this after you've finished the novel.*

The following information is the author's research and opinion. It is not a medical opinion provided by a medical professional. If you have healthcare concerns, you should consult your personal physician for medical advice. In addition, this is not meant to scare or dissuade patients from needed surgery.

### Anesthesia—Postoperative Cognitive Dysfunction (POCD)
**Bold** *below is the author's emphasis, not the referenced source's emphasis.*

The inspiration for this book is the anesthesia story and how the effects of anesthesia on a geriatric brain could stir repressed memories, as well as introduce a host of health problems, as was noticed in a close relation of mine.

The characters are fictional, but the medical circumstances, treatment, and pharmaceuticals are real situations observed by the author.

As with any work of fiction, any resemblance to persons living or dead is coincidental, meaning this is not someone's life story.

The lessons learned firsthand are not meant to exploit anyone who has suffered postoperative cognitive dysfunction. The goal is to help others avoid similar problems and to hopefully improve our communication with the medical community.

There is (in my opinion) a frightening void in the discussion of negative outcomes that can happen in a surgical procedure. The pros and cons are heavily weighted on the pro side because something has happened to the patient. The prognosis that leads up to the surgery is presented as the optimum, hopefully when all other measures have been exhausted. Many times, without the procedure, the patient might decline rapidly or die. However, if the patient has the procedure, they still might decline rapidly or die, not because their doctor or healthcare professional is a bad practitioner, but because they didn't know the real risks or have the support system they needed to improve their outcome. Again, this is purely a layperson's opinion.

It seems to be a given that any surgery could result in maiming or death if the patient read the warnings, but **where is the warning about anesthesia, especially in the geriatric brain?** Patients are given paperwork to read and sign before a procedure, but most people don't read it or understand it thoroughly. Please read the information and ask questions if you don't understand.

**The parts of the brain** that are the last to mature during adolescence are the first to **age and shrink** (https://www.webmd.com/healthy-aging/which-area-of-the-brain-is-most-suscepitble-to-shrinkage-as-we-age#1). I'm not a doctor, but this makes me wonder if an older person receiving anesthesia may have risks related to brain shrinkage?

"Several risk factors for postoperative disorders have been identified, and anesthesiologists commonly adapt their practice habits when taking care of elderly patients to try to mitigate the effects of the anesthetics on postoperative cognitive function. These practices are reasonable and prudent; yet they are **not well supported by an understanding of the aging brain and**

**specifics of how the anesthetic effects on the brain change with age**. Through functional imaging and electrophysiological studies, much is being learned about the neurophysiology and the neuroanatomy of normal aging." https://pubmed.ncbi.nlm.nih.gov/23820102/

Warnings of complications (in my opinion), usually overwhelm the patient and/or are ignored. You receive a thick handout of material to read and sign off that you read it when you didn't. Then, you'll have a discussion with the surgeon about what he does, days or weeks before the procedure. The **day of** surgery, the anesthesiologist comes in for a quick Q&A before you go under sedation.

Seriously, we just let the anesthesiologist do what he thinks best? I'm not calling anesthesiologists bad specialists, but we should talk to them ahead of time like we do the surgeon. **We're talking about the brain.**

"Postoperative cognitive dysfunction (POCD) **is a serious complication after surgery, especially in elderly patients.** The anesthesia technique is a potentially modifiable risk factor for POCD. This study assessed the effects of dexmedetomidine, propofol or midazolam sedation on POCD in elderly patients who underwent hip or knee replacement under spinal anesthesia." https://www.ncbi.nlm.nih.gov/pmc/articles/PMC6595716/

Did you know that a spinal and light sedation are safer for many elderly patients, than general anesthesia?

I didn't either, until I asked what options an elder had.

A few more notes on sedation relevant to **all ages**.

Twenty percent of dental patients use sedation to calm their fear of the dentist. If you dread the dentist, you might consider natural alternatives to sedation, like music and audiobooks. If you are not fearful, hopefully you don't opt for unnecessary sedation. (https://www.colgate.com/en-us/oral-health/anesthesia/is-iv-sedation-dentistry-right-for-you)

Remember when they put our mothers and grandmothers under during the 1950s and 1960s to pull babies out with forceps? That was considered innovative. Women were convinced they needed to be put under during childbirth, while Dad waited in the next room for the announcement of a boy or girl.

We've fallen into the same trap with colonoscopies.

The only paperwork the doctor and facility provided me or my husband prior to a colonoscopy, other than how to prep, was that a patient receiving anesthesia had to be driven home and in the care of an adult for 24 hours. There wasn't really a reason, just a requirement. I'm sure that was intended to cover anything that might happen in 24 hours. There was also a warning not to use heavy equipment or make any important decisions in that 24-hour period.

What about after 24 hours?

I had my last colonoscopy without anesthesia. I asked and got permission to have my procedure sans propofol. My doctor asked me if I could be still. That was pretty much all that was necessary. I felt nothing of the scope until two turns that made me feel like I might pass out, but they were brief. I had an inflating blood pressure cuff on my left arm and was on my left side the whole procedure. The blood pressure cuff was the biggest pain, not the scope. I had an anesthesiologist watching me if I signaled, I wanted to go under. But otherwise, I watched the television screen showing my healthy colon. Bonus, I drove myself home.

"Unsedated colonoscopies are nothing new. In fact, they used to be standard. But here in the Home of the Brave, we'd rather not prove we're badass with, um, our ass. Some data suggest that less than 20 percent of us would consider the option. Some experts think it will help if unsedated is replaced with sedation-free or medication-free, but no matter how you put it, it still comes down to where you put it." https://www.menshealth.com/health/a26828776/no-sedation-colonoscopies/

The sportscaster Joe Buck almost lost his career due to a procedure using anesthesia. Prior to that, he would get hair plugs using just topical treatments to his scalp. (https://www.si.com/media/2016/10/06/joe-buck-fox-book-hair-plugs-surgery-voice)

"A few weeks before the start of the 2011 baseball season, Buck underwent his eighth hair replacement procedure. But something went wrong during the six-hour-plus procedure. When he woke up from the anesthetic, Buck could not speak. He believes his vocal cord was paralyzed because of a cuff the surgery center used to protect him during the procedure. A doctor not part of the operation theorized to Buck that the cuff probably got jostled during the procedure and sat on the nerve responsible for firing his left vocal cord. Buck was also going through personal stress at the time, as his marriage to his high school sweetheart was ending. That stress, Buck theorizes, could have made him more susceptible to nerve damage.

"Panicked, Buck sought a voice specialist at Barnes-Jewish Hospital in St, Louis, Dr. Bruce H. Haughey, who told him he had a paralyzed vocal cord and there was no guarantee on when his voice would come back."

Comedian Joan Rivers died unexpectedly after receiving anesthesia:

"There are minor operations and procedures, but there are no minor anesthetics. This could turn out to be the one lesson learned from the ongoing investigation into the death of comedian Joan Rivers." (https://thehealthcareblog.com/blog/2014/09/08/what-happened-to-joan-rivers/

On Michael Jackson's addiction to propofol:

"Prosecutors built a strong case that the 50-year-old "king of pop" died after Dr. Conrad Murray had given Jackson a large dose of propofol (pronounced PRO-poe-fall), a powerful anesthetic, to help him sleep and then left him unattended."

The article link provides a lot of information on the drug and Jackson's death. But I found one statement odd,

"'And there is some loss of memory, which is a good thing,' explained Dr. Aglio." (https://www.health.harvard.edu/blog/propofol-the-drug-that-killed-michael-jackson-201111073772)

I've heard this loss of memory comment before by doctors. It implies that you wouldn't want to remember being cut open or going through a procedure—but knowing what I know about memory loss in people I love (from the use of anesthesia), I find the statement offensive.

Surgery isn't the same as baking a pie. There might be a recipe for knee surgery success, but each body is unique and only you and your advocate know yours. Do you have a high threshold for pain? Do you get tipsy when sipping wine? Do you bloat or perspire easily in the heat? Can you hear or see without your glasses or hearing aid? These questions won't come up in surgery, but they may in recovery. What's normal for you may seem abnormal to your nurse who doesn't know you. They may think you are fine, but you could be showing signs of confusion.

If I have surgery, I will ask my advocate to use some signals we have both rehearsed if there is a concern. I may not remember the signal while I'm under medication, but it doesn't hurt to prepare. Your advocate is your voice when you aren't coherent.

No matter your age, it's important to know more about the warnings, possible outcomes, anesthesia options, side effects of your procedure, and what medications to anticipate should you have procedural side effects.

You've heard all the side effects on commercials. Your advocate should be watching for these. Choose a family member or advocate you trust, someone who listens and doesn't cave under pressure or fear of authority figures, meaning the doctors. They're not there to make a doctor's work difficult, but to **help** the doctor understand you.

There isn't a one-size-fits-all solution to quality of life.

As for rehabilitation centers, you need to investigate them. The goal of the facility should be to help you get back home or wherever you lived prior to surgery in **better shape** than when you arrived. There are rehabilitation centers (my observation) that keep patients comfortable, and there are centers that work toward recovery. You can read the reviews but remember there are reputation management tools that websites use to squash down unfavorable reviews to lower positions on their site. Read them all!

I always Google: "Complaints about…" to see if anything surfaces. Talk to others as well.

If you've finished the book, you understand Suzy did her best to check infection rates at the hospital and rehab where Ginny was going. Hearing the following story jogged my memory about researching infection rates before a procedure:

A friend announced they were having a procedure at a particular hospital. Another friend knew the hospital had a high infection rate and counseled, "Cancel it now. That place has a high infection rate!"

The surgeon who was to perform the surgery had advised my patient friend pre-surgery, "You **will** want to get on your feet in a few days (at the hospital) and move to the rehab center to avoid infection."

That went right over my friend's head, until they matched up the warning to "cancel it" with the doctor's comment to "avoid infection."

The doctor could easily have said, "I told you so," if infection had happened and my friend complained. He wasn't a bad doctor; he was protecting himself. He works at these hospitals, and I believe he was sincere. He was being honest. He doesn't control the hospital.

We should always ask, "Why are you telling me this?" or, "Help me understand what I should know about infection," or, "What would you do if your parent or child was having this procedure?" or, "What rehabilitation center would you send your mother to?" Here is one website that shows medical ratings, including infection rates: https://www.hospitalsafetygrade.org/

Listen carefully, then ask more questions.

In the case above, the surgery was cancelled, and the patient went to another doctor and got a second opinion.

If you move into assisted living due to complications, have someone check the place first. If you move there, have someone visit often and advocate for you.

Finally, if you are wondering why I didn't have a medical expert check my facts in this book, it's because a medical expert didn't have a lot of the answers I needed when the people I love had real issues, which is why I wrote the book.

It is my hope that doctors and nurses read this book to see how a patient advocate dealt with POCD, rehabilitation, and assisted living. That's the real world. This is not about medical shaming. We, the family and advocate of a patient, form a team with the medical professionals. There are no stupid questions and no crazy answers. Sometimes, the simplest solution is overlooked.

Frontline workers see bits and pieces of our lives and do their best (we hope) with the protocols and guidelines they are provided. We can't expect them to know us, but to know the human body. That's why we must work together.

**Olanzapine**

This medicine saved a life, or I should say a mind. That's where the title *Mind Hostage* came from. It seemed anti-depressants were the only drug being considered for an elder's confusion when an anti-psychotic was needed. This person had never taken any of these medicines prior to surgery, so we must assume that the pharmacology and anesthesia involved in the surgery created the side effects that lead to the problem.

Again, it's not an indictment of the medical community, but a fact that many doctors just don't recognize the symptoms of postoperative cognitive dysfunction, POCD. Too often after a medical procedure a senior citizen's confusion is said to related to the aging process. The body breaks down. It isn't as resilient. It will take time to recover.

The quote below talks about how it may be possible to avoid POCD by taking olanzapine *before* a procedure. It's a short article and worth reading the whole article and discussing with your doctor.

> "Administration of 10 mg of oral olanzapine perioperatively, versus placebo, was associated with a significantly lower incidence of delirium. These findings suggest that olanzapine prophylaxis of postoperative delirium may be an effective strategy." (https://www.sciencedirect.com/science/article/abs/pii/S0033318210707234)

**Wills & Trusts—Weird Inheritances**

The Felps and Walcotts are my characters, not real people. I wanted a unique historical storyline to tie into Ginny's repressed memories, thus the inheritance twist. I didn't know if a future inheritance was possible, until I did some homework. See the link I've copied. This helped me shape Walcott's story: https://www.theguardian.com/world/2011/may/12/michigan-tycoon-wellington-burt-fortune

**A legacy of bitterness** Michigan millionaire Wellington Burt used his will to put his enormous wealth out of reach of his family for almost a full century. When he died in 1919, his will was discovered to specify that his vast fortune would not be passed on until 21 years after the death of his last surviving grandchild. She died in 1989 and the 21-year countdown ended on November 2010. About 12 people discovered they were beneficiaries of the strange will, described as a "legacy of bitterness", and they shared a fortune estimated to be worth $110m.

## Movies and Theaters

The Victory Theatre was an early vaudeville theatre in Tampa, Florida that eventually showed silent films and later talkies.

The Tampa Theatre around the corner from the Victory opened in 1926 is still showing movies today.

Tampa Theatre's Marketing Director Jill Witecki was kind enough to share much of the theatre's history and a behind-the-scenes tour. She explained that Tampa Theatre would not have shown *Way Down East* when the original released in 1920, because they weren't open. Even if they had been, they were a Paramount Theatre and didn't show films from other studios.

The film *Way Down East* was based on a play by Lottie Blair Parker, who was no relation (that I'm aware of) to my Blair kin. *Way Down East:* https://www.loc.gov/item/2014637179/

The play was a huge success in its day in 1897. I was personally shocked that a story about a worldly man tricking a naïve young woman into sex under the guise of a fake marriage was a hugely popular play, before it was a movie.

I saw the 1920 movie in a Film Appreciation class at St. Petersburg Jr. College. Our teacher Bill Gammage was a huge fan of the lead Lillian Gish. He even had her brought her to the college for a talk. I had a chance to meet her and get her autograph on my program afterward. It was a magical moment. She was beautiful at any age.

When I saw the movie, I was taken by the ruse and the horrible people Anna Moore encountered. This silent depiction was etched in my memory and found its way into this book by way of my characters. I didn't plan it. My characters wove it in.

My favorite scene in *Way Down East* is the baptism scene. I found it touching and extremely tragic.

I could not image what women who lived in the late 1800s and early 1900s thought of this film, other than they knew women like Anna, or they were women like Anna.

I later bought *Way Down East* on DVD and several other D.W. Griffith classics.

His film *Birth of a Nation* was highly controversial in racial content and inspired hate crimes. I am not promoting the filmmaker's first film and broke that DVD after screening it. I had seen snips of *Birth* in the same class mentioned above long ago and couldn't recall much other than how Griffith pioneered many film techniques. Griffith followed *Birth* with many more films whose content was not inflammatory, or so I've read. I do not know his full history. However, the film *Way Down East* is mindful of how women are held to a different standard. Griffith's career has been redefined by that first film, which has pretty much erased him from Hollywood, as well as much of Gish's legacy. See the articles below:

https://www.theguardian.com/film/2019/may/10/lillian-gish-the-birth-of-a-nation-controversy-name-removed-cinema-ohio

Gish Charitable Foundation https://gishprize.org/

## Romeo, Florida

We drove through Romeo many years ago. There are still family farms and a church in the area, but it is listed as a ghost town on many internet searches. This is not due to hauntings but because it's been absorbed into Dunnellon, the Marion County tax collector's office explained.

Romeo is now just a sign outside of Dunnellon, Florida. When the post office closed in 1955, it stopped existing as a town, as I understand from the tax office and several books I have perused. The neighboring town of Juliette existed from roughly 1850 to 1926. I've not found an explanation for the naming of the two towns. I'd be happy to hear from you if you find some historical records about it.

A lot of the towns in this book are fictional, but Romeo is a real place, a Florida parcel of the past that was always small. I fell in love with the town's name, then I learned of its sister town Juliette. How could you not use a real place when they have the names Romeo and Juliette? Perhaps another author would build a fictional town within their novel to romanticize the names. However, I have read enough real history to discover there isn't a romantic story behind the towns; in fact, the record is very dry and masculine.

That made it even more poignant that the women of Romeo in my book are genetically isolated from the world. They are emotionally trapped in an unnatural hereditary existence that shaped their future. A story they did not know held them back. I can personally relate to that. After some family history research and discoveries, I can see how my own family followed a limited existence.

If you've ever watched *Finding Your Roots* on PBS, you'll hear and see Dr. Henry Louis Gates, Jr. show his guests the similarities in their family history that helped shaped their future.

I wanted my people, Monica, Ginny, Suzy, Minnie, and Chloe, to have roots in a hidden rural setting where their Shakespearean-esque misfortune would be private, much like Anna Moore's *Way Down East* heartbreak. However, their stories, like many of ours, are merely a genie trapped in a bottle, until someone discovers it and unknowingly releases the genie.

# ACKNOWLEDGEMENTS

Thank you to Lisa DeSpain, my editor and book formatter. Lisa is a lifeline, a literary phone-a-friend, and all-around good human being. I owe much to Lisa! Thank you also to Tom Hillman at tomhill-mannmediadesign.com, who created and manages emilyskinnerbooks.com, and my cover designer Claudia at Labelschmiede.com. And special thanks to a new friend, Kate Rock of Kate Rock Book Tours, www.katerocklitchick.com. They are all easy to work with and keep me sane.

To my friends who read, write, and/or just encourage me: Suzy Rodenbach, Howard and Lot Whittington, Robyn Fairbanks, Susan and Ernie Zager, Elle Thorpe, Roxanne Smith, Carrie Vanerio, Roberta Terranova, Theresa Moser, Susan Brimmer, Kathy Powell, Regena Stefanchick, Angela Sanford, Becky Marble, CJ and Gregg Fisher, Kathie Fahey, Judi Burten, Gretchen Wells, Val Ross, Tracy Brandt, Doris Hurst, Glenn Ireland, Lori Garside, Muriel Savino, Pat Lynch, Pam Corkum, Peggy Sheffield, Peg Connell, Judy Roe, Joyce Huslander, Susan Logsdon, Kim Salter, Marcia Engle, Marylou Bourdow, Kathy Durnell, Elaine Duval, Stanton Holder, Laurie Williams, Ramon Mendoza, and Sheila Ramler.

Sheila Ramler entered my contest to win a character role using her real name. It was great fun creating her tow truck driver character.

257

To family members who encourage me: Barbara Williams, Tom Skinner, Blair Skinner and Caitlin Poley, Marquel and Drew Rogers, Ellen Williams, John and Kathy Williams, Cecilia Garrison, Robin Williams, Kathleen Sims, Louis Scarnechia, Mark Williams, Ruth Skinner and Selena Sieb. Thanks for the love. Forgive me if I've missed anyone.

*The following resources and individuals were extremely helpful in the historical context of the novel:*

Todd at Hillsborough County Public Library Online Resource Chat

Tampa Bay History Center, 801 Water Street, Tampa, FL 33602

Jill Witecki, Marketing Director, Tampa Theatre, 711 N. Franklin Street, Tampa, FL 33602

Sydney Jordan, Collections Specialist USF Libraries, Special Collections, University of South Florida, 4101 USF Apple Dr, Tampa, FL 33620

Melissa Sullebarger, Curator of Education, Henry B. Plant Museum, 401 W. Kennedy Blvd., Tampa, FL 33606

Susan Carter, Curator of Collections, Henry B. Plant Museum, 401 W. Kennedy Blvd., Tampa, FL 33606

Dunnellon Public Library, City of Dunnellon, 20750 River Drive, Dunnellon, FL 34431

Norma Robinson, Director, Sulphur Springs Museum, 1101C East River Cove Street, Tampa, Fl 33604

# ABOUT THE AUTHOR

Emily Skinner lives in Tampa Bay, Florida with her husband, Tom. In addition to writing, she also enjoys traveling, visiting local museums, growing sunflowers, and working with their daughters, Marquel Skinner and Blair Skinner, on their film and acting projects.

*Books by Emily W. Skinner*

Hybrid Medical Thriller/Southern Noir by Emily W. Skinner
*Mind Hostage*
Romantic Suspense Novels by Emily W. Skinner
*Marquel* (Book 1)
*Marquel's Dilemma* (Book 2)
*Marquel's Redemption* (Book 3)

Booktrailer: Marquel book trailer on YouTube—
*featuring actor Eric Roberts & Marquel Skinner*
www.youtube.com/watch?v=6e6O7iYqeVQ

---

Young Adult Novels by E.W. Skinner
St. Blair: Children of the Night—Book One
St. Blair: Children of the Night *Sybille's Reign*—Book Two
The Diary of St. Blair—Book Three

---

Historical Nonfiction by Emily W. Skinner

*Until We Sleep Our Last Sleep:*
*My Quaker Grandmother's Diary of Faith and Community*
*Amid Depression and Disability*

*The Diarist: A companion book for your inspired thoughts*

Short Memoir by Emily W. Skinner
*Master of the Roman Noir*

Sign up for email updates at:
www.emilyskinnerbooks.com

Follow Emily on:
www.facebook.com/emilyskinnerbooks
www.twitter.com/emilyauthor
www.instagram.com/emilyauthor
http://www.thefilmmom.blogspot.com/
https://www.goodreads.com/author/show/6982753.Emily_W_Skinner


Emily W. Skinner
PO Box 8590
Seminole, FL 33775-8590

*Reviews and ratings appreciated!*